MW00378537

Shakespeare Under Cover

By Erin Wade
Copyright 2/2019
ISBN: 9781796625622
Edited by Susan Hughes

Independently published by
Erin Wade
©2/2019 Erin Wade
www.erinwade.us

DEDICATION

To the one who has always supported me in everything I have ever undertaken. You have encouraged me and have always been my biggest fan. Life is sweeter with you.

Erin

Acknowledgements

A special "Thank You" to my wonderful and witty "Beta Master," Julie Versoi. She makes me a better storyteller.

A heartfelt "Thank You" to Laure Dherbécourt for agreeing to beta read for me. She has added insight and an incredible knack for catching incorrect homophones.

What I Can Promise You!

The only stars I can guarantee you
are the ones in my eyes when I look at you.
The only love I can promise you forever is mine.
The only touch I need to complete me is yours.

Shakespeare Under Cover
Erin Wade

Chapter 1

Professor Regan Shaw watched her class file into the lecture hall. For the tenth time today, she wondered why she had agreed to be the guest professor for a year. *Burn out,* a tiny voice inside her head reminded her. *You're a has-been and right back where you started.*

A noisy group of students pulled her from her reverie. "Come on, Brandy, you promised." A six-four hunk in a football jersey pulled at a blonde wearing a matching jersey.

Must be going steady, Regan thought. *They look so much alike. If he wasn't pawing her, I'd think they were siblings.*

"Keep your hands off me, Joey Sloan." The blonde yanked her arm from his grasp.

"That's not what you said last night," Joey said, grinning salaciously.

The blonde shot him a look that would have melted an intelligent man. "I have changed my mind. A woman's prerogative."

"You can't just yank me around like that," Joey growled.

"Why don't I just cut you loose?" the girl threatened. "Why don't you go find someone else to—"

"Aww. Look, Brandy, I'm sorry," Joey muttered. "I just want you to come to the frat party tonight. I like to show you off, baby."

"No, and that's final." Brandy spotted an empty chair on the front row between two geeky-looking guys and sat down, leaving Joey no choice but to sit somewhere else.

Regan stood. "Ladies and gentlemen, welcome to Discovering Shakespeare. I'm Professor Regan Shaw."

"Hot damn," a male voice called out from the back of the lecture hall. "You're really something, mama."

Brandy jumped to her feet. "Who said that?" she demanded. "Joey, was that you?"

"Miss . . ." Regan quickly scanned the class roster for Brandy's last name. She had no Brandy on her list. "I am quite capable of controlling my class," she said loudly.

Brandy whirled around to face her. "Sorry," she said as she dropped back into her seat.

"How many of you studied Shakespeare in high school?" Regan continued. Everyone's hands went up. "So, you know his plays and prose were written over four hundred years ago?"

Nods and moans were the response from her class.

"Shakespeare can sometimes be difficult to understand," Regan continued.

"That's the understatement of the day," Brandy interrupted. "Shakespeare is ambiguous."

Regan flashed her million-dollar smile. The one that always captivated her audiences. "Part of the reason Shakespeare seems so ambiguous is because he made up his own words. If he had no word to express his emotions, he simply created one. We can thank him for such words as addiction, archvillain, and bedazzled.

"I want you to read *A Midsummer Night's Dream* and be prepared to discuss the symbolism Shakespeare uses. I will see you all next week."

Regan looked at her class roster again. "Brandy, may I see you after class?"

The room emptied quickly. Brandy remained seated until Regan spoke to her.

"Are you supposed to be in my class?" the professor asked. "I don't have you on my roster."

"Brandywine," the girl said. "Grace Brandywine."

Regan smiled slightly. *Of course*, she thought. *Second name on my list.*

"I see," Regan said. She walked from behind her desk and leaned against it as she studied her student.

Grace Brandywine was movie-star beautiful. Everything about her screamed "money." *Probably oil money*, Regan thought.

Brandy tossed her head and glorious blonde hair cascaded down one shoulder and settled on her perfect breast. "I loved your last book," she said, smiling. "You're a wonderful writer. The movie didn't do it justice."

"Thank you." A slight smile played on Regan's lips. *You didn't see my last book*, she thought. *No one did. It was rejected by my publisher.*

"I can't wait to read your next work," Brandy said. "I've read all your novels. You're my favorite author. That's why I took this class."

"Oh," Regan teased, "I was certain you took the class to study Shakespeare."

Brandy made a sound between a giggle and a snort.

Damn, she's cute, Regan thought.

Suddenly, a handsome man in his midforties entered the lecture hall. "There you are! I had a feeling I would find you counseling a student. Did you forget we have a lunch date?"

"I didn't forget," Regan said. "I'm just trying to get my roster in order."

"I'll grab us a table, but hurry. The SUB fills up quickly this time of day." He squeezed Regan's arm and then left the room.

"I'm meeting Joey in the SUB," Brandy said. "Want to walk over together? You could tell me more about Shakespeare."

"I have to drop something off to Professor Fleming," Regan said. "I'll see you around."

"Want to go with me to the Delta Tau Delta fraternity party tonight?" Coach Danny Tucker asked hopefully.

"I don't think so." Regan frowned. "You know how I feel about drinking and frat boys."

Danny laughed. "Indeed, I do. The powers that be have instructed me to attend their first bash of the year. So, you're going to throw me to the wolves with no backup?"

Regan watched as Brandy and Joey strolled into the Student Union Building. Joey had his arm draped around Brandy's shoulders. His hand sneakily brushed her breast. Brandy slapped his arm away. "Joey Sloan, if that happens again, I swear . . . ."

Joey grinned mischievously. "Sorry, Babe, it really was an accident. I know how you hate PDA."

Brandy nodded and stomped away from him. She raised her head and found herself staring into the deep brown eyes of her English lit professor. A twisted smile passed across her lips.

"Professor Shaw, Coach Tucker, may we join you?" Brandy pulled out a chair and sat down. *Coach Tucker and*

Joey share the same lack of imagination when it comes to a date, she thought.

"I am trying to talk Professor Shaw into going with me to the Delta Tau Delta bash tonight," Tucker said, grinning.

"You should come," Joey said, his eyes twinkling with glee. "Brandy and I will be there. It'll be wild and crazy. It will be hot!" He let his eyes wander down Brandy's slender body.

Regan tilted her head and caught Brandy's eye. The girl shrugged. "You should come," she said softly.

"Three great recommendations," Regan said. "How can I go wrong? What time does it start?"

"Starts at seven." Tucker grinned from ear to ear. "I'll pick you up at six-thirty."

"Umm, I'll meet you there," Regan said. "I may not stay till the bitter end."

Coach Tucker looked at his watch. "We gotta go, big guy. Football practice in ten minutes. You need to suit up."

Regan watched as the two men left, mumbling to each other and laughing out loud.

"Delta Tau Delta. Is that the fraternity that has all the drug charges leveled against them?" Regan said.

Brandy shrugged. "You can't believe everything you hear."

"I was under the impression you weren't going," Regan said between sips of her iced tea.

"Joey wouldn't stop hounding me, so I agreed to go to get him to leave me alone." Brandy cocked her head and surveyed Professor Shaw. "He's the president of the fraternity. Said I was making him look bad by refusing to attend his first party."

"Are fraternity parties all Joey takes you to?" Regan asked. "I mean, what does he do when he plans something special, like dinner and a floor show?"

Brandy laughed out loud. "Joey's idea of a floor show is tableside guacamole. What about you and Coach Tucker?" Brandy raised her eyebrows.

Regan blushed. "Tell me why you date Joey," she said, desperate to change the subject.

"Probably the same reason you date Coach Tucker." Brandy smiled knowingly.

I doubt that, Regan thought.

Brandy paid extra attention to her appearance as she dressed for the party. She was in her I'm-gonna-knock-your-boots-off mood. She briefly wondered if Professor Shaw wore boots. Loud honking in front of her sorority house told her Joey was demanding her presence.

Dad would kill me if he saw me tolerating Joey's rudeness, she thought as she skipped down the stairs.

The party was in full swing when the couple arrived. Joey parked his Porsche convertible along the curb, jumped out without opening his door, and started up the sidewalk.

Brandy sighed loudly then opened her own door and got out of the car.

Coach Tucker and Professor Shaw were already at the party. A crowd of male students gathered around Professor Shaw.

"I'll get us a couple of brews," Joey yelled as he headed for the tubs of beer.

Brandy observed her professor. The woman was classy—hot, but classy. Dressed in a pair of formfitting black jeans and an open-necked, electric-blue blouse, she looked like one of the students. Her long black hair curled around her shoulders, framing a face that dreams were made of. Brandy wondered how anyone applied makeup that perfectly.

Brandy ran the numbers through her mind, trying to figure the woman's age. She came up with thirty-six. Regan Shaw was young for one who had accomplished so much.

"Here ya go, Babe." Joey held out a dripping bottle of beer to her.

"Thanks."

##

As the party grew louder and Joey got handsier, Brandy decided to leave. She had poured the beers Joey kept feeding her into the huge Mexican urn at the foot of the stairs. She was headed there when she saw Professor Shaw sneakily dump the contents of her bottle into the same urn.

An inebriated Coach Tucker staggered toward Professor Shaw. "Obviously you don't like beer." He laughed. "Let me get you a glass of wine."

Ignoring Professor Shaw's protest, he weaved his way to the bar. Pretending to text on her cell phone, Brandy moved closer to him as she saw him put his hand into his pocket. To her surprise, he pulled out something and dropped it into Regan's drink.

Is that son of a bitch drugging her? Brandy thought.

Coach Tucker swirled the wine much longer than seemed necessary and then carried the glass to Professor Shaw.

"Come on, Babe." Joey grabbed her around the waist. "Let's go upstairs to my room."

"I want to dance," Brandy insisted. "You never dance with me."

"Okay, okay," Joey huffed. "One dance then we go upstairs."

Brandy nodded. She watched Professor Shaw as the woman moved to the closest sofa and sat down. She finished half the wine and then set it on the coffee table. She leaned her head back and appeared to go to sleep.

"Joey, I think Professor Shaw is sick," she said.

"Nah, she's fine. Coach will take care of her." He shot her a malicious grin and jerked his head toward the staircase. "Come on, I'll take care of you."

"You go on up," Brandy said sweetly. "I need to visit the ladies' room first."

As Joey stumbled away, Loraine Munoz grabbed his arm and clung to him all the way up the stairs.

Brandy looked around for Coach Tucker and spotted him in the corner making out with a cheerleader. She walked to Regan. The woman was dead to the world. The blonde sat down by the professor and pulled Regan's arm around her shoulders. She slipped her arm around Regan's small waist and stood up, pulling the professor with her.

Regan was dead weight, but Brandy managed to drag her outside. She hoped the crisp night air would revive the woman. She felt in Regan's pocket for car keys and found a single fob. She pushed the button, praying a car would respond. A car across the street flashed its lights.

"Bingo," Brandy said as she dragged the smaller woman toward her car.

##

"Hold your horses," Kiki Carson yelled as her roommate continued kicking the door. "Didn't God give you hands? Just turn the knob, for God's sake. It's unlocked.

"Holy crap!" Kiki exclaimed as Brandy carried Regan through the door.

"She doesn't look like much," an out of breath Brandy huffed, "but the further I carried her, the heavier she became."

"Isn't that Professor Shaw?" Kiki whispered as if someone might hear her.

"Yeah, Coach Tucker roofied her at the frat party," Brandy growled as she gently placed the professor on her twin bed.

"You've got to be kidding."

"Does she look like I'm kidding?" Brandy demanded.

"Does he know you saw him?" Kiki frowned.

"No, and I was able to video it with my cell phone." Brandy pulled the phone from her pocket and showed the recording to Kiki. Then she turned on her laptop and copied the video from her cell phone to the computer.

Kiki took the professor's pulse. "She's fine," she declared. "Just needs to sleep it off. How did you get rid of Joey?"

Brandy grinned. "Loraine Munoz was crawling in his pants, last time I saw him."

"I bet that really upset you," Kiki said with a chuckle.

"Better her than me. He is such an ass."

Both women watched silently as Regan stretched out on the bed.

"She's truly gorgeous," Kiki commented. "Should we undress her and put her to bed?"

"Would you mind doing that while I shower?" Brandy asked. She rummaged through her dresser drawer for a couple of soft T-shirts. She tossed one to Kiki. "This should work for her tonight."

Regan woke with a splitting headache. It hurt to open her eyes. *I'm hallucinating,* she thought. *Where am I?*

The urge to find a bathroom forced her to sit up in the bed. She tried to connect the room to anything in her life and failed. Thanks to her many book tours, she was used to waking up in strange bedrooms. But this didn't look like a hotel room. *This looks like a dorm room.*

A faint light from another room caught her attention. *The bathroom,* she thought.

She placed her feet on the floor and found herself standing on something soft, but firm.

"What the hell?" A drowsy Brandy rolled away from the professor.

Regan fell back onto the bed as Brandy turned on a lamp.

"Professor Shaw, are you okay?"

The lamplight danced in the blonde's emerald-green eyes. *I have never seen a more beautiful woman,* Regan thought.

"I'm not sure," Regan said softly. "Where's your bathroom?"

Brandy took Regan's hand to lead her to the bathroom. Regan noticed a woman sleeping in the other bed. A digital clock on the nightstand between the two beds showed seven a.m., Saturday, September 15.

When Regan returned, she walked to the bed where Brandy sat cross-legged. "How did I get here?" she whispered.

"Let's go to Starbucks for coffee, and I'll tell you all about it," Brandy whispered back. She handed Regan her neatly folded clothes and put on clean clothes from her closet.

"I'll drive," the student whispered as she picked up her teacher's key fob.

Brandy parked the car and took Regan's elbow, supporting her as they entered the Starbucks.

"I didn't drink at all last night, but I feel like I've been drugged." Regan pinched the bridge of her nose.

"You were," Brandy said bluntly. "Your boyfriend roofied you."

"Coach Tucker?" Regan gaped at her student. "Surely not."

Brandy pulled her iPhone from her pocket and showed her professor the video.

"I . . . I don't know what to say." Regan frowned. "The only reason I went to that party was to protect you. I figured something like this would happen to you, not me."

Brandy gasped. "Joey? You think Joey Sloan would rape me?"

"He is very aggressive with you," Regan said defensively.

"He's no rapist."

"Whatever." Regan shrugged, distressed that the girl would so easily dismiss the danger of being at a drunken frat party with a guy almost three times her size. "If he wanted to, I doubt you could stop him."

"Who says I would want to stop him?" Brandy grinned wickedly.

"May I have a copy of that video?" Regan asked.

"What will you do with it?"

"I intend to take it to the university security chief and file an official complaint."

"Look, Professor, I don't want to get involved in anything with campus security." Brandy shrugged. "They wouldn't do anything anyway. They never take any action. They will question Coach Tucker and take his word against yours. Tucker is a winning football coach. He took the team all the way last year. They won't even reprimand him. He's raped a dozen girls, and nothing ever comes of it.

"You're a visiting professor. They will just pacify you and then tell you not to return when the semester is over."

"So we just let him get away with drugging me?" Regan whispered.

Brandy nodded. "No harm, no alarm. You're fine."

"What did Joey say when you left the party?" Regan asked, having difficulty accepting the girl's lackadaisical attitude.

"Nothing," Brandy said. "Loraine Munoz was too busy getting into his pants."

"What the . . . ?" Regan muttered as Brandy followed her gaze to the TV screen in the Starbucks. A photo of Coach Tucker filled the screen. The streamer running beneath the photo said, "Head Coach found dead early this morning."

The two women moved closer to the TV so they could hear what the newscaster was saying.

Regan gasped. "He was stabbed to death! Someone murdered him."

"Must have roofied the wrong woman," Brandy said. "He got what he deserved. He was a pig."

Regan cringed at the venom in Brandy's voice and the anger in her eyes.

##

Half of her students used Coach Tucker's death as an excuse to skip class on Monday. Regan carefully noted each one who was not in attendance. No one skipped her class without suffering the consequences.

She could see Joey and Brandy in the hall outside her room. Joey had his hands in Brandy's hip pockets, pulling the girl against him. He was whispering in her ear. She slapped him and charged into the lecture hall.

Joey rubbed his cheek as if he couldn't believe a girl had just hit him. He smiled salaciously and followed Brandy into the room. Brandy sat down between the two geeks. Joey leaned over to one of them and said a few words. The man picked up his books and moved. Joey sat down by his girlfriend.

Regan watched as Joey sketched something on his notepad. He folded the sheet and grinned as he slid the note to Brandy.

Brandy glared at her boyfriend before opening it.

"Miss Brandywine," Regan said authoritatively, "come here, please."

Still holding the note, Brandy walked to the professor's desk. Regan pulled the note from the girl's hand and opened it. She blushed slightly as she saw that Joey had drawn two stick figures copulating. He had written, "You and me, Babe," beneath the drawing.

Regan placed the note in her desk drawer. "Please return to your seat.

"Mr. Sloan," Regan said, "would you please give us a brief synopsis of *A Midsummer Night's Dream*?"

To Regan's surprise, Joey gave an in-depth summary of the play. *He's obviously smarter than he seems*, she thought. She cringed as Brandy ran her hand down his thigh and whispered something in his ear. He grinned like a fool.

Chapter 2

Regan slipped into a chair at the back of the lecture hall. The school chancellor had called a meeting of all instructors and administrators. The topic of conversation was Coach Danny Tucker.

"As you all know," Chancellor Katherine O'Brien said, "Coach Tucker was murdered last night after a frat party at the Delta Tau Delta house. Although he coaches here, he lived in Oklahoma. Since the investigation crosses state lines, I have asked the FBI to handle this case.

"This is FBI agent Peyton King." O'Brien made a sweeping gesture toward a gorgeous strawberry blonde with brilliant blue eyes. "Agent King will be questioning each of you. Please give her your fullest cooperation. Even if you didn't know Coach Tucker personally, simply answer Agent King's questions."

Peyton King walked to the podium and flashed a smile that would overshadow a spotlight. At five-ten she was intimidating and a ten on the gorgeous woman scale. "I want to make this as painless as possible," she said.

"This morning I will interview those of you whose names begin with A through L. M through W, why don't you come back after lunch." Peyton's mesmerizing voice floated from the speakers. "There's no need for you to waste time sitting around here all morning."

Brandy was waiting in the hallway when Regan emerged from the lecture hall. "What did they say?" she demanded.

"Nothing really," Regan said. "Everyone will be questioned in alphabetical order. I must return after lunch."

"Want to have lunch with me?" The gregarious blonde flashed her brilliant smile.

"I have things to do." Regan shrugged.

"I heard the killers cut off his penis," Brandy whispered.

"Seriously?" Regan gasped. "Where do you want to have lunch? Not the SUB!"

"I know just the place." Brandy led the way. "We can take my car."

##

Regan was not surprised to find that Brandy drove a BMW. She parked in front of a hole-in-the-wall diner and jumped out of her car to open Regan's door.

Everyone greeted Brandy as they entered the restaurant, and they took a seat in the back of the diner.

"Did you get a good look at the FBI agent?" Brandy squealed.

"You mean Agent King?"

"Yes, FBI Agent fricking gorgeous Peyton King. She worked that coed abduction case a couple years ago," Brandy wiggled her eyebrows. "She's something! I bet she's great in bed."

"Miss Brandywine, I don't really care to indulge in this kind of conversation with you." Regan started to stand, but Brandy caught her hand.

"I'm sorry, Professor." Brandy smiled. "I didn't mean to be offensive."

"I'm afraid I find your uninhibited attitude about sex a little shocking."

"Really?" Brandy grinned seductively. "Then I suppose you would be doubly shocked to know I find you incredibly hot. Even hotter than FBI Agent King."

A pink blush started from the center of Regan's chest and spread up her neck to color her face. She was lost for words and distraught that a student would speak to her in such a manner.

"You may take me back to the university now," she said in her haughtiest tone.

Brandy laughed out loud. "Don't be such a prude. I'm just jerking your chain." She waved to the waitress. "We're ready to order.

"I suppose you're upset over the death of Coach Tucker," Brandy continued. "We all are."

Regan raked her teeth over her bottom lip. "I didn't know him that well." She sighed. "He certainly wasn't the man I thought he was."

"They will probably question you pretty extensively," Brandy said, "since you were his date the night he was murdered."

Regan's mouth moved, but no sound came out. She hadn't thought about that.

"It's a good thing you were with me all night," Brandy said, her eyes twinkling.

"I wasn't exactly *with* you."

"You spent the night in my bed," Brandy said, clearly enjoying her professor's embarrassment.

Regan's brown eyes locked with Brandy's green ones. "I'm sure there are worse things that could happen to me."

It was Brandy's turn to blush. She couldn't stop the warm feeling that spread over her body.

The blonde cleared her throat. "You know I'll verify that you spent the night in my dorm. You have a solid alibi," she said seriously. "I think we should show Agent King the video on my cell phone."

Regan smiled slightly. She knew she had won this round with her student. "I believe we have to."

"Can you believe Coach was mutilated?" Brandy squealed as she salted her burger.

"Where did you hear that?"

"Joey told me," Brandy replied. "Joey knows everything that goes on around here."

"Yes, I'm certain Joey is a trustworthy news source," Regan huffed.

"Tell me about your next book," Brandy said, changing the topic as she took a bite of her burger.

"Right now I don't have a next book," Regan said. "I'm taking a hiatus from the computer."

Brandy threw back her shoulders. "I know a thing or two about writers."

"Do tell."

"I know you always have several books working at one time." Brandy plunged ahead, undeterred by her professor's look of disgust. "I know you haven't released a book in about eighteen months, and the literary world is expecting your next book to be your best."

Regan fought back the urge to shake Brandy and tell her she didn't know squat about the publishing business or writers. She didn't know how much it hurt when your agent returned the book you had poured your heart and soul into with a note that read, "This would kill your career."

"I know you're filthy rich and don't need the money," Brandy said, still chattering. She knew Regan was miles away. "And I know for sure I'd like to go to bed with you."

"What? What the hell are you babbling about?" Regan stared at her.

"About your next book." Brandy's innocent look was laughable.

"The last thing you said." Regan glared at her.

"I was just checking to see if you were listening." Brandy stuffed a French fry into her mouth. "Apparently you were."

Chapter 3

"Professor Regan Shaw," Peyton King read from the list in her hand. She blushed slightly as her heart skipped a beat when a beautiful brunette stood and walked toward her.

Calm down, Peyton chided herself. *It's been too long.*

"Thank you, Professor." Peyton flashed her sweetest smile. "I appreciate you taking the time to speak with me."

"Did I have a choice?" Regan raised a perfectly arched brow.

"No, ma'am, you didn't. Please have a seat. This shouldn't take long."

Regan sat down and crossed her legs. Her skirt slid up to midthigh. Peyton couldn't pull her eyes away from the shapely legs. She blushed when her eyes locked with Regan's.

Peyton flipped open a file folder marked *Regan Shaw* and stared at the sheet of paper in it. "You were on a date with Coach Tucker last night?"

"Yes."

"Did you quarrel? Have a lover's spat?"

"Hardly," Regan huffed. "It was my one and only date with Coach Tucker. I assure you he was very much alive and falling-down drunk when I left the party."

"A fraternity party?"

"Yes."

"You left the party without him?"

"Yes."

"So, you did quarrel," Peyton insisted.

"Agent King, please stop putting tongue in my mouth." Regan scowled then blushed profusely when she realized what she had said. "Words. Please stop putting words in my mouth."

Peyton tried to suppress her smile as Professor Shaw struggled to recover from her faux pas.

"We didn't have words," Regan said. "He roofied me, and a student got me out of there."

"Drugged you? Coach Tucker drugged you?" Peyton was aghast. None of her prior interviewees had hinted at such activity on the part of the popular football coach.

"Professor Shaw, did anyone see him drug you?"

"The student who saved me. She also videoed him doing it." Regan pulled her cell phone from her purse, queued the video, and handed it to Agent King. "She sent me a copy. I didn't believe it at first either."

Peyton watched the video. It turned her stomach to think that the demure professor could be in an entirely different situation today, if not for her student.

"May I have a copy of this?"

"Of course." Regan reached for her cell phone.

"I'll just add my number to your contact list," Peyton said, smiling. "Is it okay if I send myself the video?"

Regan nodded.

"I assume you'll be around campus if I have any more questions for you." Peyton bit her bottom lip.

"I . . . uh, am I a suspect?" Regan asked.

"No, the question I have in mind is, would you join me for dinner?"

"I'm not sure I should," Regan hedged. "I was his last date and all and—"

"You can say 'no' if you wish. Although I've worked cases in this area, I'm not very familiar with the dining establishments. I thought you might be able to direct me to some good Chinese or Italian. It's not like I'm asking you out on a date. Since you were on a date with Coach Tucker, I'm assuming I'm not your type."

Regan laughed. "Of course. I'm just a little rattled. It's not every day one's date from the night before is found mutilated the next morning."

Peyton squinted at her. "How do you know he was mutilated?"

"I . . . I don't know. Wasn't it on the news this morning?"

"No, that's one of the things we're keeping out of the news." Peyton stood and walked around the room. She returned to stand in front of Regan. "That is something only the killer would have known."

Regan was quite aware of who had given her the information. Brandy had tossed it out to entice her to have lunch.

"Who gave you that information?" Agent King's flirty demeanor was gone. In its place was a no-nonsense FBI interrogator.

"One of my students, I think." Regan didn't want to implicate Brandy, but King's chameleon-like change had disoriented her.

"Which one?"

"Uh, um, I'm not certain," Regan sputtered. "I don't want to give you a wrong name."

"Why don't you give me a name, and I'll sort out whether or not it's wrong?"

"Grace Brandywine," Regan mumbled.

"Brandywine? Of course." Peyton snorted. "I've dealt with her before."

Chapter 4

Brandy watched the door of the building Peyton King had confiscated for her headquarters. She knew the FBI agent would be on campus until she caught the killer. King was tenacious. When she went after something, she always got it.

Brandy shifted her Beemer into drive and eased forward as Professor Shaw walked out of the building and started down the sidewalk. She pulled alongside the professor and rolled down the passenger-side window.

"Professor Shaw," Brandy called. "Want a ride?" She leaned over and pushed open the passenger-side door.

Regan hesitated then sat down in the car.

"You look like you've seen a ghost," Brandy noted. "Was Agent King that hard on you?"

"Brandy, I mentioned that Coach Tucker had been mutilated, and she went berserk. She demanded the name of the person who gave me that information."

"So, you threw me under the bus?" Brandy quipped. "Is that the reason you're white as a sheet?"

"I feel awful. I would never try to get you into trouble." Regan scowled. "I didn't tell her Joey told you. I'm certain she will interview you."

"I would expect her to interview me," Brandy said, wrinkling her nose. "I saved you from a fate worse than death. I'm sure she'll want to know about my relationship with you."

"We have no relationship," Regan scoffed. "I'm your English lit professor, and you're my student. That's it."

"Yes, that's all it'll ever be." Brandy's woeful tone made Regan look at her in time to see a sly smile cross her face.

"Brandy, sometimes you worry me."

"That's good." Brandy laughed out loud. "Where to for dinner, Professor?"

Pat Sawyer pulled the pocket file folder containing complaints filed on Coach Danny Tucker. She debated shredding the incriminating evidence she had gathered during her past ten years as the university police chief. Always acting the part of the southern country gentleman in public, Tucker was a vile human being in private. Now Tucker was dead, and there was no need to publicize her complicity in protecting the sexual predator.

Almost like clockwork, Pat received at least one, and sometimes two, complaints every month from coeds claiming that Tucker had raped them. Over 150 complaints had been filed against the winning coach. Some of the complaints had been so severe that Pat had instructed the victims to file a report with the Austin Police Department. Of course, the overworked APD had filled out a report and then informed the women they had to deal with the campus police force.

Pat was ashamed to admit that she had been forced to look the other way to keep her high-paying job as the police chief at the university. With over 500 commissioned police officers serving under her command, the UT System police department was the third-largest statewide police force in Texas, behind the Department of Public Safety and Texas Parks and Wildlife.

Tucker's death would allow her to wash her hands of the whole sordid mess and start over. She would never again compromise her ethics or standards. She tried not to think of what had led her down the dark, dismal road she had taken.

Heads would roll—including her own—if Tucker's file ever fell into the wrong hands. FBI Agent Peyton King would nail her to the wall if she ever found out the extent of her involvement.

A loud knock on her office door interrupted her debate, and she slid the file folder into the bottom drawer of her desk.

The door swung open, and Peyton King—in all her glory—charged into Pat's office.

"Come in, Agent King." Pat smirked. "How can I help you?"

"I need to see your file on Danny Tucker." King never wasted time on niceties.

Pat eyed King as one would a wild animal about to pounce. "What makes you think I have a file on Coach Tucker?" Pat watched King's eyes to see if she was just guessing or had hard evidence.

"I already have a search warrant." Peyton's twisted smile told Pat she was in trouble. She decided to call the agent's bluff.

"Go ahead and serve it. We've no secrets to hide. You'll find nothing, so I'd appreciate it if you'd keep your suspicions to yourself until you find something to justify them. May I see your search warrant?" Pat held out her hand.

"It's on its way," Peyton said.

"Then you won't mind waiting in the lobby until it gets here?" Pat stood and walked toward the door. "I'm trying to solve a murder case."

"You're off the case," Peyton barked. "It's my case now, and I don't have anyone's ass to protect or kiss."

Pat's eyes flashed. "Are you insinuating that I would look the other way when a crime is committed on campus?"

"It's been known to happen," Peyton said. "That's why universities shouldn't police themselves."

Pat shifted uneasily from one foot to the other and then opened the door for Agent King to leave her office.

King was as tenacious as a pit bull. She had arrived on campus two years ago when newly elected chancellor Katherine O'Brien had requested the FBI investigate the disappearance of four coeds. King had moved swiftly, calling in all the personnel at her disposal, and located the women in the boxcar of a train headed for Mexico.

Both O'Brien and King had been heralded for their quick action, while Pat had spent the following months wiping egg off her face for failing to take the disappearance of the four women seriously.

Pat's intercom buzzed. "Chief, Chancellor O'Brien is on the phone."

Pat groaned as she mentally prepared to deal with the Irish spitfire waiting on her line. She decided to let O'Brien take the lead. "Chief Sawyer."

"Good morning, Chief. Please fill me in on your investigation of Coach Tucker's death."

Katherine O'Brien never wasted words on cordiality when her university was under attack.

"The case is out of my hands, Chancellor. The FBI are confiscating my files as we speak."

"Cooperate with them," O'Brien ordered. "Don't make them get a search warrant. That will make it look like we have something to hide, and we do not. Do we?"

Pat gulped. "No, ma'am. We've nothing to hide."

"Good. That's what I wanted to hear."

When O'Brien ended the call, Pat leaned her head back against her chair and closed her eyes. She knew it was going to hit the fan when Peyton King found Tucker's file.

She looked around her office for a place to hide the incriminating files but decided King would find it no matter where she hid it. That would make her look worse than ever. She decided to hand the file over to Agent King. She pulled all the complaints from the file except the last four and hid them in another file.

Chief Sawyer opened her office door and stepped into the waiting room.

"We don't have our warrant yet," Agent King said, looking up from whatever she was typing into her cell phone.

"You don't need one." Pat tried to look amiable. "Chancellor O'Brien said to give you Coach Tucker's file." She held out the thin file.

"Is this all there is?" Peyton asked.

"Yes."

##

"FBI Agent Peyton King to see Chancellor O'Brien."

"Do you have an appointment?" the prissy secretary said.

"Seriously?" Peyton growled. "What part of FBI Agent did you not understand?"

The secretary jumped to her feet and led the way to the chancellor's office. "FBI Agent Peyton King to see you, ma'am."

Katherine O'Brien drew herself to her full height of five-seven and walked around her desk to greet Peyton. "Agent King. How may I help you?"

"I wanted to thank you for the phone call that resulted in this." Peyton handed Danny Tucker's file to the auburn-haired beauty.

Katherine motioned for Peyton to sit as she returned to the chair behind her desk. "It's very light. I was afraid there would be more."

"Four complaints," Peyton said. "It doesn't exactly jibe with this file from the Austin police." Peyton placed a file that was over two inches thick on Katherine's desk.

"She's withholding evidence," Katherine said.

Peyton shrugged. "We'll find it. My people are going through her office with a fine-tooth comb."

"May I see what you find before you release any information?" Katherine asked. "I have a feeling this is going to be bad."

"Sure," Peyton said as a smile cut across her face, "if you'll have dinner with me while I wait for my folks to finish. I have a video you need to see. I don't want you to be blindsided."

"That sounds like a fair trade," Katherine said. "Some place outside of town."

"I know just the place." Peyton opened the door and let her hand rest on the chancellor's lower back as she ushered her out of the office.

##

Harvard-educated Katherine O'Brien was the epitome of success. The University of Texas's first woman chancellor/president and the first Irish immigrant to head a comprehensive research university in the United States, her track record was incomparable.

The offices of chancellor and president had always been held by two different people, but Katherine had insisted she hold both positions to avoid the constant infighting that went on at the highest levels of academia.

Under Katherine's leadership, the Texas Advanced Computing Center had launched Stampede, one of the largest computing systems in the world for open science research, which had led to mind-boggling discoveries in DNA by compiling input from genetic scientists all over the world, allowing them to consult and work together on their theories. The computer system saved universities worldwide from wasting valuable research funds duplicating work already finished by other scientists.

Katherine's most lauded accomplishment recently was landing the National Science Foundation grant to establish an Engineering Research Center (ERC) for research into nanomanufacturing, the first ERC designated at UT Austin and only the second in Texas.

At forty-five, Katherine O'Brien was exactly where she wanted to be, but she knew things weren't as they seemed. She was aware that beneath her firm foundation, something was wrong. Something was always causing a ripple that never quite reached her. The Texas good-old-boy confederate always seemed to close ranks, preventing her from getting a clear view of seething problems. She feared that Coach Danny Tucker's death was only the tip of the iceberg.

Chapter 5

Regan downed her last bit of coffee and got out of her car. She had spent a restless night thinking about Danny Tucker and Brandy's insinuations that he had raped several coeds over the years. She debated on whether she should tell Agent King.

A movement in a shadowy alcove caught her attention. Joey Sloan had someone pinned against the wall and was running his hands up and down her sides. The girl wasn't trying to fight him off. *God, don't let it be Brandy.*

She started to call out Joey's name but decided she didn't really want to know who he was crawling all over. She hurried to her classroom.

As she slipped her transparency into the overhead projector, Brandy and Joey entered the room. They were arguing loudly.

"You promised you'd go home with me this weekend," Joey whined. "My folks are dying to meet you."

"It's too early to meet the parents," Brandy argued. "You know how parents get all excited when they think their offspring has landed a real catch."

"You are a real catch." Joey grinned as he placed his hands on her hips. "You're the only girl I want to catch."

"I bet you said that same thing to Loraine Munoz while you were banging her last night," Brandy huffed.

"I did not. Babe, you know you're the only girl I love."

"I'll think about it," Brandy promised, "but we sleep in separate rooms. And no sneaking into my room after your parents go to bed."

The bell rang, and they continued to argue.

"Miss Brandywine, Mr. Sloan, would it be possible for you to find a seat and let me teach my class? Or I can just give you both a zero for today."

Brandy shot Joey a disgusted look and took a chair on the front row.

Regan waited while her class settled down. "I know that there is a lot of speculation about Coach Tucker's death."

A murmur ran through the room.

"I'm going to give you Wednesday off to finish reading *A Midsummer Night's Dream*. I'll post your study guide tonight, so you will know what to expect on Friday's test."

Joey held up his hand. "Professor, do you grade on the bell curve?"

"Yes."

"What if we have a failing grade but all of our other grades are good? Will you allow us to throw out one grade every report period?"

"Yes," Regan replied. "Any other questions? If not, class is dismissed."

Regan wanted to avoid the SUB, so she walked across campus to the nearest kolache shop. She was surprised to see Brandy sitting alone in a booth, reading a textbook.

Brandy looked up and smiled as Regan entered. She motioned for Regan to join her. Regan stopped at the counter and ordered coffee and a kolache before walking over to the booth.

"I don't want to bother you," Regan said. "Obviously, you're studying."

"Spanish." Brandy shrugged. "I was just brushing up. I heard the professor is going to give us a pop quiz this afternoon and a test on Friday. She's not as nice as you."

"She probably wants to see the level of her students, so she will know where to start teaching."

"Duh, Professor, it's beginner's Spanish 101. You can't get much lower than that."

Regan was fluent in Spanish, but Brandy didn't need to know that.

"So, join me?" Brandy gestured toward the seat across from her, and Regan sat down.

"Has Agent King questioned you yet?" Regan asked as the server placed her order on the table.

"After lunch she's going to start interviewing students who had contact with Tucker. Joey is at the top of her list. He's captain of the football team."

"Does he know anything?" Regan couldn't hide her curiosity.

"Help me study for my Spanish test Friday, and I'll tell you." Brandy's impish grin made Regan's heart skip a beat. She couldn't pull her gaze away from her student's beautiful face.

"Okay," Regan mumbled.

"What time?" Brandy beamed.

"What time for what?" Regan furrowed her brow in confusion.

"What time should I come to your place, so you can help me study?" Brandy looked up at her through long lashes and smiled.

"I meant right now . . . right here."

"No can do." Brandy stuffed her Spanish book into her backpack and stood. "I have to get to class. See you tonight. Six at your place."

"You don't know my address," Regan replied.

"Yes, I do." Brandy waggled her eyebrows. "You can cook dinner for me, if you'd like."

Regan watched the girl as she sprinted out the door. *Oh God. What have I gotten myself into? The last thing I need is Grace Brandywine in my home.*

"Joey Sloan, is that correct?" Peyton King watched the cocky young man sprawled out in the chair in front of her desk. Joey Sloan certainly overpowered the room. "You're dating or going steady with Grace Brandywine?"

"Yes, ma'am." Joey grinned, his blue eyes twinkling.

"Did you see Coach Tucker Friday night?"

"Yes, ma'am."

"Do you know what time he left your fraternity party?"

"No, ma'am." Joey hung his head and blushed slightly.

"What time did you last see him at your party?"

"A little after midnight. He was falling-down drunk and groping the girls."

"Do you know the names of the girls he groped?" Peyton had a feeling there was a brain beneath Joey's mop of unruly blond hair.

"No, ma'am. It all sorta runs together in my mind."

"Your date was Grace Brandywine, right?"

"Yes, ma'am."

"Did you leave the party around midnight?"

"No, ma'am."

"If you were at the party, why didn't you see Coach Tucker leave?"

Joey's blush deepened. "I was upstairs with someone."

Ah, I think I've just caught Brandy and Professor Shaw in a lie, Peyton thought.

"Who were you with upstairs, Joey?"

"I'd rather not say." Joey ducked his head lower.

"I'd rather you did." Peyton's stern voice was flat. "We're you with Brandy?"

"Oh, no, ma'am. Brandy left early. She took Professor Shaw to her dorm. I later found out that Tucker had put drugs in the professor's wine."

"So, who was with you, Joey? Who can provide you an alibi for the time of Coach Tucker's murder?"

Joey locked gazes with Peyton. "Surely you don't think I killed Coach Tucker?"

"If you don't have an alibi, I'm going to assume—"

"Loraine Munoz," Joey blurted. "Please don't tell Brandy. She'll kill me."

Peyton shoved her notepad in front of Joey and handed him a pen. "Please write Miss Munoz's phone number on here. I'll need to call her to verify your alibi.

"Joey, who told you Coach Tucker was mutilated?"

"I really can't say, ma'am. Everyone was talking about it in the frat house when I came downstairs that morning."

"Did Miss Munoz come down with you?" Peyton asked.

"Yes, ma'am. We spent the night together. Please don't tell Brandy."

##

Regan had stopped by the supermarket on her way home. She had decided on spaghetti and meat sauce with French bread and salad. It was her go-to meal in a pinch, and her meat sauce was to die for, even if she did say so herself.

Her home was immaculate, and wine was already chilling in the refrigerator. She put on her sauce to simmer while she took a shower. Everything was ready when Brandy rang the doorbell.

Regan wiped her palms on her apron. She was surprised at her excitement. The thought of spending the evening with Brandy was appealing to her. She opened the door.

Regan couldn't hide her smile. It was obvious that Brandy had taken extra care to look her best for their dinner. *This is beginning to feel like a date,* Regan thought.

"Wow! You're so hot." Brandy scanned her professor from the top of her head to the tips of her painted toenails. "I love the way those jeans hug your hips, and that sweater accentuates all your gorgeous curves." Brandy ran the tip of her tongue along her lips, trying to moisten them.

Regan stared at the brazen young woman without moving. *This is a bad idea,* she thought.

"I brought wine." Brandy moved into the foyer and closed the door behind her. "I pegged you as a red wine drinker. Of course, it might not go with what you've prepared for dinner."

Regan looked at the bottle of Bordeaux. "This is a Chateau Lafite Rothschild Pauillac. You shouldn't be spending this kind of money for wine."

"I didn't." Brandy giggled. "I took it from my dad's wine cellar."

Regan cocked an eyebrow. "Why does that not surprise me?"

"So, will it go with our dinner?" Brandy's smile was infectious.

"Yes, it's perfect. Give me your jacket. I'll hang it up."

Brandy followed Regan into the kitchen. "If you'll give me a corkscrew, I'll open the wine and let it breathe while we get dinner on the table."

"Top drawer on your left," Regan directed as she stirred the spaghetti sauce.

"Oh my God!" Brandy sniffed the air. "That smells like heaven. How can you be so damn gorgeous and cook too?"

"Brandy, I don't think—"

"Sorry, Professor. I was way out of line. It won't happen again. I didn't mean anything by it. I just have a knack for saying what I'm thinking. If it's in my mind it comes out my mouth.

"Are we going to study Shakespeare the entire semester?" Brandy teased as she poured their wine.

"It is a course on Shakespeare," Regan reminded her. "Or I could give you a break and have the class do a report on *The Purloined Letter.*"

"No! No! Shakespeare is just fine. Don't give us Poe." Brandy groaned as if mortally wounded.

"You don't like Poe?"

"Some of his stuff is great. I mean, the story lines. Like *The Pit and the Pendulum, The Tell-Tale Heart,* and *The Masque of the Red Death.* Oh, and you must love *The Cask of Amontillado.* But *The Purloined Letter* is a trip to boredomville."

"Boredomville isn't even a word, Brandy."

"If Shakespeare could make up his own words, so can I," Brandy jested. "Honestly, Professor, if Poe submitted his writings to a publishing house today, they'd rubber stamp 'Rejected' on all of them."

Regan frowned. "I suppose you like *The Fall of the House of Usher* too?"

"It was interesting," Brandy said.

"Do you know what I find interesting?" Regan held out her glass for more wine. "That you're drawn to the ones where the main characters were obviously demented."

"So, what does that say about me?" Brandy made an evil face. "I could be a serial killer?"

"I doubt it." Regan chuckled. "You're way too pretty to . . ." She stopped as she realized she was flirting with Brandy.

"You think I'm pretty?" Brandy's eyes twinkled. "Are you attracted to me?"

"You're too pretty to be in your professor's home flirting with her." Regan shook her head. "Let's get this over with."

Regan stood and walked to the living room. "Where's your Spanish book? Do you have a study sheet?"

"I should go," Brandy said, heading toward the door. "Thank you for the best meal I've had in a long time and the most stimulating conversation I've ever had." She leaned down and kissed Regan on the cheek. "Good night, Professor."

##

The next day, Brandy tossed a thick envelope onto Peyton's desk.

"What's this?" Agent King asked.

"Just in case you haven't found them yet, it's over a hundred reasons why Coach Tucker was murdered and that many people with motives."

King rolled her eyes. "I picked these up yesterday. What compelled you to get them?"

"I don't want you looking at Joey for Tucker's death." Brandy sat down in the chair across from the FBI agent. "He told me you really grilled him on that point."

"I've marked your boyfriend off my list," Peyton said. "It seems he has an airtight alibi."

"Let me guess. Loraine Munoz?" Brandy snorted.

Peyton nodded. "She swears they were awake all night."

"Yeah, Joey could do that." Brandy chortled. "He has the stamina of a racehorse."

"Do you know anyone who was molested by Tucker but didn't report it?"

"If I did, I wouldn't tell you." Brandy's eyes darkened. "The bastard got what he deserved. If he'd raped Professor Shaw, I would have killed him myself."

Chapter 6

Pat Sawyer paid visits to three people: Athletic Director Bob Radford, Chief of Staff and Executive Senior Associate Athletics Director Robin Chase, and Assistant Head Coach Clint Brand. She had one message for all of them: "Keep your mouths shut and swear you knew nothing about Tucker's activities."

The problem was that all three of them not only knew about Tucker's escapades, they had participated in some of them. If one of them went down, they all went down, taking Pat with them.

Pat sat in her vehicle and waited as Peyton King's officers went through her files. She wondered if they would be there all night. She had hidden the files on Radford, Chase, and Brand, along with Danny Tucker's.

Maybe that wasn't the smartest thing to do, she thought. *If they find one of them, they will have all of them.*

It was after midnight when King's agents called it a night and locked up the police chief's office. The customary yellow tape declaring, "Police line. Do not cross," crisscrossed the door.

Pat waited until she was certain everyone was gone and then entered her office. She stood on her office chair to slide back the ceiling tile hiding the files and breathed a sigh of relief when she saw them.

She stuffed the files under her uniform shirt and left the office. She drove the fifteen minutes to her home and pulled her car into the garage. Only then did she feel safe enough to remove the files from under her clothing.

She pitched the files on her kitchen island and pulled a cold beer from the fridge. She sat down and began reading the reports.

The earlier reports were of mild misconduct—fondling, groping, exposure of genitals—nothing she considered dangerous. When the girls had reported an incident, she'd merely taken their reports and assured them the perpetrators would be punished. She'd called the coaches involved and warned them about the complaints. The football team had been on track to win the national championship. Pat knew she would lose her job if she rocked that boat.

Danny Tucker had reported directly to the university president. There had been no doubt in Pat's mind who would lose in that confrontation.

When Chancellor O'Brien had merged the positions of chancellor and president, Tucker had continued to report to the president. Pat had often heard him curse because O'Brien questioned the behavior of his team and his coaches.

"They're males," Tucker had hooted. "If you suppress their natural instincts, you suppress them on the football field."

O'Brien had made headlines and a few enemies when she expelled members of the team for criminal sexual conduct. Overestimating his popularity, Tucker had challenged the chancellor in public. He had lost the confrontation and almost lost his job.

It was no secret that O'Brien would have loved to fire the aggressive football coach but refrained from doing so because she knew the backlash she'd get.

Pat separated the files into two categories: rape and assault. Often, the coeds had fought back and escaped being raped but had been badly beaten.

The more she reviewed the files, the more disgusted she became with herself. *How could I let this happen on my watch?*

But she knew how it had happened. Sadie had happened. Danny Tucker had introduced them at a pep rally. Blonde, beautiful, and built like a brick outhouse, Sadie had steamrolled Pat and provided her a weekend she'd never forget. She'd also provided Tucker a video that would ruin Pat's career.

Pat still remembered the cold fear that had embraced her when Tucker dropped the video by her office. "I thought you might enjoy reliving this." His cruel smile had turned her stomach. She knew what it was without looking. *How could I have been so stupid?* she thought for the thousandth time.

The video could only be classified as hard-core porn. They had experimented with every toy on the market, in every position. Being a lesbian was one thing, but watching their sex acts with a little S&M thrown in, including up-close shots, was disgusting.

The football staff had continued to molest whatever gender they preferred, and Pat had looked the other way. Things had almost come to a head the year before O'Brien accepted the chancellor/president position.

A celebration for the football team and athletic staff had resulted in a lot of drinking, drugs, and sex. Jamie Wright, one of the girls attending the party, had been reported missing the next afternoon.

The girl's roommate had filed the report. Pat could still remember the wave of dread that had washed over her when the roommate informed her that her friend had been at the athletic celebration the night before.

Three days later, the girl's body had been dragged from a stream that ran behind some campus apartments. The autopsy had been the thing nightmares were made of. Pat shuddered as she pulled the report from her file. Numerous men had engaged in sex with the girl—probably against her will. Cause of death had been asphyxiation. Semen DNA had been matched to Tucker and three football players. All four men swore the girl had left the party under her own power and that she had willingly engaged in sex with them.

Pat still recalled the faces of the girl's parents when they were informed of her death. She hadn't told them the results of the forensic report, only that their daughter had been strangled by persons unknown.

The girl's roommate had gone to the *Austin Statesman* and given them everything she knew. The local police department had been called in, and the parents had sued the university.

Tucker had stormed into her office. "You've got to fix this! You can make this go away. Do it quickly, or your little video goes to the president. He'd love something to take the heat off the athletic program."

Pat had revisited the spot where Jamie Wright's body had been pulled from the stream but found nothing. It was obvious the girl's body had been dumped.

A local homeless man had followed her to the water's edge. "Whatcha doing?"

"I'm looking for a student," Pat had replied.

"Pretty, dark-haired girl?" the bum had asked.

"Yeah. Did you see her down here?" She'd pushed on her cell phone to record their exchange.

"Yep," he'd said with a snicker. "We wrestled."

"She wrestled with you?"

"Yep."

"I bet she whipped you, didn't she?" Pat had baited him.

"Nah, I won," he'd said, flashing a toothless grin.

"Did you choke her?"

"Sure did. She started screaming and yelling for the police," the derelict had said. "I had to shut her up, but she got away from me and ran, so I hid." Pat had turned off her cell phone. She had enough to pin the murder on the vagrant.

"She was alive when you ran?" Pat had asked.

"Yeah, but some big guys took her. She struggled to get away from them, but they shoved her into their car."

Pat pulled another beer from her fridge, unscrewed the top, and took a long pull on it. *The vagabond's better off in prison than living on the streets,* she reasoned as she recalled how she had edited the recording she gave the police to implicate the man in the coed's murder.

She wondered if her job was worth her soul.

Chapter 7

Regan read her email as she waited for her class to be seated and the bell to ring. The email from the chancellor's office received her immediate attention. Katherine O'Brien was hosting a formal reception for all the department heads to kick off homecoming week at the university.

The email directly under O'Brien's was from the chairman of the English department, Matthew Bolen. "Please do me the honor of accompanying me to the chancellor's department head reception?"

Regan immediately replied, "Yes, I'd be delighted to."

Twenty-one years her senior, Matthew had been her first English professor at UT. They had established a friendship that had lasted over the years. Regan had been his beard on many occasions. The chancellor's reception would be one such occasion.

"I'll call you tonight," Matthew emailed back.

"Why do you go with the old guys?" Brandy muttered.

Regan jumped and quickly closed her laptop. "Miss Brandywine, it isn't polite to read other people's mail. Why are you looking over my shoulder anyway?"

"I wanted to see what you were doing." Brandy's honesty was both refreshing and disarming.

Regan suppressed a smile. "Please be seated. I have a class to teach."

Regan addressed her students. "How many of you finished your reading assignment?" Everyone raised a hand.

"Good." Regan surveyed her class. "Shakespeare's use of symbolism is well known in academic circles. Who can tell me what symbolizes absurd fickleness in *A Midsummer Night's Dream?*"

The silence from the class caused Regan to frown. "No one? What did you get from reading *A Midsummer Night's Dream?*"

"Bored," a voice called from the back of the room.

Brandy swiveled around in her chair to see if it was Joey being a smart ass, but she couldn't spot him.

"What about you, Brandy? Any thoughts on Shakespeare's symbols?"

"The love potion," Brandy declared. "Just like love does in real life, it made asses of all of them."

"Excellent," Regan said. "Do you have a favorite line from the play?"

"Yes. It was stated by the fellow who was turned into a jackass. He said, 'Reason and love keep little company.'" Brandy held Regan's gaze as she recited the line. "Do you believe that, Professor?"

Regan couldn't pull her gaze from Brandy's. She couldn't control the heat she felt sweeping her body. She shook her head, breaking the trance induced by Brandy's emerald eyes.

"If you haven't read *A Midsummer Night's Dream,* make sure you do. You will be tested over it when our class meets again," Regan instructed. "Class dismissed."

Regan shoved her papers into her computer bag and fished her keys from her purse.

"Coffee?" Brandy made the two-syllable word sound like a seductress's enchantment.

"No, I . . . um, have things to do."

Brandy caught her by the arm. "Regan, have I done something wrong? Are you angry with me?"

"No, I'm not angry with you, Brandy. I truly do have a lot to do."

"Can we have dinner? My treat," Brandy said. "To pay you back for the delicious meal you cooked for me."

"I . . . I can't tonight. I have a date."

"Oh! Maybe another time, then."

Regan couldn't bear the hurt in Brandy's voice. "It's the chancellor's reception."

Brandy frowned. "That's just for VIPs and department heads."

"I'm a plus-one," Regan explained.

Brandy raised her eyebrows.

"Dr. Bolen," Regan added. "Chairman of the English department."

Before she could reply, Joey charged into the room. "Brandy! I've been waiting for you. I was afraid something happened to you."

"Joey Sloan, you skipped my class," Regan said, challenging her student. "Why?"

"I . . . uh . . . we gotta go. We're going to be late." Joey grabbed Brandy's arm and pulled her toward the door.

"I told you I can't go to your frat party tonight," she insisted as Joey dragged her out the door.

Chapter 8

Regan pulled a stunning dress from her closet. The black, fitted evening gown was perfect for the chancellor's reception. It hugged her curves and showed just enough cleavage to make one's mouth water. The material shimmered in the light from her dressing table.

She finished her makeup and was applying lipstick when the doorbell rang. Matthew was always prompt.

She grabbed her clutch and walked to the front door. She liked going out with Matthew. He was tall enough for her to wear high heels.

"Oh, be still my heart," Matthew said, whistling as he appraised his date. "Lord help you, woman. If I weren't gay, you'd be in trouble."

Regan laughed out loud. "You've always looked handsome in your tux, and you've always been so good for my ego."

He nodded and held out his arm for her.

##

"How does it feel to be back in the classroom?" Matthew asked as they fastened their seatbelts.

"Interesting," Regan said. "Students are more forward than in my day."

"Yes, it's a little frightening." He laughed. "They treat sex so casually that they will offer anything for an *A*."

"I haven't been propositioned yet, but I have noticed how freely they exchange favors with one another, like it's no big deal."

"It's still a big deal to me," Matthew said. "I don't take relationships lightly."

"Speaking of relationships . . . how is Phillip?"

"Wonderful as ever," Matthew exclaimed. "He'll be at the reception. He's chairman of the engineering department. He wants us to have you to dinner soon."

"Let me get things under control, and I'd love to. Coach Tucker's murder has caused an uproar on campus, and my students are having trouble settling down."

"I understand you were his date," Matthew noted.

"Yes. He tried to drug me. One of my students saw him and took me away from the party."

"It's a nasty business, athletics." Matthew shook his head. "There's a different attitude now. All that matters is winning. It's not like it was when Darrell Royal was coach.

"The new philosophy is win at any price. Money, drugs, cars, women—the athletic directors will use anything to attract and keep the best players. Of course, they partake of the goodies too."

"What about Chancellor O'Brien? I understand she expelled some top players for molesting coeds."

"She's doing her best, but they keep things from her," Matthew explained. "She's in the loop in other departments, but athletics is a different animal."

Matthew pulled his car to the curb, where valets rushed to open their doors. "Professor Shaw," the valet said, "you look . . . amazing."

"Thank you, Nathan," she said as she recognized her student. "You look very dashing in your tux." The young man blushed, hung his head, and stopped just short of doing an "aww shucks" routine.

##

Matthew was the perfect date. He steered her around the room, introducing her to anyone he deemed important. She soon had a following of groupies as people realized she was *the* Regan Shaw, author of many top-sellers, with eight award-winning movies based on her books.

"I forget what a celebrity you are." Matthew laughed as he handed her a glass of champagne.

Regan felt it, the shift in the air, the electricity that filled the room. She turned to face the ballroom entrance as attendees made a path for the most handsome couple she'd ever seen. The man was over six feet tall, with broad shoulders that tapered to a narrow waist and hips. His hair was the same glorious golden color as his date's. He smiled. He knew he had the prettiest woman in the room on his arm.

Regan was light-headed. Probably because she had stopped breathing. The woman wore a white, fitted evening dress like her own. It was cut a little lower, exposing more cleavage than Regan dared. The slit up the side opened and closed with each step she took, treating onlookers to slim, shapely legs.

The couple disappeared as the crowd closed around them, and everyone began talking at once.

"Who is he?" Regan said, nearly choking on the words.

"Gorgeous, isn't he?" Matthew giggled. "That is Grayson—"

"You must be Professor Shaw." The man materialized from the crowd and lightly touched Regan's elbow.

Regan turned to face Grace Brandywine and her date.

"Professor,"—Brandy's eyes twinkled with mischief—"I had no idea you would be here."

It took Regan a few seconds to find her voice. "I didn't expect to see you here. I see you're a plus-one also."

"Sort of." Brandy wrinkled her nose. "I'd like to introduce my dad, Grayson Brandywine."

Grayson held out a well-manicured hand to Regan and smiled. His green eyes were as spellbinding as his daughter's. "Brandy has told me so much about you. She loves your class."

"Yes, Brandy is a lover of Shakespeare," Regan said as Matthew gouged her in the back. "May I introduce my date, Professor Matthew Bolen. Matthew is the chairman of our English department."

The four exchanged pleasantries for a few minutes before one of Regan's groupies found her.

"I knew I had this in my car," the woman gushed. "Would you mind autographing it, Professor?" She held up Regan's latest—and last—novel.

Regan smiled and sat down at an empty table to sign the book. She looked up as Matthew and Grayson walked away.

"They went to get us fresh drinks," Brandy informed her. "Regan, you're gorgeous. I mean, I've always thought you beautiful, but you're breathtaking."

Back at you, Regan thought, stealing the vernacular of the snowflake generation. "You're quite stunning too." *So stunning I'm having trouble breathing.*

"I thought you were looking for a dinner partner tonight," Regan managed to say.

"Just you." Brandy smiled and waved at someone across the room. "I would have kicked Dad to the curb if you'd said yes to my dinner invitation."

"Your father is extremely handsome. His hair is the same color as yours." Regan laughed. "I had assumed your hair was the product of a very skillful hairdresser."

"Either that or Dad and I use the same beauty salon." Brandy's impish grin made Regan laugh.

"I'm betting on au naturel."

"You'd win the bet," Brandy assured her.

The men returned with their champagne and joined them at the table. Chancellor O'Brien was working the room, making a point to speak to everyone. Matthew and Grayson stood as she approached their table.

"Dr. Shaw," O'Brien said as she caught Regan's hand between her own. "It's a pleasure to have someone of your stature on our faculty. You have brought the university a lot of good press and increased recognition for our creative writing curriculum. I'm an avid fan and can't wait to read your next book."

Don't hold your breath on that book, Regan thought. "Thank you, I'm very proud to be a part of the faculty. You have done some amazing things for the university."

"Katherine, there are some people here you need to meet," Grayson said, touching her arm. "May I introduce you?"

"Of course." She linked her arm through Grayson's. "Thank you for coming tonight," she said to them before turning away.

"Go mingle, Matthew. I'm going to sit and visit with Brandy."

"Let's get out of here," Brandy whispered once they were alone. "I have my own car. I met Dad here."

Regan frowned. "I can't do that. I can't walk off and leave Matthew."

"He's found the one he wants to be with," Brandy whispered in her ear. Her warm breath sent shivers down Regan's spine.

"Brandy, I'm closer to your father's age than yours," Regan said, sighing. "You're my student. I can't—"

"How old are you?" Brandy demanded.

"Thirty-six," Regan answered. "Fourteen years older than you."

"You checked on my age?"

"I was checking your academic record and noticed you are twenty-two"

"Dad's forty-eight," Brandy volunteered. "Would you date someone older than you?"

"Yes, of course."

"Dad's twelve years older than you. Would you find that acceptable?"

"Yes."

"You're fourteen years older than me," Brandy pointed out. "I find that acceptable, but—"

"You're also a woman." Regan scowled. "I don't find that acceptable."

Brandy jumped back as if Regan had slapped her. "I thought you were a lesbian."

"You thought wrong," Regan snapped. She stood and searched the room for Matthew.

"Looks like your date went home with his friend," Brandy huffed. "Come on, Professor. I'll give you a lift home."

Before they could leave, Robin Chase, the women's athletic director, pulled out a chair at their table. She was taller than most men, with a muscular physique and short, black hair. "Brandy, where's Joey?" she asked.

"He didn't receive an invitation," Brandy said with a smirk.

Robin looked around the room. "Who's your date? I can't believe he'd be fool enough to leave you unattended."

Brandy was slow to answer. "I'm Dad's plus-one."

Regan was surprised to see Brandy being cautious. Then she noticed Robin had placed her hand on Brandy's leg where her dress fell away, exposing her thigh.

"Are you and Joey coming to the team's beer bust tomorrow night?" Robin asked.

Brandy furrowed her brow. "I won't be there. I have tutoring."

"Ridiculous." Robin pulled her chair closer to Brandy and slipped her arm across the back of Brandy's chair. The girl stiffened. "Everyone knows you're a genius."

"Except in English," Regan said, jumping into the conversation. "Unfortunately, tomorrow night is the only time I have available to tutor Miss Brandywine. As you know, homecoming week requires all of the faculty's time."

Robin scanned Regan as if seeing her for the first time. "Well, aren't you something?"

"Umm . . . and more your age," Regan muttered.

Brandy stood. "Come on, Professor. You promised me a ride home since my father has found more interesting company."

"I can take you home," Robin volunteered.

"I've already had the valet pull my car around," Regan said. The lie slipped easily through her lips. "It was nice to meet you, Miss Chase." *How appropriate is that name?*

Robin caught Brandy's arm. "You really should accompany Joey to more of the team's parties. It would help his career." She leered at Brandy.

"I doubt that Joey's career needs my help," Brandy hissed. "He's pretty spectacular on his own. He does hold the quarterback passing record in the division." She jerked her arm from Robin's grasp and caught Regan's hand. "Let's go, Professor."

Regan was surprised to see Brandy's BMW pulled in front of the valet's desk.

"I held it here for you, Brandy," Nathan said.

"You're the best, Nat." Brandy palmed a tip to the young man as he opened the door for Regan.

Brandy laughed as she pulled away from the curb. "Who would have guessed that Robin Chase would be my wingman?"

Regan couldn't keep from laughing at the young woman. "You're incorrigible."

"Thank you for saving me from the viper." Brandy's solemn expression surprised Regan.

"What's going on, Brandy?"

"I'm not sure. I know Joey is not happy that everyone keeps pressuring him to bring me to their activities."

Regan placed her hand on Brandy's arm. "Please be careful. There is something terribly wrong happening on this campus."

"I know."

"Brandy, I find your generation so confusing. You're practically engaged to Joey, but I know you're attracted to me."

"Yeah, I'm not too good at hiding that," Brandy admitted. "You're just so damn gorgeous and intelligent and nice. I find that I'm happiest when I'm around you. You engage my mind and my fantasies."

"Hmm. I would like to be friends with you. You challenge me mentally. No student has ever told me Edgar Allen Poe was boring and validated the statement."

Brandy pulled her car into Regan's driveway. She was at Regan's door as it opened.

Brandy snorted. "So, all you're interested in is my mind?"

"You do intrigue me." Regan smiled. "But I'm not—"

Brandy caught Regan's face between her hands and kissed her. Of its own volition, Regan's body melted against the other woman, basking in her softness, engulfed by her scent. She let her arms slip around Brandy's waist and pulled her closer, as Brandy deepened the kiss and wrapped her arms around Regan. *Dear God, this feels so good*, Regan thought.

Brandy's tongue eased its way past Regan's lips and pushed between her teeth. Regan pulled her closer as their tongues met for the first time.

Breathless, Brandy released Regan. "You're not what, Professor?" she murmured, a sly grin slipping across her face.

"Not going to invite you in." Regan gently pushed her away. "Good night, Brandy." She hurried up the walk to the security of her home.

Regan closed the door and leaned against it, reliving Brandy's kiss. No one had ever kissed her like that.

Chapter 9

Regan read the text from her agent. "Have you come to your senses?" She shook her head as she deleted the message.

She was recognized internationally as a top-notch writer and had many best sellers and awards to prove it. Eight of her novels had been made into movies, and her name was on two television series. She felt that she had earned the right to write and publish whatever moved her. Unfortunately, her agent and publisher didn't agree with her. She was still smarting from their refusal to publish her last novel.

"Publishers don't like genre hoppers," her agent had informed her.

"J. K. Rowling changed genres," Regan had pointed out. "Moving from young adult to murder mysteries."

"She also changed her name," her agent reminded her. Rowling's adult books were written under the name of Robert Galbraith.

Regan didn't want to change her name. She had spent a lifetime making the name Regan Shaw synonymous with good murder mysteries. She wasn't going to hide behind a nom de plume just because someone didn't like her subject matter.

She stared at her laptop screen. *This is the book I was destined to write*, she thought.

A knock on her office door broke her reverie. "Come in," she said, closing her laptop.

"I hoped I'd find you here." Brandy bounced into her office. "Are you going to the bonfire tonight?"

"I thought the bonfire was discontinued years ago." Regan wrinkled her brow, trying to recall how long ago the practice had been abandoned.

"It's not school sanctioned," Brandy said as she sat on the edge of Regan's desk. "The Greeks sponsor it. All the sororities and fraternities make it happen."

"Let me guess," Regan scoffed. "It's just another excuse for a big, drunken shindig."

Brandy grinned. "It's more than that. There's also a lot of food and dancing and gratuitous sex."

"I believe I'll pass on it. Surely you aren't going?"

"I wouldn't miss it for the world," Brandy chirped. "I love to dance and eat, and who knows . . . maybe I'll get lucky."

"As if you have to try." Regan shook her head in disbelief. "Joey hangs all over you every chance he gets."

"Who said anything about Joey?" Brandy wiggled her eyebrows. "There's someone else I want to be gratuitous with."

"Oh, I see." Regan looked down at the top of her desk. Her stomach lurched when she thought about Brandy having sex with anyone . . . else.

Where the hell did that come from? she thought.

Brandy scooted along the side of the desk until she was beside Regan. "Go to the bonfire with me, Professor."

"I . . . don't think that's a good idea." Regan cleared her throat.

"If you don't go with me, I'll have Joey crawling all over me. If you're with me, he'll behave in public."

Regan couldn't stop her head from nodding.

"Awesome!" Brandy clapped her hands and leaned down to hug Regan as the brunette looked up. For the briefest, electrifying moment, their lips met.

Brandy jumped back as if she had been burned. "Professor, I'm so sorry. I didn't mean to . . . I only meant to hug you. I'm so—"

"I know it was an accident," Regan said. "No harm done." *Except that now I can't get the taste of your lips out of my mind.*

"I'll pick you up at six." Brandy backed toward the door. "Thank you for . . . everything."

##

Regan knew she was courting trouble. She couldn't recall anyone who had attracted her like Grace Brandywine. Brandy was beginning to visit her dreams. *The last thing I need is a professor/student scandal.*

"Professor?" Agent King said as she stuck her head into Regan's office. "I was hoping I'd catch you."

Peyton King made Regan uneasy. She could never tell if King was making polite conversation or covertly questioning her. She motioned for King to have a chair and waited for the agent to state her business.

Peyton looked around Regan's office. It had a temporary feel to it. Nothing about it was personal. No photos, no knickknacks that belonged to Professor Shaw.

Peyton smiled. "I know this is a bit like a groupie, but I'd be very appreciative if you'd autograph your last book. It's my favorite." She pulled a copy of Regan's latest published novel, *Deadly Romance,* from her jacket pocket.

Regan couldn't hide her delight. She loved autographing her books for fans. She pulled her favorite pen from her purse. "What would you like me to say?"

"It's for a friend." Peyton blushed. "A special friend. Would you mind writing, 'The world is perfect when two hearts beat as one?'"

Regan tilted her head and appraised the FBI agent. "I never pegged you as a romantic," she teased.

"Some people can change your life forever." Peyton chuckled.

"Yes. Yes, they can." Regan recalled Brandy's soft lips brushing against hers. "Unfortunately, it's not always for the better. Are you going to the bonfire tonight?"

"Yes! Chancellor O'Brien asked me to go, just to make certain everything is under control," Peyton said. "Are you going?"

"Yes, Grace Brandywine and I are going. I think Joey Sloan is going with us. Why don't you join us?"

"Thank you for the invite. I'll meet you there. I have to stay until the last dying ember," Peyton said, laughing. "I'm sure you'll want to leave before I do."

"Are you getting any closer to catching Coach Tucker's killer?" Regan asked.

Peyton frowned. "No, but at least no one else has died. The heathens calmed down for a while, but homecoming week has fired them up. Three cases of rape have been filed this week."

"Doesn't Chief Sawyer handle campus lawbreakers?"

"She's supposed to, but she seems more intent on protecting the perpetrators than prosecuting them. I don't know why Katherine . . . uh, Chancellor O'Brien keeps her."

"I'm sure the chancellor has her reasons," Regan said. "She seems extremely capable."

"She is that," Peyton said. "It would help me tremendously if she'd give me more insight into her employees."

"I heard she gave you complete access to all personnel files."

"True," Peyton mumbled, "but access to files and her thoughts are two different things."

A bell rang, setting off a stampede of students. "They're out for the day." Regan laughed. "Time to get ready for the bonfire."

Chapter 10

"What do you think?" Brandy beamed as they parked in the field half a mile away from the bonfire. They could see the pile of dead trees, old barns that had been bulldozed, and planks stacked high, waiting to light up the night sky.

"I think it's going to get hot here tonight," Regan said.

"All the more reason to drink beer." Brandy grinned.

"You're not going to ply me with liquor tonight, are you?"

"Would it help my cause?" Brandy's impish smile made Regan look away from her glorious green eyes.

I could lose my soul in those eyes, she thought. She stumbled over a clod of dirt in the field, and Brandy caught her.

"Hold my hand," Brandy said, "at least until we get out of this field. It's pretty uneven."

Regan welcomed the closeness of the other woman. Brandy's hand was strong and her steps confident. *She is amazing,* Regan thought.

The half-mile hike over uneven terrain passed quickly as the two discussed campus events, laughed, and teased. They clung to each other to keep from falling in the plowed field. Brandy continued to hold Regan's hand when they reached the caliche-covered area that served as a hard surface for the partiers. Temporary bleachers were set up a safe distance from the bonfire.

Food trucks lined the perimeter of the area, and music blared from a dozen different directions. It looked like half the student body was there, and it wasn't even dark yet.

"Are you hungry?" Brandy asked hopefully.

"Starved," Regan replied. "What do you suggest?"

"There's Tex-Mex, pizza, Italian, Chinese, wraps, tacos, cheese fries, Subway . . . you name it."

"You choose." Regan laughed. Brandy's enthusiasm was contagious. Regan was enjoying herself.

"So much great food, so little time," Brandy said, groaning as if mortally wounded. "How about a Subway? I'm really not a big fan of the greasier fare."

"Subway sounds great." Regan tugged on the blonde's hand, leading her toward the Subway truck.

"Why don't you grab us a seat at one of the picnic tables?" Brandy suggested. "I'll battle this crowd for food."

Regan reluctantly released Brandy's hand and found a small picnic table away from the milling crowd. Half an hour later, Brandy joined her bearing Subways, chips, and cold drinks.

"Wow! It's a madhouse up there. I'm glad we arrived early."

They'd barely gotten started when they heard Joey hailing his girlfriend as he and another man approached them. "Hey, Brandy! I thought you weren't coming tonight."

"You convinced me I should support you," Brandy said as she stood and kissed his cheek.

"Y'all know Coach Clint Wayne, the assistant head coach." Joey took a huge bite out of Brandy's Subway.

"Hey, get off my sub." Brandy wrestled her sandwich away from him. "Go get your own. The truck's right over there."

"You never give me anything anymore," Joey groused as he looked around for the truck. "Want me to get you another one since I ate half of yours?"

"Yeah, that would be the gentlemanly thing to do," Brandy scoffed.

"Get me a couple too," Coach Wayne said. "And a couple bags of chips and a beer." He didn't offer Joey any money to pay for his order.

Brandy pulled a crumpled twenty from her pocket. "Here, I'll pay for my own." She glared at Wayne, who ignored her hint.

Joey grinned at Brandy as he cast a sidelong glance at Wayne. He leaned forward and whispered in her ear. "He's a cheapskate."

"Joey Sloan," Brandy slapped his arm. "Is that all you think about?" She pretended he'd whispered something risqué to her.

Joey laughed out loud and trotted to the food truck.

"You coming to the beer blast after the bonfire?" Wayne asked the two women.

"No, I have to prepare a test for class," Regan answered.

"And I have to study for her test." Brandy snickered.

"You're on the faculty here?" Wayne said as he gaped at Regan. "You look more like a student."

"Coach Wayne, this is Professor Shaw," Brandy said.

"You're the one Tucker roofied," Wayne snorted. "I can understand why."

Fury flashed through Regan. "Seriously? You think it's easier to roofie a woman than to ask her permission?"

"Nah, I didn't mean that," Wayne drawled. "I meant I could understand why he wanted to get it on with you."

Regan stood. "Honestly, Coach Wayne, the more we talk, the more I dislike you. It pains me to think you influence young men." She stomped away, disappearing into the crowd.

"Neanderthal," Brandy snapped at Wayne before sprinting after Regan.

"Where'd the girls go?" Joey asked when he returned from the food truck a few minutes later. "I got Brandy a sub."

"Just more for us." Wayne snarled as he tore into the wrappers.

"Regan. Regan!" A firm hand wrapped around Regan's upper arm. "Don't let that caveman ruin our evening," Brandy said as she turned the professor to face her.

"Where in God's name did the university find these misogynistic bastards?" Regan railed. "This is like stepping back into the Stone Age."

"Men's attitudes don't change," Brandy huffed. "They just learn to hide them better. Present a little better façade."

"Your father isn't like that."

"No, but Dad was raised by two women. My grandmother and her lover. He is much more genteel than most men. I suppose that's why my mother chose him."

"Your mother wasn't with him at the reception."

"We lost her in a boating accident when I was twelve. Talk about trial by fire. I'm sure my dad thought the world was coming to an end. I was so angry that she was gone. Hurt that she would leave me." Tears began to trickle down Brandy's cheeks.

"What did he do?" Regan comforted her, pulling Brandy into her arms.

"The same thing you're doing." Brandy sniffed. "He just held me and let me cry or curse until I finally got it out of my system and realized how lucky I was to have a father who loved me."

Brandy dried her eyes on her shirtsleeve. "We must go find Joey. They'll get him into trouble if we don't."

They walked back to the picnic table, but Joey and Wayne were gone.

"Let's split up," Brandy suggested. "You start on this end of the bleachers, and I'll start at the far end. We'll meet in the middle. If you spot Joey, call me on my cell phone. Don't try to get him to go with you. I don't know how much he's had to drink. He can get belligerent when he drinks."

It took Regan thirty minutes to spot Joey under the bleachers. He was throwing up. Clint Wayne and Robin Chase were with him. *Too much to drink*, Regan thought.

Regan called Brandy's phone, but it went to voicemail. She left a message describing where they were and then walked toward the three.

"Is he okay?" Regan asked as she approached.

"He's fine," Wayne grumbled. "We'll take care of him. He's had a little too much to drink." He began to lead Joey away as Chase stepped in front of Regan to prevent her from following.

"Joey's fine," Robin Chase's feral grin didn't convince Regan that Joey was fine.

"Maybe I should take him home," Regan offered, although she had no idea where home was. She just wanted to get Joey out of their clutches.

"Maybe you should mind your own business, Professor." Chase continued blocking her way.

"He's my student," Regan countered. "He is my business." She sidestepped Chase and moved around her.

Chase caught Regan's arm and twisted it behind her back. She overpowered Regan, pushing her deeper under the bleachers. She shoved Regan's arm higher up her back, causing the brunette to scream out in pain.

"You're hurting me," Regan howled. "Let me go."

"Oh, I think you like it." Chase's hot breath burned Regan's ear as she shoved her hard against the crossbars supporting the bleachers and used her body to pin Regan against them. "I've got something else you'll like too." She shoved her hand under Regan's sweater and reached around to grope her breast before snaking her hand into Regan's jeans.

"Help me! Someone help me!" Regan screamed but knew she couldn't be heard above the cheering crowd who had begun to stomp their feet on the bleachers. The roar was deafening. She knew no one would save her from Robin Chase.

Robin's head snapped sideways from the force of the blow as Brandy hit her with her fist. Brandy hit her again, and Robin crumpled to the ground. She continued to attack with the fury of a wild animal, kicking Robin over and over.

It took Regan a minute to realize what was happening. She caught Brandy's hand and pulled her away from the body of Robin Chase.

"Stop, Brandy," Regan commanded. "Stop! You'll kill her."

"I want to kill her," Brandy growled. "She was trying to rape you."

"But she didn't. Thanks to you, I'm fine."

"We need to find Joey," Regan yelled above the noise. "They gave him something that made him throw up. Probably a drug or something. Wayne has him."

Chase moaned, and Brandy kicked her again.

"The athletic department has a motor coach on the other side of the food trucks. They probably took him there." Brandy caught Regan's hand. "Watch for security as we go. We'll need all the help we can get."

"Go on without me," Regan instructed. "I think Robin cracked my rib or something. It hurts to breathe."

"I'm not leaving you alone," Brandy said. "We'll take it easy."

They walked hand in hand past the food trucks and headed for the motor coach with LONGHORN FOOTBALL emblazoned on the side.

Suddenly, Peyton King stepped in front of them. "Regan, where are you two going?"

"I'm glad you caught up with us, Peyton." Brandy quickly explained what was happening.

"Where'd you leave Robin Chase?" she asked as she punched in a number on her cell phone.

"Beneath the west-side bleachers," Regan replied.

"Sawyer," Regan barked into her phone. "Pick up Robin Chase. She's under the west bleachers. She's pretty beat up. Arrest her."

Peyton listened as Pat Sawyer repeated the information. "We'll be at your office as soon as possible," Peyton added. "I'm picking up Joey Sloan."

The three waded through the football players milling around the motor coach and opened the vehicle's door. Joey was lying on the sofa. His face was pale, and his breathing was shallow.

Peyton immediately called for an ambulance as Brandy rushed to Joey's side. She fell to her knees and caught Joey's face between her hands.

"Joey, wake up. Wake up, baby. It's me, Brandy." Tears ran down her cheeks as she tried in vain to get a response from him.

"Peyton, what's wrong with him?" Brandy cried. "I can't rouse him."

Before Peyton could reply, Clint Wayne and a male student came out of a bedroom wearing only their jockey shorts. "What's going on out here?"

Peyton took a picture of the almost-nude men with her cell phone. "Your star quarterback has OD'd on something," Peyton said. "We're trying to save his life."

"You have no business in here," Wayne fumed.

"This says I do." Peyton pulled back her jacket, exposing her badge and Glock.

The wail of a siren stopped everyone in their tracks. Pat Sawyer burst through the door, assessing the situation. "In here," she yelled to the ambulance attendants.

The men quickly placed Joey on a gurney and rolled him into the back of the ambulance. Brandy looked from Joey to Regan. "I want to go with him," she said between sobs.

Regan nodded, and Brandy jumped into the back of the ambulance with her boyfriend.

Peyton watched the ambulance speed away and then turned to Pat Sawyer. "I told you to take care of Coach Chase."

"I looked for her under the west bleachers," Pat said. "She wasn't there. She must have left under her own steam."

Peyton was suddenly aware of the circle of behemoth football players surrounding them. For the first time in ages, she felt uncomfortable. She knew three attractive women in the midst of drunk and drugged brutes was a powder keg waiting to ignite. She reached for Regan's hand and whispered to Pat, "Call for backup. ASAP."

Peyton unsnapped the strap over her gun and slowly pulled it from the holster. Pat did the same. "Shoot anyone who even looks like they will rush us," Peyton instructed as they backed out of the circle.

"Get them," Wayne yelled as he jumped from the motor home, still in his underwear. "They'll destroy everything we've worked for."

Peyton shot Wayne in the leg. "My next shot goes into his head," she yelled as they continued to back away from the crowd.

Flashing blue-and-white lights accompanied by sirens announced the arrival of campus police and a SWAT team in full regalia. One of the officers began speaking through the public address system built into his car. "You all need to move along. This party's over."

The men continued to mill about, and the officer spoke again. "Move on out," he commanded. "Anyone still standing here after I count to ten will be arrested."

The men began to leave and disappeared into the crowd of homecoming partiers.

"I called an ambulance for Coach Wayne," Pat informed Peyton.

Peyton nodded and started to walk away. "Agent King," Regan called out. "Can you give me a ride home? It seems I've been deserted."

"Sure, come on." Peyton never broke stride as Regan ran to catch up with her.

##

Regan gasped as the bonfire went up in flames. It lit the night sky like the sun. Peyton stopped her car and watched the spectacle. "Impressive," she snorted then turned to Regan.

"I need to run by the chancellor's home and inform her that I shot her assistant head coach. She's not going to be happy with me, but I want to assure her that he'll be able to coach the big game Saturday."

They rode in silence until Peyton pulled her sedan into the circular drive of a multimillion-dollar home. "Wow!" Regan gasped. "The university provides nice housing for its top brass."

Regan smiled. "No, Katherine O'Brien owns this home. She said she plans to spend the rest of her days in Austin, so she purchased her home instead of using the one provided by the university."

"It's impressive and beautiful," Regan mumbled.

Peyton got out of the car and walked to Regan's door to open it. "Aren't you coming in?"

"No, I'll just wait for you."

"Please come in. The chancellor will be pleased to see you. She's a big fan of yours."

"I'm dressed for a bonfire, not a visit with the chancellor." Regan reluctantly got out of the car, gasping as the pain in her side increased. She just wanted to get home, take a half dozen aspirin, and put ice on her injuries.

"Chancellor, how many times do I have to tell you not to answer the door yourself?" Peyton scolded softly when Katherine O'Brien greeted them.

"Everyone has the day off except Marisa." O'Brien laughed. "I am the only door opener available. I thought you were . . . Professor Shaw. What a pleasant surprise. Do come in."

"This is a line-of-duty visit," Peyton explained as they followed O'Brien into the library. "I'm afraid there's been some trouble at the bonfire."

"Please, sit down," Katherine said. "I'll have Marisa bring us coffee, and you can tell me all about it."

As Peyton related the events of the day, Regan scanned Katherine O'Brien's bookshelves. She had the usual academic tomes, an entire bookshelf of finance-related hardbacks, and all of Regan's novels—even her last book, *Deadly Romance*.

Katherine caught Regan looking at her collection. "As you can see, I'm a fan of yours," she said. "You have such interesting plot twists. Things I never expect."

"Thank you," Regan replied. "I'm flattered that you make time in your busy schedule to read my novels."

Katherine returned her attention to Peyton. "Agent King, you say my assistant football coach commanded the team to attack you, and Women's Athletic Director Robin Chase tried to rape Professor Regan?"

"Yes, ma'am."

"Will you file charges against them?"

"Yes, ma'am."

"Good," Katherine said.

"I will begin the search for a new head coach, assistant coach, and women's athletic director. The athletic department has needed a good housecleaning for a long time."

"What about the game Saturday?" Regan asked. "Who will coach the players through that?"

"Athletic Director Bob Bradford can surely handle that." Katherine smiled and sipped her coffee. "We select the weakest team in our division to play for homecoming. That guarantees a win, so it should be a no-brainer for Bradford. I'll call him after you leave. I hope he's sober."

Peyton thanked the chancellor for her time and rose to leave.

"Where are you going now?" Katherine asked.

"The hospital." Peyton grimaced. "I need to find out how Joey Sloan is doing and check on Clint Wayne. I also need to know if Robin Chase showed up in the emergency room. From what I heard, Grace Brandywine gave her a good beating."

"Please keep me informed," O'Brien instructed Peyton. "And it was good to see you again, Professor.

She walked them to the door and watched as Peyton's vehicle disappeared.

##

"Do you mind riding to the hospital with me?" Peyton asked. "If I'm right, you will have some bruising on your back and arm where Chase manhandled you. I'd like to have you examined and all injuries photographed and detailed as evidence against her."

"I could do that while you check on Joey," Regan said. She didn't want to see Brandy and certainly had no desire to see Brandy and Joey together. *I've been a fool,* Regan thought. *I was falling in love with Grace Brandywine. Obviously, she's sowing her wild oats before settling down with Joey. I just caught her fancy.*

"Penny for your thoughts," Peyton teased.

"I was just wondering if you have any persons of interest in Coach Tucker's murder," she said. She had no interest in sharing her true thoughts with the agent.

"Honestly, not a soul," Peyton huffed. "We'll start interviewing all the people who filed assault charges against him and see what shakes out."

"Women he molested?"

"Dear Coach Tucker showed no favoritism," Peyton said. "He was an equal-opportunity rapist. I have complaints in his file from women and men."

"Tucker was a big man," Regan said. "I'm guessing his killer would have to be strong and big to overpower him."

"Remember, he was falling-down drunk," Peyton reminded her.

Peyton pulled into a reserved parking space close to the hospital entrance and tossed her federal government identification parking card on the dash.

Regan followed her to the hospital information desk and looked around while Peyton got Joey's room number. "I need to speak with someone about collecting evidence for an FBI investigation," Peyton said.

The attendant nodded, punched a number into the phone, and handed the receiver to Peyton. The agent explained what she wanted, repeated a floor and room number, and then thanked the attendant.

"I'll take you to the third floor and go over what we need with the nurse," Peyton said as they headed for the elevators.

Peyton explained that someone had physically assaulted Regan. "She wasn't raped but was handled very roughly. I need shots of any bruising or cuts. I must check on someone else here. How long do you think this will take?"

"No more than an hour." The nurse handed Regan a hospital gown and motioned for her to change into it. "She can call you when she's finished."

"Put the gown on backward so it opens down the front," the nurse instructed. "Oh honey, someone did a number on your arm."

"It's okay," Regan said. "It's a little painful to move it, but I'm sure that will go away."

"Was your arm shoved up behind your back?"

"Yes, how did you know?"

"Classic domestic violence." The nurse shook her head. "The bastards always twist the women's arms behind their backs, threatening to break them if they don't comply with their sick demands. Was he demanding anal sex?"

"What? Uh, no!" Regan squeaked. "It was a woman."

"A woman? Are you a—"

"No! It wasn't like that. She attacked me because I wanted to help my student."

"Humph," the nurse snorted. "As I said, put the gown on opening down the front. I need to take pictures of your torso. You're black-and-blue."

Regan complied, feeling almost as degraded by the exam as she had been by Robin Chase sticking her hand down the front of her jeans.

"Did she shove you against something?" the nurse asked as she took pictures of the X-shaped bruise on Regan's breasts and stomach.

"Yes," Regan whispered. "The crossbars beneath the bleachers."

"Are you having pain?"

"Yes. I feel like a train ran over me. I ache all over."

The nurse called a doctor on duty, and he arrived as she finished her examination of Regan. He looked at the photos and X-rays.

"Do you have someone to drive you home?" the doctor asked.

"Yes. Agent King," Regan answered.

"Then I'm going to give you something for pain. It will make you sleepy. In about thirty minutes you'll feel no pain."

When the exam was finished, Regan called Peyton, who requested that she join her in room 210. "I'm almost finished. Just wrapping up Joey's statement. What did your exam show? Any broken bones?"

"No, just a lot of bruising," Regan replied. "I'll wait in the hallway outside Joey's room." She didn't want to watch Brandy fawn over Joey.

Weariness overcame Regan as she rode the elevator down to the second floor. The entire day had been a rollercoaster of emotions. She felt like the rodent in Brandy's game of cat and mouse.

I know better than to get involved with a student, Regan thought, chastising herself. She propped her back against the wall and pulled out her cell phone.

A text dinged into her phone as she stepped from the elevator. "Will you have a late supper with me?" The message was from Brandy.

Regan typed, "No." Then she reread Brandy's message.

"Why not?" This time, the question was whispered into Regan's ear, making her jump and eliciting a grunt of pain.

"Joey needs you," Regan scoffed.

"His father is with him," Brandy informed her. "He'll be okay now. Besides, you must be starving. We didn't get much to eat today. Please? I feel badly about how the day ended. It started off so good."

"Then your boyfriend was drugged or whatever," Regan reminded her. "Honestly, Brandy, I'm physically and emotionally drained. I just want to go home."

"I'll take you home," Brandy volunteered.

"Your car is still at the bonfire," Regan reminded her.

"Agent Peyton had an officer bring it to the hospital. I believe it's parked next to hers. Let me tell her I'm taking you home. Give me a minute."

The refusal died on Regan's lips as she looked into clouded green eyes.

Brandy disappeared into Joey's room and returned in less than a minute with a smile on her face. "We're good to go," she said, pulling Regan's arm through hers.

Regan relaxed into the seat of Brandy's car. She couldn't recall ever being so exhausted. Her body ached as if she'd ridden a rough horse on a long trail ride. Every inch of her hurt.

Brandy glanced at her passenger and was surprised to find Regan sleeping. She knew Regan had experienced a traumatic day.

When Brandy pulled into Regan's driveway, she gently shook Regan awake. "You're home," she announced.

Regan looked around, trying to focus on her location. Her attempt to move brought a low moan to her lips.

Brandy rushed to the passenger's side of her car and helped Regan out. She supported her to the door.

"I can make it from here," Regan mumbled as she unlocked the door and then stumbled into Brandy's arms.

"Easy, Professor," Brandy whispered as she led Regan to her sofa and gently helped her lie down. Regan's eyes closed as soon as Brandy covered her with the light blanket from the back of the sofa.

Brandy found a soft T-shirt in Regan's closet. She eased Regan's sweater off and unfastened her bra. She pulled the bra away and gasped at the bruising on the brunette's breasts and abdomen. "I'll kill Robin Chase for this," she mumbled.

Chapter 11

Regan lay on the sofa trying to figure out why she wasn't sleeping in her bed. As sleep receded and her mind cleared, she recalled the awful events of the preceding day. She groaned as she moved the arm Robin Chase had twisted behind her back. She wondered if Robin had damaged her rotator cuff.

She ran her hand up her stomach and flinched when she reached her breasts. "God, that's sore," she muttered.

Finally, she opened her eyes. She wasn't ready to sit up. She simply lay on her back, staring at the ceiling and wondering what Brandy was doing. *She's probably at the hospital holding Joey's hand.*

As daylight began to filter into her living room, she turned her head to look around. She was surprised to see the silhouette of a person sitting in the chair closest to her. It took her a minute to realize it was Brandy. The blonde was watching her.

"How do you feel?" Brandy asked.

"Like I was caught in a stampede." Regan tried to sit up, but cried out in pain when she put weight on her elbow.

Brandy was at her side immediately. "Let me help you. You're black-and-blue all over."

"How do you know? Oh, you undressed me," Regan said as she realized she was wearing only a soft T-shirt and panties.

"I . . . um, thought you'd sleep more comfortably out of your sweater and jeans." Brandy slipped her arm under Regan's shoulder and gently pulled her into a sitting position. "Would you like some coffee? I'll make a fresh pot."

Regan blushed. "What I need most right now is the bathroom."

"Let me help you." Brandy moved to the side with the uninjured arm and sat down. "Please put your arm around my shoulder. I'll pull you up as I stand. I'll have to put my arm around your waist. Is that okay?"

"Yes, but please hurry." Regan's need to reach the bathroom was becoming more urgent.

Brandy lifted her from the sofa and slowly walked her to the bathroom door. "Can you make it from here?"

"Yes."

"Yell if you need me," Brandy told her. "I'll wait right here by the door."

After a few minutes, Regan opened the door. "Would you mind brushing my hair?" she asked.

"I'd love to," Brandy said honestly. She followed Regan to the chair in front of her dressing table and steadied her as she lowered her body to the stool.

"It's a mess," Regan mumbled, still feeling the effects of the Tramadol the doctor had given her the night before. "I can't raise my arm high enough to brush it."

"It's beautiful," Brandy murmured as she ran the brush through Regan's silky black hair. "It's so soft."

Brandy brushed Regan's hair as the brunette studied her student in the mirror. The look of concern on Brandy's face was sincere. "Why aren't you at the hospital with Joey?"

"He's hell-bent on playing today. You needed me more." Brandy shrugged. "He's fine. They pumped his stomach, and now he wants to eat everything in sight." A smile crossed her face.

"There." Brandy made a final, gentle stroke with the brush and placed it on the dressing table. "If you want to lie back down, I'll make coffee and fix our breakfast."

"I think I need to work out this soreness." Regan moved her arm and turned her head from side to side. "I'll sit at the island and visit with you in case I need to tell you where something is."

"I'd like that better." Brandy grinned. She reached to put her arm around Regan.

"Just let me hold your arm as I walk," Regan said. "I'm not steady yet."

Regan sipped her hot coffee. "This is delicious," she said with a sigh. "You make a great pot of coffee, Miss Brandywine."

Brandy curtsied. "Thank you, ma'am. I aim to please." She slid a plate of scrambled eggs and bacon in front of Regan and turned when the raisin bread popped up in the toaster. She placed the toast and her own plate on the island and sat down on the stool next to Regan.

"This is nice," Brandy said. "Having breakfast with you. I wouldn't mind doing this every—"

"Please don't, Brandy," Regan whispered. "Don't say 'every morning.'"

Chapter 12

"Dammit, one of those little shits stole a Mule last night." The foreman of the bonfire cleanup crew scowled as he looked around for his missing Kawasaki 4x4 vehicle. "It'll show up somewhere wrecked.

"Let's get this mess cleaned up," he instructed as his workers mounted front-end loaders and bulldozers to clean up the smoldering remains of the bonfire. He pointed to five workers standing nearby. "You take the Mules and start cleaning up the trash under the bleachers."

The first dozer driver made a pass through the rubble and stopped when his equipment upended the charred Mule. He killed his engine and ran to find his boss.

"Mac, I found the Mule," he gasped. "You gotta see this."

The two of them climbed into a Mule and followed the path cleared by the dozer.

"Son of a—"

"Boss, look closer," the dozer driver urged. "I think there's a—"

"Fricking body!" Mac yelled. "Jesus Christ, the little shit drove it right into the middle of the bonfire. What the hell was he thinking?"

Pat Sawyer ran her hand through her short hair. "This place is going to hell in a paper bag," she fumed. "Do we know who it is?"

"No, ma'am," her deputy answered. "We're waiting to hear from the medical examiner's office. They took the body about thirty minutes ago. The workers only found part of the body—from the waist up. They're still combing the ashes for the rest of it."

"Male or female?" Pat barked.

"We don't know. The skeleton was all that remained. "Clothes, flesh, jewelry . . . all disintegrated. You know how hot those bonfires get. The coroner's office said it's difficult to ascertain the sex without the pelvic region. Did you know that male and female bodies are almost identical except for the pelvic area?"

"Yeah, that's one of the first things they taught us in forensics.

"I must break the news to Dragon Lady." Pat fretted as she donned her hat and jacket. "I just hope she doesn't kill the messenger. You stay at the coroner's office, and call me the minute they know anything."

"Yes, ma'am." The officer hurried out the door.

Pat dreaded the next few days. It was always horrific to notify a parent of their child's death. They paid big bucks for their offspring's education and couldn't fathom that the student had died in the care of the university.

Pat had reached Chancellor O'Brien's office when her deputy called. "They found the rest of the skeleton. It's a female."

Pat thanked him and entered the area that housed and protected the chancellor. The receptionist recognized Pat and raised an eyebrow. "A visit from you can't be good," she said.

"Is Chancellor O'Brien in her office? Pat asked. "It's urgent that I speak with her."

The woman nodded toward Katherine's secretary, who flashed Pat a pleasant smile.

"Chief, let me notify the chancellor that you're here."

Katherine waited for Chief Sawyer to close the door behind her. Pat shuffled her feet and Katherine pushed aside her thoughts about the grim reaper.

"What's wrong?" she asked.

"The cleanup crew found a woman's body in the bonfire," Pat blurted.

Katherine inhaled deeply then breathed out slowly. "Do we know who she is?"

"No, ma'am, but we'll leave no stone unturned until we do."

"Thank you, Chief." Katherine stood. "Please keep me informed. I want to know the minute you know anything."

"Of course." Pat stumbled as she backed from the room. She wondered how Katherine O'Brien could always reduce her to a gawky teenager.

O'Brien waited until Pat shut her door to dial Agent Peyton King. "Agent King, a body has been found in the charred remains of the bonfire. It's a woman."

"Do they know who it is?" Peyton asked.

"No, but I'd like you to keep an eye on Chief Sawyer's investigation. She worries me."

"I will, Chancellor," Peyton promised.

Chapter 13

"Aren't you going to the big homecoming game?" Regan asked Brandy as the blonde settled into the recliner in her TV room.

"I'd rather stay with you. Just in case you need anything."

Regan nodded and hugged herself as a chill engulfed her body.

"Are you cold?" Brandy stood. "Tell me where you keep your throws, and I'll get one for you."

"No, I'm tired. Sleeping on the sofa wasn't very restful. I hope you won't think me rude if I take a nap in my bed."

"I won't think you rude," Brandy assured her. "Just call me if you need anything. Um, is it okay if I watch the game on your TV?"

"Of course."

Regan slept through the day-long hullabaloo leading up to the homecoming game and awoke just in time to hear the kickoff. The announcers were giddy about the news of Joey Sloan being in the hospital the night before but rallying to lead his Longhorns.

Regan listened as Texas received the ball, and Joey quickly moved his team down the field for a touchdown. The crowd went crazy. She realized she liked knowing Brandy was in the other room watching television. She liked having Brandy in her home.

She sat up on the side of her bed and waited for a bout of dizziness to pass before trying to stand. She thought about changing into something more presentable but decided to go with the sweatpants and Henley she had on. She walked to the TV room, where Brandy was stretched out on the sofa, resting comfortably against the overstuffed arm. She had kicked off her shoes and pulled the throw over her.

##

Brandy looked away from the TV as Regan entered the room. She couldn't stop the look of open desire that crossed her face. Regan was heart-stopping with her long black hair tousled from sleep. She wore no makeup, and her features were soft and sweet. She looked so vulnerable.

"It's chilly," Regan said. "I need to light the fireplace."

She walked to the mantel and flicked the switch that ignited the gas logs. "It'll take a few minutes for it to warm the room," she said.

Brandy pulled back the throw and motioned for Regan to join her on the sofa. "Just slip right in here and lean back against me." Regan settled between her legs and leaned back into arms that were warm and welcoming.

"I'll be careful not to squeeze you or hurt you when we make a touchdown. Joey is tearing up the other team. They can't stop his passing game."

##

Regan watched in awe as Joey fired pass after pass to his receivers and marched his team down the field to a touchdown every time they had the ball. The score was embarrassing, and Regan wondered why Bob Radford wasn't putting in the second-string quarterback so Joey could rest. There was no way the other team could beat the Longhorns.

"Why is Radford running up the score so high?" Regan asked.

"I don't know. That's not the sportsmanlike thing to do. Especially on a homecoming game."

"He needs to take Joey out," Regan declared.

"Joey will take care of it," Brandy assured her. "He's all about being a good sport."

Almost as if he had heard his girlfriend's declaration, Joey began calling only running plays. The Longhorns made no score in the last quarter.

Regan developed a whole new appreciation for the young Adonis. He was an exceptional athlete, and she knew he was extremely intelligent. *I suppose I do understand what Brandy sees in him,* she thought. *He really is a good guy.*

"Do you want to watch another game?" Brandy asked. "I could order a pizza. Is there another team you follow?"

"I do love the Crimson Tide." Regan giggled.

"Oh, that's like an arrow through my heart," Brandy said, groaning. "But I have to admit, they are one hell of a football team. So, is pizza okay?"

"Uh-huh, a supreme with extra cheese."

Brandy laughed. "I swear, Professor, you are the woman I've been searching for all my life."

They were still eating pizza when the Alabama-Auburn game broke for halftime. A newsflash streamed across the bottom of the screen during halftime activities: "Woman's body in University of Texas bonfire identified as UT Women's Athletic Director Robin Chase."

"Oh dear God!" Regan gasped. "Did you know they found a body in the bonfire?"

"No." Brandy frowned. "This is the first I've heard about it. Let's switch to cable news and see if we can learn more details."

Skipping through news channels, Brandy caught a live interview with Chancellor O'Brien. The anchor was introducing Katherine and did a quick review of her impressive credentials. "Chancellor O'Brien is in our Austin affiliate's studio speaking with us live. Chancellor, this is the second death on your campus in a month. Do you have any leads?"

"We've turned the investigation over to the FBI," Katherine replied. "Head Coach Danny Tucker was brutally murdered earlier this month. Although he coached for UT, he made his home in Shawnee, Oklahoma, so his murder investigation crosses state lines, making it a federal case."

"Is it true the charred remains of a woman found in the UT bonfire are those of Women's Athletic Director Robin Chase?"

"The remains have been positively identified as those of Robin Chase," Katherine affirmed.

"You were brought in two years ago, after the former chancellor was fired because of sexual improprieties in the football program involving both coaches and players. Is that correct?"

"I was hired for many reasons." Katherine flashed her thousand-watt smile. "One of them was to clean up corruption in the athletic department.

"Both Coach Tucker and Coach Chase had complaints in their files. As everyone knows, a university can't simply fire winning coaches without first investigating allegations against them. Coach Tucker and Coach Chase were under investigation. If we had confirmed that the complaints had merit, we would have had no choice but to relieve them of their duties."

"Was Robin Chase's death a horrible accident or another murder? Are you going to delve deeper into the misconduct of the athletes and coaches?" The anchor pushed Katherine.

"We will do whatever is necessary to make certain that the University of Texas provides a healthy, safe atmosphere for all our students." Katherine was emphatic. "We are waiting for the forensics report on Coach Chase. At this point in time, no ruling has been made on her death."

"Is it true that Coach Chase was a lesbian?" the man asked.

"I'm not privileged to information concerning Robin Chase's sexual preferences," Katherine said, her pleasant expression never changing, "but even if she were, that's not grounds for dismissal. As long as individuals conduct themselves properly, we don't care how they identify sexually. And I must add that I don't see how that has any bearing on her death. Why did you ask that question?"

"I . . . uh, um . . . Thank you, Chancellor O'Brien, for taking the time to visit with us tonight."

The local news manager rushed to Katherine. "I apologize for his rudeness," she exclaimed. "Those New Yorkers are embarrassing sometimes."

"No apology necessary," Katherine said. "I appreciate you giving me the opportunity to state our position on national TV."

"Our driver is off work now, but I'd be delighted to return you to your home," the station manager declared, walking Katherine to the front door of the station.

"That won't be necessary," said a tall blonde who strode toward them. "I'll drive Chancellor O'Brien home, if that's alright with her."

##

Brandy turned off the TV. She'd lost interest in the game. "This isn't good," she said. "I gave Robin a pretty good beating when I caught her trying to—"

"She was alive when we walked away." Regan caught Brandy's hand. "And you certainly didn't throw her into the bonfire. You never left my side. I doubt anyone will think you're guilty of murder."

"How did she get into that bonfire?" Brandy pondered. "I'm certain we will hear from Agent King tomorrow. I'd better get to my dorm. Kiki will be worried sick."

"You can call Kiki," Regan suggested. "I'd feel safer if you stayed with me tonight."

The look that crossed Brandy's face made Regan add, "You can sleep in the guestroom."

Brandy snickered. "I knew that was what you meant."

Chapter 14

"You did an outstanding job with that interview," Peyton said as she walked Katherine to the car. "You always say just the right thing."

"Um, yes, but I must admit I was thrilled that the news media hasn't gotten the information that a gorgeous blonde FBI agent shot my assistant head coach. I would have had trouble fielding that one."

Peyton chuckled as she opened the door for Katherine. "The truth would have been unpleasant."

Peyton started her car and turned to the chancellor. "You're beautiful. I love that dress. You're too stunning to take home. Let me take you to dinner?"

Katherine gazed into eyes so blue she felt she could swim in them. "I'd enjoy that."

Peyton drove to a quaint Chinese restaurant outside Austin. It was expensive, which guaranteed it wouldn't be overrun with UT students. "Chief Sawyer is going to have her hands full tonight," she mused. "Texas won the homecoming game, and every frat and sorority on campus will have a drunken celebration that will eventually spill onto the streets."

Katherine nodded. "Maybe we should initiate a campaign encouraging sobriety. Next year we could bring in several popular bands and hold dances without alcohol. I will begin with my own administration. A zero tolerance for public consumption of alcohol. We need to set an example for our students, especially in the athletic department.

"Tucker was a big guy. Sober, I doubt anyone could have overpowered him. Do you have any more news on the cause of Robin Chase's death?"

Peyton smiled and took the chancellor's hand, pulling it into her lap. She knew Katherine's rapid-fire barrage of ideas and questions was her way of dealing with difficult situations.

"She was dead when she was put into the fire." Katherine's hand tightened on Peyton's. "Her neck was broken," Peyton continued. "Someone had to put her in the Mule, drive it into the fire, and jump out in time to avoid burning themselves. My job is to figure out how they did it without being seen."

"Do you think the two deaths are connected?" Katherine asked.

"I'm not certain, but there is one common denominator in both deaths."

"What?"

"Not a what," Peyton said, "a who. Both victims made an assault attempt on Professor Regan Shaw."

"You think Professor Shaw is involved?" Katherine gasped.

"No, but I think someone who cares about Regan Shaw might be a wee bit overprotective."

"I love this place." Katherine looked around the Chinese restaurant. "I'm glad you selected it."

Peyton smiled. "It's quiet and intimate. I thought we could talk without interruption. I found Chief Sawyer's files on the athletic department."

"From the dark clouds I see in your blue eyes," Katherine said, frowning, "I have a feeling I'm not going to like this."

"It looks like Sawyer devoted most of her time to cleaning up the messes made by the athletic department. She made DWIs go away and dropped theft charges on athletes daily. The thing she was losing control of was the sexual assault complaints.

"There are hundreds of complaints filed by coeds against the members of UT's athletic department. I have a dozen complaints about your athletic director. They range from rape to assault with his fist."

"Go after him hard," Katherine insisted. "I want to be rid of him. His attitude has poisoned the entire coaching staff and the players."

"Do you have anyone in mind to replace him?"

"I'd love to have someone with the morals of Peyton Manning." Katherine laughed. "Wouldn't that be a coup?"

"Why not go for Manning?" Peyton giggled as she emptied her wine glass. She refilled it and Katherine's before proposing a toast. "Here's to getting Peyton Manning as the UT athletic director."

"Could you bring your files to my home tomorrow, so we can see if I have enough cause to fire Bob Radford?"

"I'd be willing to work on that tonight." Peyton smiled devilishly. "I have the files in my apartment, if you'd like to go over them there."

"Are you inviting me to see your etchings?" Katherine laughed. "I'd like that." She lost herself in the blue ocean of Peyton's eyes.

Chapter 15

Campus Police Chief Pat Sawyer panicked when she realized Agent King had the files she had hidden. She knew it was just a matter of time before Chancellor O'Brien requested her presence. O'Brien had been reasonable with Pat so far, but the police chief had seen the chancellor almost dismember those who displeased her. Pat was certain O'Brien would be livid over her collusion in the cover-up of criminal activities within the athletic department.

Pat chose two o'clock Sunday morning to search Athletic Director Bob Radford's office. She had to find the photos and any copies of the video of her wild night with Sadie. She pulled on her gloves and conducted a three-hour search that turned up nothing.

"Dammit, where did he hide them?" She searched Radford's laptop but found no traces of the video. She wondered if Agent King had taken Danny Tucker's laptop. Tucker had always done Radford's dirty work. The evidence she wanted was probably in Tucker's office, which was sealed off with FBI tape.

Throwing caution to the wind, Pat made another of her epic bad decisions. She carefully left Radford's office as she'd found it and headed for Danny Tucker's office.

Pat slipped under the FBI tape and used her master key to open Tucker's office. It looked like a Texas cyclone had ripped through it. Desk drawers were hanging open, and files were dumped in a heap on the floor. Every file drawer had been pulled from its cabinet and emptied. Tucker's laptop was gone.

Pat knew that Peyton King's team had left no stone unturned. *I'm so screwed*, she thought as she relocked Tucker's office and slipped from the athletics building.

The first rays of the sun were turning the campus buildings into glorious shades of gold, pink, and yellow as Pat entered her own office.

"I wondered what hours you kept."

Peyton's voice stabbed Pat's heart, and she turned to face the FBI agent. "I was just—"

"I know what you were just doing," Peyton scoffed. "You were looking for this." She held up the video. "I see the coaches put an appropriate label on it—*Sadie Does the Police Department*."

Pat choked back the bile that rose in her throat. "The police department?" she croaked.

Peyton pulled a dozen more video CDs from her pocket. "At least a baker's dozen. Twelve here, plus yours. That makes thirteen."

"Are you going to turn those over to Chancellor O'Brien?" Perspiration was popping out on Pat's brow.

"I answer to a higher power than Chancellor O'Brien," Peyton huffed. "O'Brien would just fire you and hope you'd slink away, but you've committed federal crimes. You do know that intercepting the chancellor's mail is a crime? And then there's the matter of framing an innocent homeless guy for murder when you knew the culprits were football players and coaches."

Pat gulped. She could feel the noose tightening around her neck. "Look, Peyton, I was being blackmailed. I had no choice. I had to do those things."

"Who, specifically, was blackmailing you?"

Pat hesitated. *If Peyton didn't know, maybe she hadn't found all the files,* she thought.

"Was it Bob Radford?"

"No. The buck stops with Clint Wayne . . . slimy little prick."

"I'll need you to testify against everyone involved in this mess," Peyton said. "I need detailed information from you that will put them all behind bars. Did Radford have any knowledge of what was going on?"

Pat's hesitation let Peyton know she was about to hold back important information.

"Don't lie to me now, Sawyer. This is the only chance you'll get to make a deal. If you hold out anything, I'll personally see that you go to jail with your buddies in the athletic department."

"Yeah, Radford knew," Pat mumbled.

"Did he participate in the team's little orgies?"

"Sometimes." Pat hung her head.

"Did you ever try to stop them?"

"Of course! That's why they slipped Sadie in on me." Pat avoided Peyton's gaze. "They wanted something to hold over me."

"And you gave it to them?" Peyton huffed.

"Yeah!"

Peyton pushed a lined yellow pad toward Pat and pulled a pen from the holder on her desk. "Write down what you know," she instructed the police chief. "This needs to sound like a sincere apology. If you help me prosecute Radford and Wayne, I'll get you into the witness protection program. You can go somewhere else and start over."

Pat scowled and picked up the pen. "How should I start it?"

"If you're truly sorry, start with that," Peyton scoffed. "I'll help you. Write, 'It is with a heavy heart that I must put on paper the evil deeds I've been a party to.'"

Pat began writing and committed to paper the things she had been involved in over the years. Two hours passed, and her hand began to cramp. "I can't write anymore," she grumbled.

Peyton encourage her to continue. "I need information on Radford and Wayne. Write that your hand is cramping, and you will continue on video. Then you can record the rest on your phone."

"Works for me." Pat shrugged. "I'll be glad to get this off my chest. You're doing me a favor, Peyton. I appreciate it."

"I just want to get this mess cleared up," Peyton replied. "Where were you when Robin Chase was murdered? Did you see anyone suspicious?"

Pat stiffened. "I was with you and Professor Shaw."

"No, I called you to pick up Robin," Peyton said, furrowing her brow. "I asked you to arrest her. You joined us about thirty minutes later, saying you never found Robin."

Pat glowered at Peyton. "I haven't murdered anyone," she rasped. "Don't try to pin this mess on me, King."

"I'm not," Peyton said. "I just can't figure out who did it. Professor Shaw and Brandy were with me. Joey was passed out in the motor coach. Maybe Radford and Wayne are killing off anyone who could incriminate them."

"They'd have to kill off the entire football team . . . and me," Pat said.

Peyton thought about it for a moment. "I should put you in protective custody. You're my star witness. I can't afford to lose you."

"I can't see those two killing anyone," Pat said.

"You may be right. Clint Wayne was in his skivvies when we reached the motor coach. I think he was with another male."

"Yeah," Pat muttered, shaking her head. "He does like the younger boys. He always calls dibs on the freshmen."

"Do you have any thoughts on who might be killing your coaching staff?"

"I haven't a clue," Pat snorted. "Do you want me to record on your phone or mine?"

"Yours would be more appropriate." Peyton looked over the written confession Pat had made and then shoved it back to her. "You need to sign the last page and initial all the others."

Pat signed and initialed the sheets of paper. She couldn't believe she'd been sucked into such a mess.

Chapter 16

Killing Robin Chase had been easier than expected. Grace Brandywine had kicked the hell out of her, and she was still dazed when the Mule pulled up beside her and a figure dressed in a Batman costume leaped from the 4X4 and helped her stand. "Can you walk?"

Robin leaned heavily against Batman. "Let me sit in the back of the Mule in case I pass out," Robin whimpered. "That little bitch. I'll make her pay for this in ways she'd never imagine."

Batman helped her into the bed of the Mule and slid her as close to the driver's seat as possible before closing the tailgate.

"Let me look at your face." Batman tilted Robin's head to get a better look. With a hand on each side of Robin's head, it had been easy to snap her neck. Her limp body slid down into the bed of the Mule.

No one noticed them as the bonfire exploded into flames. Batman drove the Mule as close to the fire as possible, got out, weighted down the gas pedal, and pushed the Mule into drive. It shot forward and disappeared into the flames.

No one paid any attention to the athletic figure dressed as a superhero. It was easy to slip under the bleachers where the clothes were hidden, pull jeans and a sweater over the black unitard, and stuff the Batman mask under the bottom bleacher step for later retrieval. *Now to catch up with the others.*

Chapter 17

Regan dozed, vaguely aware of the mouthwatering aroma of coffee and bacon. For a moment, she was back in New York. Back in the apartment she'd shared with Leslie Winters. Her first two years with Leslie had been pure heaven. The beautiful blonde newscaster had been charming and vivacious and refused to take no for an answer. Regan had fallen hard for her and thought her life was set. Leslie would cover hard news, and Regan would write fiction loosely based on the real-life stories Leslie uncovered.

It had taken Regan another two years to force herself to admit that the woman she had fallen in love with was a raging alcoholic who wouldn't admit she had a problem. Even after Leslie was fired for showing up at a live interview stumbling drunk, she had refused to get help.

As job opportunities dried up for the blonde, she became depressed and turned to the bottle more and more. She became belligerent and finally abusive. It had taken Regan one more year to realize there was no future with Leslie and to muster the courage to pack her things and leave. Finding her in bed with another woman had been the last straw.

She spent the following year writing her masterpiece and another year coming to terms with the fact that her publisher had rejected the novel.

"Hey, sleepyhead," Brandy said, easing into her bedroom carrying two steaming mugs. "Want a cup of coffee?"

"Oh yes!" Regan stretched and pulled herself into a sitting position. She accepted the cup of coffee and took a sip. "Oh, this must be the nectar of the gods, and you must be a goddess." She smiled at Brandy. *An extremely beautiful goddess.*

Brandy giggled at the compliment and blushed profusely. "I thought we'd eat breakfast at home. The restaurants will be filled with puking college students trying to cure hangovers."

Regan tamped down her desire to pull Brandy into her bed and make love with her. She closed her eyes against the vision of Brandy slowly lowering her body to cover hers and Brandy's lips moving closer to capture Regan's.

The shrill ring of Brandy's phone yanked Regan from her fantasy.

"Joey, of course I watched you win the game yesterday." Brandy giggled. "I was most impressed with the last quarter." She listened as Joey talked.

"I thought that was what happened. I knew you had refused to run up the score on them and . . . I know. . . . Tonight? . . . Sure, I'll call you later. . . . Love you too."

Brandy slipped her phone into the hip pocket of her jeans. "How do you like your eggs, Professor?"

Regan washed her face and dressed as Brandy put the finishing touches on their breakfast. "Love you too" still burned into Regan's heart. Grace Brandywine was a shameless flirt, Regan decided. One of those women who casually tossed out a glorious smile that stole one's breath away, only to turn that same smile on someone else as you watched.

She's fourteen years younger than you, Regan reminded herself as she entered the kitchen and sat down at the island where Brandy was placing juice and a plate of toast. *But damn she's gorgeous.*

"How are your bruises today?" Brandy inquired as she placed bacon and scrambled eggs in front of Regan.

"Not nearly as sore as yesterday," Regan replied. "This looks delicious. You're a good cook."

"Only an idiot could mess up scrambled eggs and bacon," Brandy said with a laugh. "But I'm afraid that's the extent of my culinary capabilities. How about you? Are you a one-trick pony?"

"I don't understand." Confusion darkened Regan's eyes.

"Is spaghetti the only meal you can cook?"

"Oh, no, I love to cook," Regan reassured her. "I have many wonderful recipes."

They ate breakfast and discussed foods they liked. "I exaggerated a little," Brandy confessed. "I'm actually a pretty good cook. What's your favorite?"

"I make a mean stuffed chicken marsala," Regan said.

"I love stuffed chicken marsala." Brandy beamed. "You can cook that for me Wednesday night."

Regan stared at her. She always felt she was not quite in the same conversation as Brandy.

"When I come over so you can help me study for the Spanish test I have on Thursday."

Regan racked her brain, trying to recall when she had made the commitment to help Brandy. Then she shrugged as the young woman put the last of the dishes in the dishwasher.

"Right now, I must go home and study for the test my sexy literature teacher is giving my class tomorrow."

"I'm going to postpone that until Wednesday," Regan informed her. "I'm certain no one studied for it this weekend, and I see no reason to set up students for failure. I'll post it on the assignment board after you leave."

Chapter 18

Agent King placed Pat Sawyer's written confession in a file folder and locked it in her desk drawer. Pat had promised to record the rest of the evil deeds perpetrated by the athletic department on her computer and email the sound file to Peyton. *Now to tell Katherine that her chief of police framed a simpleminded homeless man for murder,* Peyton thought.

She tapped Favorites and then touched the number that would dial the chancellor's direct line.

"A call from you in the middle of the day can't be good." Katherine's melodic voice sent a tremor through Peyton.

"We could combine business with pleasure, and I could give you my report over dinner tonight," Peyton suggested.

"I'd like that," Katherine said. "I'll make reservations where we won't be disturbed. Pick me up at seven."

Before Peyton could respond, Katherine had ended the conversation. *She knows I'll be there*, Peyton mused.

##

Katherine O'Brien had flitted through Peyton's thoughts all day. She pictured the fiery redhead as she drove toward her mansion.

Fanatically guarded about her private life, O'Brien's professional career was an amazing chain of successes. Her husband had been killed in an auto accident shortly after their marriage, and Katherine had never remarried, choosing to devote herself to her career.

She was fiercely protective of the university and all of its programs and traditions. She had agonized over the athletic program and often told Peyton she felt like an outsider whenever the school's sports programs were discussed. "They intentionally keep me in the dark," she'd confided to Peyton.

As Peyton pulled her sedan into the circular drive, Katherine came out the front door and walked to the car. Peyton leaned over and pushed open the passenger's door for her.

Peyton cast an approving glance at the chancellor. "You look like a twenty-something student instead of the leader of the university," she teased. "I do love tight-fitting jeans."

Katherine laughed. "Agent King, if I didn't know you better, I'd swear you're letching after me."

Peyton grinned. "Uh-huh. Let me see . . . fitted designer jeans, UT sweatshirt that stops right above the firmest derrière I've ever seen. The only thing you aren't torturing me with is your beautiful cleavage."

"I'm saving that for later," Katherine said seriously.

Peyton moistened her lips with the tip of her tongue. Her entire mouth had gone dry. She moved the conversation to safer ground. "I'm having trouble reaching your athletic director."

"Bob Radford," Katherine huffed. "I'll make sure he's in your office at nine in the morning." She pulled her phone from her purse and stabbed at the name *Radford*. His wife answered the call.

"Marion? Hello. This is Chancellor O'Brien. Is Bob around? . . . No, I won't bother him there. Please give him a message for me. He needs to be in FBI Agent Peyton King's office on campus at nine in the morning, or she will issue a warrant for his arrest. She's working out of Eldon Hall, Room 105. . . . Yes, it is extremely important. Thank you, Marion."

"If he isn't there at nine sharp, call me. I'll send officers to bring him to you."

"He's the only one I can't account for at the time of Robin Chase's death," Peyton informed her. "Sawyer thinks he might be killing off the athletic staff to rid himself of anyone who might testify against him. But then she reasoned that he would have to kill the entire football team and her in order to silence all the people who have seen him in compromising positions."

"It makes me sick to my stomach to think of all those coeds who have been scarred for life and that poor girl who was murdered. I still believe Tucker and some of the football players raped her, and that homeless man—"

"Didn't kill her," Peyton said.

"What do you mean? Pat Sawyer had his confession on an audio."

"Pat framed him," Peyton mumbled. "She edited the audio. She intentionally framed him. She admitted it."

"Oh Peyton, how do I clean up this mess?" Katherine clenched her fists. "This is the kind of stuff that gets universities blackballed. If the news media gets hold of this, my career will be over—all because a bunch of testosterone-saturated apes can't keep it in their pants."

"Maybe I can scare Radford enough that he'll resign and go away," Peyton suggested.

"I hope you can, Peyton. That would be best for everyone concerned."

"Don't worry, Katherine. I'll take care of it."

Chapter 19

In an act of defiance, Bob Radford waited until three in the afternoon to show up at Peyton's office.

"Mr. Radford, I appreciate you coming to talk with me."

"I had no choice after you ran crying to the chancellor," Radford snorted. "What's so important you got her all riled up?"

"Two deaths in your department," Peyton said, glaring at him in disbelief. "Perhaps you aren't aware that your head coach and women's athletic director have been murdered."

"Of course, I'm aware," Radford growled. "I just don't see why you want to drag me into this mess."

"This mess is of your making." Peyton glowered. She was tired of Radford's pompous attitude. "If you handled your job properly, I doubt we'd have accusations of rape and doping against your staff and players."

"I have no idea what you're talking about." Radford flopped into a chair across from Peyton.

"Perhaps this will jog your memory." Peyton pulled one of the complaints from Pat Sawyer's files.

"This was filed six weeks ago after the football team held a preseason practice. It was filed by a waitress at Hooters. According to her, half a dozen players entered the restaurant and began drinking. When they became drunk and rowdy, the manager instructed her to stop serving them.

"The players were belligerent and refused to leave. According to the waitress and the manager, you showed up, ordered another round for them, and joined them at their table. You made lascivious remarks to the waitress and argued with the manager. Austin police were called to remove you and your boys from Hooters. As you were leaving, you threatened the waitress. Early the next morning, two men broke into the woman's apartment and raped her. She identified both attackers as two of the athletes who had gotten into your car when you left the restaurant."

"Of course, they got into my car. I took them back to their frat house. They were too drunk to drive. That doesn't mean I condoned what they did later," Radford groused. "I had nothing to do with what happened to that girl."

"According to the Austin police report, both football players claimed that you suggested they should pay the woman a visit."

"I don't recall," Radford said flatly. "Do I need to get my attorney?"

"No, I'm not going to arrest you, but I will be reporting what I have found to Chancellor O'Brien."

"Don't do that," Radford whined. "That bitch is just looking for a reason to fire me."

"You don't have a good rapport with the chancellor?" Peyton did her best to look shocked.

"No, she's a man-hating tyrant," Radford declared. "If she had her way, UT would have no football program."

"I doubt Chancellor O'Brien would ever shut down something that has been such an institution at UT. She is all about tradition. She's also all about obeying the law."

Peyton thumbed through the files on her desk. "I have enough evidence to file criminal charges against you. If I were you, I'd resign before the press gets hold of the sordid stories involving you."

"Seriously?" Radford made a guttural sound deep in his throat. "I have three years left on my multimillion-dollar contract. I'm not walking away from that. Chancellor O'Brien doesn't have the balls to fire me. The publicity would be bad for her reputation and the college."

"It doesn't bother you to tarnish the university's reputation?"

"Hell no! One university is as good as another. I'd file a lawsuit claiming O'Brien's fight with me is over my refusal of her advances."

"I . . ." Anger electrified Peyton's body. "If I were you, I'd have a heart-to-heart talk with Chancellor O'Brien and work out what is best for the university."

"What would be best for the university would be to get rid of O'Brien and put a man in that job who understands about football. She thinks the English department is as important as my sports programs."

"Imagine that." Sarcasm dripped from Peyton's lips.

After Radford left, Peyton separated the complaints against the coaches and players. Complaints against the coaching staff had escalated over the past two months. She called O'Brien's office and was told the chancellor was in a meeting. "Please give her a message that I'll contact her in the morning. I'm leaving my office for the day."

Peyton locked all the files in the office wall safe and locked the door. As she was walking to her car, she spotted Regan Shaw strolling toward her.

"Professor Shaw, are you looking for me?"

"No, I'm walking to that little Greek restaurant across from Acorn Hall," Regan answered.

"If you're hungry for good Greek food, don't waste your time there," Peyton said. "I was just going to dinner. Why don't you join me, and I'll show you a great Greek restaurant?"

Regan considered the invitation and then nodded. "That sounds delightful."

As they drove, Peyton questioned Regan about Grace Brandywine. "Did she leave your sight the day Robin Chase was murdered?"

Regan gave careful thought to the question. "No. After she pulled Robin off me, she held my hand, supporting me as we searched for the coaching staff's motorhome. It took us thirty or forty minutes to locate it. You met us just before we reached it, and we were with you until Brandy left in the ambulance with Joey."

"I, uh, hate to say this," Peyton said, "but you are the common denominator in both murders. Coach Tucker and Coach Chase both tried to molest you."

"Surely you aren't one of those law enforcement officers who places the blame on the victim," Regan raged. "I can assure you, my skirt wasn't too short. I was wearing jeans on both occasions, and I was not wearing low-cut sweaters.

"I've lost my appetite, Agent King. Please take me home."

"I'm sorry," Peyton mumbled. "Please do stay and have dinner with me. I'm just chasing around in circles on this case. The only one I can't account for is Chief Sawyer. I called her on the phone for backup, so she wasn't with any of us."

Peyton parked her car and turned toward Regan. "I don't mean to be abrasive. I've never had a case like this where so much is at stake. Chancellor O'Brien's reputation, the athletic program, and the campus police force will all come under review if I can't solve this quickly."

They got out of the car and were silent as they entered the restaurant. Peyton requested a table in a private area. They gave the server their order and waited until she walked away to continue their conversation.

"Maybe it isn't anyone who's in our lives now," Regan suggested. "Maybe it's one of the students who was molested or a relative of the young woman who was murdered. I'd certainly hunt down the person who got away with killing my daughter."

"But a derelict was charged with that murder," Peyton said, wondering why Regan thought justice hadn't been served in that case.

"Oh, yes, of course," Regan mumbled.

"I'll begin working my way through the victims tomorrow. Tonight, let's discuss more pleasant things, as friends do."

"I'll vote for that." Regan laughed.

"Let's talk about you, your books, and all the exciting things going on in your life." Peyton opened her menu. "I read in one of the magazines that your last book is being made into a television series."

"Yes. In June I'll be returning to New York and then heading to Hollywood."

"That book was set in Dallas, as I recall," Peyton said, gazing into eyes warm with laughter.

"It was. I imagine I'll be back in Texas once the filming begins."

"Will you have any input in the selection process when they decide who will play your main characters?" Peyton signaled for the waitress. They placed their order and then continued discussing Regan's career.

"Yes, that's one thing that is stipulated in all my contracts," Regan answered. "I've met so many beautiful people on this campus. I'd love to have an unknown play the part of Victoria in the new series. I'm discussing it with my producer right now."

"Anyone I know?"

Regan laughed. "I'd rather not say. She probably won't do it anyway."

"Speaking of the devil," Peyton whispered as a group of diners entered the restaurant.

Regan turned to watch Joey and Brandy crowd around a table with their friends. "I wasn't thinking about Brandy," Regan said. "I was thinking about Katherine O'Brien."

"O'Brien?" Peyton gasped. "Yes, she'd make an incredible police captain."

"An incredibly beautiful police captain," Regan said.

Both women laughed as they thought about the staunch chancellor running a police department. "She could do it," Peyton added.

Chapter 20

Regan was glad her back was to the rowdy college students. She didn't want to watch Joey put his hands all over Brandy. Even the thought made her nauseous.

Peyton leaned close to Regan so she could hear her over the chatter coming from the students' table. "You know we have to walk past them to leave," she said.

Regan nodded and pulled her wallet from her purse to pay her half of the check. "My treat," Peyton said, handing the waitress a credit card. "Dining with you was so much nicer than taking home a burger or ordering-in pizza. We should do this more often."

The two women stood talking as they pulled on their jackets and gathered their things. The students quieted when they realized the FBI agent and professor were in the restaurant.

"Professor, Agent King, what a surprise meeting you two here." Joey rose to his feet as he greeted the two women. He introduced them to his companions and ended with, "Of course, you know Brandy."

Brandy tried to hold Regan's gaze, but the brunette looked away. "Don't forget to study for your test Wednesday," Regan reminded them.

Peyton placed her hand on the small of Regan's back and gently moved her toward the door.

"Miss King," the waitress called. "You forgot your credit card."

As Peyton walked back to their table to retrieve the card, Brandy stood to face Regan. "Don't forget you're tutoring me tomorrow night."

"I haven't forgotten." Regan suppressed her smile. *That's all I can think about.*

Peyton returned and resumed her efforts to usher Regan from the restaurant.

Brandy narrowed her eyes as she watched the possessive way Agent King touched the professor.

Regan scolded herself for being so excited about cooking dinner for Brandy. The alluring young woman had been on her mind all day. Everything was ready to go into the oven an hour before Brandy's arrival.

Regan poured a cup of fresh coffee and strolled into her home office. The blank screen of her computer beckoned to her. *Maybe I should start a new book,* she thought.

She pushed the button that would take her into a new world. A world that existed in her mind and manifested itself on the computer screen. She had been toying with the idea of writing about the campus murders. *I think I'll title it "Insanity in Academia,"* she thought.

Regan opened the manuscript of her unpublished book. 429 pages of her personal best opened onto the screen. It still disturbed her that the book had been rejected. She had never received a rejection letter before. Her first book had skyrocketed to a bestseller, as had every book following it.

She jumped when her doorbell rang. She checked her watch. It was too early for Brandy. She wondered who it was as she hurried to the door.

"Peyton! What a pleasant surprise. Please come in."

"I'm sorry to show up unannounced." Peyton glanced around the room as Amazon Alexa's alarm reminded Regan it was time to take her chicken marsala from the refrigerator.

"Alexa, off," Regan commanded. "Would you like a cup of coffee, Peyton?" Regan motioned for the agent to follow her into the kitchen. "It's fresh."

"That's the best offer I've had all day." Peyton grinned. "I've had better days."

Regan poured a cup of coffee for Peyton and refilled her own cup. She checked the temperature of her oven and pulled the chicken marsala from the refrigerator.

"Either you're expecting company, or you cook incredible cuisine for yourself."

"I'm tutoring Grace Brandywine for her Spanish test tomorrow," Regan explained.

"An English lit professor who doubles as a Spanish tutor? You're multitalented, Professor Shaw. How fluent are you in Spanish?"

Regan laughed. "Fluent enough."

They continued their conversation in Spanish, and the blonde agent impressed Regan with her command of the language.

"You've obviously immersed yourself in the language too," Regan said.

"I dated a hot Latina for several years," Peyton said, smiling at the memory. "She dumped me for a Latin lover."

"Oh, I'm sorry."

"It's okay," Peyton said. "I saw her last year. She was with her husband and three children."

"Did that hurt?"

"No. There's something about seeing your ex trucking 300 pounds in spandex that makes you know you dodged a bullet. How did you become so fluent in the language?"

"My mother," Regan said. "She was from Mexico. My father met her when he was assigned to Mexico City. He's with the state department, and she's an attorney."

"Ah, that explains the raven hair and flashing brown eyes," Peyton murmured.

Regan put the chicken marsala in the oven and began slicing and buttering French bread. "If I'd known you were coming, I would have prepared more chicken."

"Oh, no, I just dropped by to return these." Peyton held out a pair of sunglasses. "You left them in my car."

"It's been raining all day. I haven't missed them. Thank you."

The doorbell announced the arrival of Brandy. Peyton downed the last of her coffee. "I'd better be going. I have a couple more stops to make, and the weather's getting worse."

Peyton led the way to the door and opened it as an impatient Brandy pushed the ringer again. Shock registered in Brandy's eyes as she stood face-to-face with the agent. "What are you doing here?" Brandy demanded.

"That's really none of your business," Peyton huffed as she turned her collar up against the rain and darted to her car.

Brandy left her umbrella on the porch and followed Regan into the house. "Mmm. Something smells good."

"Your favorite." Regan smiled as Brandy opened the drawer and pulled out the wine opener. She tried to overcome the pleasure she felt at Brandy's familiarity with her home.

"A nice chardonnay to compliment an exceptional chicken marsala," Brandy said as she pulled the cork from the bottle and filled their glasses.

"I hope it's exceptional." Regan sighed, accepting the glass Brandy held out to her.

Brandy clinked her glass against Regan's. "Everything you do is exceptional, Professor."

"Thank you." Regan turned away. She didn't want Brandy to flirt with her. She surmised that Brandy had spent the night with Joey.

"So . . . you and Agent King?"

Brandy let the statement hang in the air, and Regan left it there, refusing to play games with her gorgeous student. "We have twenty minutes until dinner is ready. Do you want to start on your Spanish?"

"I'd rather hear about your day." Brandy slid onto the stool at the end of the island. "What was Agent King doing here?"

Regan gazed at her inquisitive guest. *Is that jealousy glinting in those green eyes?*

"Returning my sunglasses," Regan replied. "I left them in her car when we went out."

Brandy inhaled deeply, gathering her thoughts. "Are you two dating?"

"Brandy, your questions are out of line. There is a separation between my private life and my professional life."

"Of course. You're right," Brandy acknowledged. "I'm sorry, Professor. I sometimes move faster than I should. Don't you find society's dictates frustrating?"

"What do you mean?"

"I mean, for instance, when I meet a gorgeous woman who completely overwhelms me, I just want to pull her into my arms and kiss her. I hate all the posturing and dancing that goes on."

Regan laughed. "I'm certain you'd be a big hit at lesbian parties if you walked through the room kissing every gorgeous woman you saw."

"You took my statement out of context," Brandy said seriously. "I said, 'a gorgeous woman who completely overwhelms me.' I've only met one such woman in my lifetime."

Regan looked away from the fire flickering in Brandy's eyes. "This is not a conversation we should be having."

Brandy pushed for answers. "Is Agent King a part of your private life?"

"Is Joey Sloan a part of your private life?" Regan countered.

The oven buzzer sounded, ending the uneasy conversation.

Brandy followed Regan to the oven. "That smells delicious," she said, sniffing the air. "What can I do to help?"

Regan welcomed the shift in Brandy's mood. "Refill our wine glasses, and we'll be ready to dine."

As Regan served their dinner, the rain increased from heavy to a torrential downpour. "Wow! Listen to that," Brandy said as she walked to the large picture window that overlooked Regan's pool. "It's coming down in buckets."

Regan joined the blonde at the window. "If this continues, I'll need to pump water from the pool before it overflows."

A flash of lightening lit up the black sky. Thunder shook the house, and the lights flickered then left them in darkness. Regan jumped into the arms of the other woman.

Brandy's strong arms wrapped around her, and Regan marveled at how safe she suddenly felt. "I . . . um, I didn't mean to—"

"It's okay," Brandy murmured. "It's always nice to have someone to hold on to in the midst of the storm." She tightened her arms around Regan as the brunette relaxed against her. "Consider me your shelter in the storm, Regan."

The lights flickered again but refused to stay on. "I have a flashlight," Regan mumbled as she pulled away from Brandy. She quickly located it and pulled candles from another drawer and placed them in holders on the table.

"A candlelight dinner," Brandy teased. "How romantic is that?"

Regan studied the blonde. The candlelight danced in her hair, creating a halo affect around the girl's beautiful face. Regan caught her breath as she gazed into green eyes reflecting amber flames. "You are the most gorgeous woman I've ever met," she whispered as Brandy pulled her into the haven of her arms again.

"And you're the most desirable woman I've ever met." Brandy continued to hold Regan in her arms but leaned back to look into her eyes. "How long are we going to play this game, Regan?"

"I'm not the one playing games," Regan said, her voice barely more than a squeak. "You're the one sleeping with Joey Sloan and then coming on to me."

Brandy released the brunette. "Of course, you're right. I've overstepped the line here. I apologize, Professor." She returned to the table and began eating the meal Regan had prepared.

They ate in silence. The darkness outside the circle of light cast by the flickering candles made their dinner more intimate than planned.

"Brandy, I don't want there to be awkwardness between us," Regan said softly. "I value your friendship and find you quite interesting. I know you are committed to Joey, so we need to move past whatever this attraction is and accept each other as friends."

"I agree." Brandy flashed her dimpled smile and placed her warm hand over Regan's. "Friends it is." She raised her wine glass in a toast as the lights flickered and came back on.

"Does Agent King have any idea who our campus murderer is?" Brandy asked.

"She's no closer than she was the first day. She has uncovered evidence that would put the entire coaching staff and half the football team in jail for sexual misconduct."

Brandy released a low whistle. "Wow! That will destroy Chancellor O'Brien."

"I don't think so," Regan puzzled. "There was an intricate plan to keep all information concerning the shenanigans of the athletic department from Chancellor O'Brien."

Brandy frowned. "The press will still crucify her. She's ruffled some of the good-ol'-boys' feathers, and they will jump at the chance to throw her under the bus."

"Peyton isn't certain the two murders were the work of one person," Regan continued. "She's looking at a conspiracy."

"That would make sense too," Brandy said, picking up their empty plates and carrying them to the sink.

"I'll clear the table." Regan stood too quickly, knocking over her glass and watching helplessly as wine splashed onto her white blouse. "I'll never get this out."

"Go," Brandy said as she gave her a gentle shove toward the bathroom. "Wash it out in cold water. I'll finish up here while you change."

She quickly placed the dishes in the dishwasher and cleaned up the spilled wine from the table and floor. She poured fresh wine for them and carried it into Regan's office.

Regan's computer dinged as an email entered her mailbox. Brandy smiled to herself as she decided to look at the computer. If Regan didn't want her to read what was on the screen, she should have turned it off.

It took Brandy a few seconds to realize that it wasn't an email on the screen, but the first page of Regan's newest book. Her curiosity got the best of her, and she began to read.

The book was fascinating. Although it deviated from Regan's usual murder mystery fare, it had her panache and technique. Brandy didn't hear her professor return to the study. She jumped when Regan placed a hand on her shoulder.

"Regan! I . . . I didn't mean to invade your privacy. I was just so enthralled by your book that I got carried away. This may be your best book yet."

Regan closed her eyes and counted to ten. She was furious with her student for snooping but lapped up the compliments Brandy heaped on her rejected book. She fought to gain control but burst into tears.

Brandy jumped to her feet and slowly pulled Regan into her arms. "What's wrong, honey?" she cooed, moving the brunette to the sofa. She sat down, pulled the smaller woman onto her lap, and rocked her like a baby. "Regan, it's a riveting story—at least the part I read. Why haven't you published it?"

"My publisher and my agent rejected it," Regan sobbed. "I agreed to teach at the university for a year to get back in touch with real life. Instead, I've found murders and a woman I can't drive from my mind."

"Was it rejected because it's lesfic?"

"Yes." Regan sniffed, trying to dry her tears.

"And you are a lesbian, aren't you?"

"Yes, and I've fallen in love with you." Regan's sobs started again. "And you're my student. I'm fourteen years older than you. There are so many things wrong with this scenario."

Brandy continued to rock the brunette in her arms and whisper soothing words to her. "It's okay, because I've fallen in love with you too."

Regan gasped. "What? What about Joey?"

"He's my brother." Brandy giggled.

Regan stopped crying. "So, you're not sleeping with him?"

"Nope. Never have. Never will," Brandy declared. "But I'd sacrifice everything to sleep with you. Why don't I make coffee while I explain?"

Chapter 21

Regan couldn't take her eyes off Brandy as the blonde moved around the kitchen as if she lived there. The Keurig gurgled and filled the room with the aroma of coffee as the dark-brown liquid dribbled into a cup. Brandy placed the steaming coffee in front of Regan and pushed the button to fill her own cup.

"This is an involved story. We might be more comfortable on the sofa," Brandy suggested. Regan followed her into the study.

"Joey is my brother and my partner," Brandy began. "He is at UT on a football scholarship, and I enrolled here because they have a great law school. He's younger than I am, and this is his last year to play college ball, so we desperately need to wrap up our case.

"My senior year, the FBI recruited Joey and me for several reasons. I was at the top of my class, and they needed someone entrenched on the UT campus. They were quietly investigating the disappearances of young women from the university. They needed someone already active in campus life. Joey and I are very active on campus, so we were good choices for the job.

"That was three years ago, and we have been compiling evidence that incriminates the athletic staff. We had enough to start making arrests. That fell apart when someone started killing the coaches—our perps. When Chancellor O'Brien requested Agent King for the investigation of Coach Tucker's death, it threw a monkey wrench into our entire operation. After Peyton questioned me and grilled Joey, our handler decided to bring Peyton into our investigation. Peyton was made our field supervisor and was updated on our investigation. She's as baffled as we are about the case.

"Peyton came here two years ago at the request of Chancellor O'Brien to investigate the murder of a girl named Jamie Wright. She stayed long enough to wrap up that case. The girl's body was dragged from the creek that runs behind some off-campus apartments. She'd been raped and strangled. Chancellor O'Brien was convinced the coaches and members of the football team were involved in her death because of the DNA from semen on her body, but Chief Sawyer arrested a homeless man who confessed to Jamie's murder, and Agent King returned to Dallas."

"You're an FBI agent?" Regan said, wide-eyed.

"Yes."

"So . . . you're not really involved with Joey. The two of you pretend to be a couple to gain acceptance inside the coaching circle."

"Yes," Brandy said. "I didn't want to work that closely with a hetero male agent, because I knew he'd get a crush on me. I'm a lesbian, so Joey was perfect."

Brandy tried to look into Regan's eyes, but the brunette turned away. "Is that a problem?"

"I . . . I'm not sure," Regan mumbled. "I don't really know you at all."

"So, does that mean you haven't fallen in love with me?" Brandy placed her cup on the coffee table. Then she reached for Regan's and set it down. "Because I'm irrevocably in love with you."

Brandy tipped up Regan's chin, so she could look into her eyes. She slowly placed her lips on Regan's and increased the pressure when the brunette leaned into her.

Without breaking the kiss, Regan slid her arms around Brandy's neck and pulled the younger woman onto her as she stretched out on the sofa.

"Are you certain this is what you want?" Brandy murmured as she caressed Regan's breast.

Regan gasped as Brandy slipped her soft hand beneath her sweater. "Right now, this is all I want. We'll discuss your multiple personalities tomorrow."

"And my age," Brandy muttered.

The rain was still tapping a staccato rhythm on her bedroom roof when Regan turned over and snuggled into the warm body in her bed. *Warm body in my bed?* She froze as she recalled the amazing night she had spent with Brandy. Brandy—her student. Brandy—a much younger woman. Brandy—an incredible lover.

Regan recalled her years with Leslie. In their five years together, Leslie had never touched her the way Brandy had. No one had ever made her feel the way Brandy made her feel. Not just the sex—that had been indescribable—but the sweet reassuring things Brandy whispered in her ear. The tender way Brandy ran her hands all over her body, as if worshipping a celestial being.

A spark of fire ignited the arousal in the pit of Regan's stomach. She wanted the blonde woman again. Her breath caught when Brandy threw her arm and leg across her body. Brandy nuzzled her hair and whispered in her ear, "Are you thinking what I'm thinking?"

"If you're thinking about driving me out of my mind like you did last night . . . ."

"Um, I'm thinking about breakfast." Brandy laughed, tightening her arms around Regan. "Satisfying you makes one work up an appetite."

Regan nipped her on the neck and rolled out of bed as Brandy yowled. "I don't have any breakfast food in the house. I hadn't planned on you spending the night. We'll have to go out for breakfast."

"I might be persuaded to make love to you again." Brandy reached for the brunette as Regan ran into the bathroom.

"Nope, I'm up and raring to go," Regan called out as she closed the bathroom door and turned on the shower.

Brandy gave her a minute and then followed her into the shower. The hot water felt good, and they clung to each other as they kissed beneath the rainforest showerhead.

"I love your body," Brandy murmured as she lathered soap on Regan's back. She smoothed soap down Regan's sides then slid her arms around the brunette, cupping her breasts. "God, you are perfect in every way."

Regan leaned back against her young lover as Brandy nipped and kissed her neck and shoulders. "Are you certain you want to go to breakfast right now?" Regan asked.

Brandy turned her around and rinsed the soap from her body before turning off the shower. "The only thing I want to do right now is get you back into bed." She helped Regan from the shower and pulled her toward the bedroom.

Regan squealed as Brandy pushed her onto the bed and slid down beside her. "We need to dry off. We're all wet."

"The better to make love to you, my dear." Brandy bared perfect, white teeth mischievously, and Regan squealed louder as the blonde straddled her waist.

Chapter 22

Peyton thumbed through Paula Lambert's file one more time. She looked at the photos and interviews that had been taken during the girl's case. Pat Sawyer had closed the case, stating that Miss Lambert had dropped the charges. Peyton wondered what had compelled Lambert to contact her.

Her office door opened, and a determined-looking woman stepped into the room. "I'm looking for Agent Peyton King," she said.

"I'm Agent King." Peyton stood and held out her hand. "You must be Paula Lambert."

"Yes, yes, I am." For a second the woman's self-confidence slipped, but she pulled back her shoulders and tossed her shoulder-length blonde hair away from her face. "I wanted to talk to you about the rape I reported four years ago."

Peyton gestured toward the chair across from her. "Please have a seat, Miss Lambert. I have Dr. Pepper, Coke, ginger ale, and 7-UP. Which would you like? Please select one. I hate to drink alone."

"Dr. Pepper, please." Paula smiled for the first time, and a playfulness danced in her hazel eyes. "I wouldn't want you to drink alone."

Peyton popped the tops on two cans and handed Paula a paper towel and the cold drink. "I appreciate your willingness to talk to me." Peyton took a long drink from her Dr. Pepper can. "I know it took a lot of nerve for you to come here today."

She opened the file on her desk. "I know this isn't easy for you, so I'm not going to ask you to relive the events leading up to you filing the charges against Athletic Director Bob Radford. I do want to ask you why you dropped the charges and have come forward now?"

Paula shifted in her chair and looked down momentarily. Then she raised her chin as if she were used to taking on the world.

"I dealt with Chief Sawyer during the investigation," Paula said, staring past Peyton. "She convinced me it would be better to drop the charges and get on with my life. She shared scenarios of what it would be like on the witness stand. How the defense attorney would make me look like a whore and a party girl who was asking for what I got.

"She said that even though Radford raped me, I would be the one on trial. My mother was in ill health, and I didn't want to drag her through that. My father died when I was four, so it's always been Mother and me.

"Chief Sawyer said I had taken a shower and had washed away valuable DNA evidence that would be needed to convict Radford, so there was no reason to waste the money or hospital time on a rape kit. She said I'd end up looking like a slut, and Radford would walk away without even a slap on the wrist. My reputation would be ruined, and he wouldn't even lose a night's sleep over the entire incident."

"Why now? Why four years later?" Peyton frowned. "The evidence is even less now. Somewhere along the way, Sawyer allowed it to disappear.

"This file is the only thing I found in the evidence box. There's Radford's statement that he didn't even know your name and had certainly never been intimate with you.

There are photos of you with bruises on your wrists and face, indicating someone held you down and hit you. Apparently, there was a dress with Radford's DNA on it, but it's gone. I have nothing that would prove Radford raped you."

Paula closed her eyes for several seconds. She pressed her hands together and leaned her forehead against her fingers as if praying. Peyton gave her time to compose herself.

"My mother passed away last year." Her hazel eyes watered, and she blinked repeatedly to clear them. "I'll graduate from law school this year and take the bar in July. It took longer than it should have, but I had responsibilities. I received a payout from Mother's life insurance, and I earn income clerking for Judge Crawford. Before I join a law firm, I want to get this settled."

Paula's eyes darted around the room as if looking for some way to escape what she knew she must do. "Radford didn't just rape me. He left me with his child to raise. Irrefutable proof of his DNA."

Peyton's mouth dropped open as she stared at the stunning blonde. "You have his child?"

Paula nodded. "A son. It's been hard."

"Why didn't you have an abortion?" Peyton asked.

"I'm Catholic. I don't believe in abortion. All the time I was carrying Trent, I hated him. He wasn't even in the world yet, and I despised all he stood for. I couldn't sleep. I had nightmares about what Radford did to me. But when they placed that baby boy in my arms, he stole my heart. I couldn't possibly love him more. He is my life."

"You know that if you testify against Radford, all of this will be dragged through the news media. You and

Trent will be ridiculed, and he'll eventually become aware that he is the result of you being raped by Radford."

"Believe me, Agent King, I've agonized over it, but this is the right thing to do. I can't remain silent and let men like Radford continue ruining the lives of innocent coeds. We come to college so full of hope and ambition, and the Radfords of this world steal our souls."

"I could put you into witness protection," Peyton thought out loud. "You have no ties here. I could give you a new name and have all your identifying paperwork reissued. You and Trent could start a new life."

Before Paula could respond, Joey burst into Peyton's office. "Agent King . . . oh, I'm sorry. I didn't realize you were interviewing someone. I'll come back."

"No, it's fine, Joey," Peyton said. "I'd like you to meet Paula Lambert. She's working with us on the sex scandal the athletic department has laid at our feet. Paula, Joey Sloan, our star quarterback."

Joey blushed and dipped his head. Peyton waited for the "Aww shucks" to come, but it didn't.

"I'm meeting Brandy and Professor Shaw for lunch," Joey said, grinning. "Why don't the two of you join us?"

"Oh, I'd better not," Paula said as she got to her feet.

"Please?" Joey flashed his little-boy smile that made women want to cuddle him. "It isn't often I get to lunch with four beautiful women."

Paula nodded. "I'd like that."

"I would too." Peyton pulled out her keys. "Let's lock up this place and join the others."

Chapter 23

"Thanks to you, Professor Arturo let me make up my Spanish test," Brandy said as they commandeered a table in the SUB. "What did you tell her?"

"I told her that you had been in bed all week with a high fever." Regan wrinkled her nose. "It wasn't a complete lie."

"Um, you do give me fever," Brandy whispered in her ear.

"Miss Brandywine, kindly keep your distance in public," Regan teased. "You know the effect you have on me."

"The feeling is mutual, I'm sure." Brandy intentionally brushed Regan's breasts as she reached across her for a napkin.

"You are evil, Grace Brandywine. Pure evil."

Suddenly, Joey's voice rang out across the room. "There they are! I told you they'd get us a table." He pulled up an extra chair for Paula as Peyton made the introductions.

"How's your investigation?" Regan asked.

"I'm beginning to see a light at the end of the tunnel," Peyton said. "I hate cases where so many innocent people are hurt, and it's only going to get worse."

"Do you like Reuben sandwiches?" Joey asked Paula. "They make the very best Reuben in the world."

"I do." Paula laughed at his enthusiasm. "With fries?"

"Of course." Joey beamed.

They placed their orders and launched into a discussion of the upcoming Thanksgiving break.

"What are your plans?" Peyton asked Regan.

"I'll be in town. This is my home, remember? What about you, Agent King? What do you have planned?"

"My parents and younger sister are visiting me for the weekend. I'm looking forward to that. My mom is a great cook."

"You aren't cooking for them? What kind of hostess are you?" Brandy chided.

"The worst kind, I'm afraid," Peyton said.

"How about you, Paula?" Joey asked.

"We lost my mom last year, so it will just be my son and me," Paula said. "He loves drumsticks."

"Why don't we all get together for Thanksgiving at my home?" Regan suggested. "It would be fun to have a group of good friends around for the holiday."

"Sonidos mucho bueno, senorita," Brandy said, showing off her Spanish. Everyone laughed.

Regan couldn't hide the sparkle in her eyes. She had the sudden need to take Brandy home with her.

"I'll cook the turkey and cornbread dressing," Regan said. "I have my grandmother's recipe, and it's to die for."

"I'll bring dessert," Paula chimed in.

By the time lunch was finished, the five had put together a menu fit for a king.

Peyton laughed. "My parents will be so impressed. I've never introduced them to friends before."

"You're hanging out with a better class of people now," Brandy teased. "An award-winning author, a star football player, two attorneys, and . . . well, I'll be an attorney someday."

"It's settled then. Thanksgiving at my house," Regan declared.

"Uh, Professor Shaw, you do know Thanksgiving Day is also a big football day," Joey pointed out. "We need to arrive at your home around eleven and stay until around nine."

"Perfect," Regan said. "We'll plan dinner for around one and then eat leftovers and watch football the rest of the day."

Joey grinned. "Sounds like my idea of heaven."

"Will anyone be bringing a plus-one?" Regan asked as she made a list of people to cook for.

"I might bring one extra," Peyton said. "For sure my parents and sister, but I may invite a friend."

"Ooh, Agent King, do you have a significant other hidden in the wings?" Brandy wiggled her eyebrows.

"Hardly," Peyton huffed. "Just someone who is very lonely. I may invite her to join us."

"Alright"—Joey clapped his hands—"then we'll reconvene at Professor Shaw's home at eleven o'clock Thanksgiving Day."

Chapter 24

Joey followed Paula from the SUB. "May I walk you to your car? We've had some unpleasant incidents on campus lately."

"I . . . um, don't have a car," Paula stammered. "I came on the bus."

"Please let me drive you home."

A look akin to fear flashed across Paula's beautiful face.

"I promise, I'm harmless," Joey said. "I'm just concerned for your safety."

Paula could see the sincerity in Joey's eyes, and he did have the cutest dimples she had ever seen. For some reason, she trusted the blond Adonis. She hadn't trusted anyone in so long. It was like a breath of fresh air.

"I'm really one of the good guys," Joey said, his grin deepening his dimples.

"I'd appreciate that," Paula said. "I don't live on campus."

"All the more reason I should drive you home."

"Just speak your address into my navigator," Joey instructed as he fastened his seat belt. "It'll tell me where to go, and we can talk without fear of missing a turn." He pulled out of the parking lot and onto the main road before he spoke again.

"I'm surprised I haven't noticed a woman as pretty as you on campus."

"I'm no longer on this campus," Paula said, cringing slightly. "I transferred to SMU four years ago to finish my law degree."

"Our loss and their gain," Joey bantered. "What kind of law?"

"Family law," Paula replied. "In addition to practicing law, I want to do pro bono work to help women who find themselves in bad domestic situations."

"Ahh . . . a champion."

"What's your major?" Paula asked.

"Engineering. Electrical engineering, to be exact. I have a mission too," Joey said. "The American power grid is just one terrorist away from plunging the US into total darkness. I've already been hired to work with the men and women who are working around the clock to put a backup grid in place. It's a mess."

"That's fascinating," Paula said. "Tell me—"

"You have arrived at your destination," the auto navigation system announced.

Paula laughed. "Oh, I had no idea the trip was so short."

"Time flies when you're having fun," Joey said, repeating the age-old axiom as he jumped from the car and hurried to open Paula's door.

As Paula stepped out, a towheaded tot ran toward her with his arms outstretched. "Mommy!" he hollered.

Paula scooped him up as he squealed and wrapped his arms around her neck. He shyly looked at Joey. A fifty-something woman joined them.

"Joey, this is Wanda Riley and my son, Trent. Trent, this is Joey, my new friend."

"You Joey Sloan," Trent said, pointing a stubby finger at Joey. "Me and Mama see you on TV."

"Wow!" Joey's eyes opened wide. "I'm surprised you know me."

"Football." Trent wrinkled his nose as if Joey should already have the information.

"Do you like to play football?" Joey asked.

Trent wiggled from his mother's arms and ran around the corner of the house, returning with a football. "We play."

"Not now, little man." Paula laughed. "Joey has places to be, and I need to fix your dinner."

"You and your mom are going to have Thanksgiving dinner with me and some friends," Joey told the boy. "Bring your football and we'll play then."

"Can I, Mommy? Can I?"

"Of course." Paula mouthed a thank you to Joey.

"Great! I'll pick you up at ten fifteen Thursday morning." Joey stepped back from the boy. "For right now, you could give me one good throw."

Trent held the ball over his head with both hands and threw it as hard as he could. Joey's height and long arms allowed him to easily catch the wobbly, wildly thrown ball. "Hey, big guy, you're pretty good," he said, laughing as the little boy grinned at him.

Chapter 25

Brandy rolled over and reached for Regan, but the other side of the bed was cold and empty. She rolled onto her back and listened. She could hear the object of her affections humming happily in the kitchen. She sniffed the air and picked up the aromas of spices and apples mingled with all the smells of a Thanksgiving dinner.

This is what I want my life to be, she thought as she marveled over the past two weeks she had spent with Regan. Professor Regan Shaw was everything a woman should be and more. She was smart, entertaining, exciting, interesting, and beyond gorgeous. She had lived a charmed life and was one of the top contemporary authors of the twenty-first century. Brandy knew that Regan was at a crossroads in her life. Her five-year relationship with Leslie Winters was over, and her agent and publisher had rejected her latest book because the main characters were lesbians.

Brandy hoped she wasn't getting Regan on the rebound and was just a pleasant distraction. She knew Regan had accepted the guest professor position at the university to reconnect with reality. She desperately hoped that when things settled in Regan's life, she would still be a part of it.

Brandy showered and dressed and joined Regan in the kitchen. She leaned against the doorjamb and watched the brunette as she loaded the dishwasher. As Regan closed the dishwasher door, Brandy slipped her arms around her waist and placed soft kisses on the back of her neck.

"I wondered when you would join me." Regan leaned back against her lover.

"I was disappointed to wake in an empty bed," Brandy murmured against her ear.

"I'm just getting a jump on tomorrow." Regan moaned as Brandy's arms tightened around her. "I knew I'd better get up before you tempted me to stay in bed with you all day."

"Oh, so now I'm a temptation." Brandy chuckled. "That's good to know."

Regan turned in her arms and tilted her head back for a kiss. "You know I have a weakness for you," she whispered.

Brandy was the first to pull away. "What can I do to help get ready for tomorrow?"

"I've made the cornbread dressing, so all we have to do tomorrow is put it in the oven. Can you make deviled eggs?"

"I'm sure I can, with a little bit of instruction from you."

Working together, they soon completed the task of getting their Thanksgiving offerings ready to go into the oven the next day.

"Our work here is done," Regan said, leaning her shoulder against Brandy's. "Would you like breakfast? I've already had toast and coffee, but I'd be happy to fix whatever you'd like."

"Um, I may have devoured three boiled eggs while you weren't looking." An impish grin deepened Brandy's dimples. "There is something I'd like you to do for me."

"Anything." Regan tiptoed to steal a kiss.

"Anything?" Brandy wiggled her eyebrows ominously and pulled Regan into her arms. "Promise?"

"Anything," Regan repeated in her sexiest voice. "I promise."

"Good." Brandy beamed. "I want you to read to me. I want you to read your latest—but unpublished—book to me."

"I . . . I didn't—"

"You said anything," Brandy insisted.

"Very well. Let me download it to my iPad. It will be easier to read from than my laptop."

"You download and I'll make fresh coffee." Brandy stole a kiss, gleeful that she had won the debate.

##

Regan moved her manuscript to her iPad as Brandy stretched out on the sofa and motioned for Regan to join her. "Sit here between my legs so you can lean back against me and not strain your voice. We can take turns reading."

Regan briefly wondered why Leslie had never been as thoughtful as Brandy. She settled between Brandy's legs and leaned back against the softness of the woman who was stealing her heart.

The more Regan read, the deeper Brandy fell in love with her. "You're an amazing writer," she whispered into the brunette's ear. "I can't believe anyone in their right mind would turn down this story. It's incredible. Did they even read it?"

"As I said, they rejected it because my two main characters are lesbians." Regan shrugged. "They thought it would tarnish my image if a spotlight was trained on my private life."

"You really did keep you and Leslie Winters a secret," Brandy noted. "When I read your first novel, I started digging to find out all I could about you."

"Why?" Regan asked.

"I thought you were beautiful. I saw you on talk shows promoting your books. You were so poised and laughed so easily. I loved your sultry, rich voice. It made shivers run down my spine. I think I fell in love with you then. I devoured your books, and when I heard you were going to be a guest professor at the university, I immediately signed up for your course. You could have taught mud wrestling, and I'd have signed up."

Regan laughed out loud. "You are good for my ego, Miss Brandywine. I hope I can live up to your image of me."

"Oh, Regan. Don't you know you have surpassed my schoolgirl fantasies about you and turned my world upside down? I love you more every day.

"Just being here with you like this—preparing for Thanksgiving, being together and sharing our thoughts and ideas—is stimulating in more ways than one."

Regan trailed her fingers up and down Brandy's inner thigh. The blonde moaned loudly. "That's just one of the stimulations I'm talking about."

"I think it's time you acted on it." Regan closed her iPad, let it slide to the floor, and turned over to face Brandy. Their kisses were soft and gentle as they fanned the flames that had flickered during the reading of the manuscript. "I'm afraid I'm falling deeper in love with you, Grace Brandywine. So afraid."

"You have nothing to fear from me, Regan. I would rather die than hurt you. I promise I'll be worthy of everything you have to offer."

"Are you going to take what I'm offering you right now?"

"Yes, ma'am, I am." Brandy giggled as she pulled the brunette to her. "Good Lord, you're an armful of woman. Have I told you how much I love your breasts?"

"Uh-huh, you've made that utterly clear."

"Did you just do a little play on words, Professor?" Brandy murmured as she pulled Regan's sweater over her head.

"Maybe." Regan's deep, sultry chuckle filled Brandy with an unquenchable desire.

Chapter 26

The sound of running water woke Regan. She floated in and out of sleep as she listened to Brandy singing in the shower. The sound of the hairdryer prompted her to join the blonde in the en suite bathroom.

"You have no clothes on," Brandy said breathlessly.

"I believe you left them somewhere between the sofa and the bed." Regan smirked as she turned on the shower.

Brandy leaned down and kissed her sweetly. "Thank you for last night."

"My pleasure." Regan's voice sent tremors through Brandy as she pulled the brunette into her arms.

"Don't even think about getting me back into bed," Regan chided. "I don't want to be there when our guests arrive."

"Later." Brandy raised a perfectly arched eyebrow.

"I can't wait," Regan said, laughing as she stepped into the steaming shower.

Joey arrived carrying Trent in his arms, as Paula juggled the boy's small travel bag and a dessert called Mississippi Mud Pie.

"Oh my gosh," Brandy drawled as she took the dish from Paula. "This is my favorite pie. I haven't had this since . . . in a very long time."

"It is delicious," Joey assured her.

"Yes, I can see where you've stolen a spoonful." Brandy hip-bumped him as she placed the pie on the kitchen island.

##

Joey sat on the sofa and removed Trent's coat and gloves. "It's colder than a well digger's . . . uh, a witch's heart out there." He beamed as he rumpled the hair of the cutest little boy Regan had ever seen. With his blond hair and green eyes, he looked like a tiny Joey.

Trent shyly looked around the room, clutching Joey's sweatshirt in his tiny fist and snuggling into the man.

Confident her son was in good hands, Paula turned to Regan. "What can I do to help, Professor?"

"You can begin by calling me Regan. We have everything ready. We're just waiting for Peyton and her family."

As if on cue, the doorbell rang, and Peyton's family entered with a gush of cold air. Introductions were made, and everyone crowded around the fireplace as Brandy took their coats and jackets to the extra bedroom.

Joey followed Brandy as Trent trotted along behind him. "Are you sleeping here now?" he whispered.

"Maybe." Brandy frowned. "How'd you know?"

"Kiki called me two days ago and said you hadn't been in your dorm room for a couple of weeks. She was worried about you. She thought you were shacked up with me."

"What did you tell her?"

"I said, 'I can neither confirm nor deny your suspicions.'" Joey snickered.

"That works for me." Brandy looked down as a tiny hand caught hold of hers.

"Hey, little man, are you doing okay?" Brandy dropped to her knees and hugged the little boy. "Joey, he looks just like you. If I didn't know better, I'd think . . . ."

Joey scooped up Trent and held him in the air as the little boy squealed with delight. "Higher," he shrieked.

"If I put you any higher, you'll stick to the ceiling," Joey said. "Let's go see what Mommy's doing." He turned to see Paula watching them from the doorway. She was wearing a smile that lit up her face and her eyes.

"Our Thanksgiving feast awaits," Regan announced as she entered the bedroom. She let the others go ahead and hung back to ask Brandy a question. "Who knows that you're an FBI agent?"

"Just Joey, Peyton, and now you. We still need to be in deep cover until we apprehend the murderer of Coach Tucker and Robin Chase."

They returned to the dining room as the doorbell rang. Everyone looked expectantly at the others, wondering who could be disturbing their Thanksgiving.

"That's my plus-one," Peyton said, smiling as she rushed to the door. "I'll get it."

Everyone went back to talking, playing with Trent, or filling glasses with ice. The group fell silent when Peyton and her guest entered the room.

Regan was the first to find her voice. "Chancellor O'Brien! What a delightful surprise."

Katherine turned to Peyton. "I shouldn't have come. I always dampen the spirit of a party."

"Nonsense." Regan took her elbow. "Come meet everyone, Chancellor."

"My friends call me Kate," Katherine said. "I'll stay on one condition: everyone must call me Kate."

"It's a deal, Kate," Regan said. She liked the elegant, attractive woman and suspected the chancellor could be fun when she wasn't busy being the stoic leader of the university.

Peyton took Katherine's arm. "Why don't I introduce Kate to everyone while you and Brandy get the last-minute things on the table?"

"That was perfect timing, Kate," Brandy called from the other side of the kitchen. "I just finished carving the turkey." She proudly carried it to the dining room table.

Joey whistled softly to get the guests' attention. "Everyone to the table. The game starts in one hour."

They took their places at the table, and Peyton's father said the Thanksgiving prayer before everyone started passing dishes in all directions.

After eating, Paula cleared the table as Joey settled into a reclining chair in the TV room. Trent climbed into his lap and was sleeping soundly when the others joined them. "He went out like a light," Joey whispered, grinning at Paula. "Here, sit beside me." He motioned to the recliner beside his.

Regan's TV room boasted two levels of five reclining chairs. With only the huge, wall-mounted TV lighting the room, it was cozy and relaxing. A gas fireplace burned in the corner. The men armchair quarterbacked as the women rooted for their teams in a quieter fashion.

"Why don't they pull that quarterback?" Kate asked Peyton as they watched the same player pile up one delay-of-game penalty after another.

"The big money is on the other team to win," Peyton commented. "I suspect the quarterback and offensive line coach are throwing the game."

"Big money? What do you mean?" Kate frowned.

"Gambling. Betting." Peyton shrugged. "There are millions bet on college games every weekend."

"Legally?" Kate scowled, realizing how little she knew about the ugly underbelly of college football.

"Legally in Vegas," Peyton said. "And through thousands of illegal bookies all over the US."

"I want to know more about this later," Kate hissed.

Peyton whispered something in her ear, and she settled down.

Brandy placed her warm lips next to Regan's ear. "I want them all to leave. I only want to be with you," she whispered.

Regan caught Brandy's hand and squeezed it in agreement.

##

The friends cheered for their favorite teams, had heated discussions on referee calls, and devoured all the desserts and leftovers. It was almost nine when Paula pointed out that she needed to get Trent home for a bath and bed.

Regan stood at the door and bid her guests goodbye.

"Aren't you leaving, dear?" Kate said to Brandy.

"Yes, ma'am," Brandy assured her. "I'm just going to help Professor Shaw clean up. I'm afraid we have destroyed her kitchen."

"We're going to follow you home," Peyton informed Katherine. "I'll feel better if I know you're home safe with the doors locked."

"It's really not necessary, Agent King," Katherine said, restoring their rightful places in the academic world.

Necessary or not, Peyton persisted. "Your safety is my responsibility, Chancellor."

"If you insist," Katherine said.

Regan closed the door on their last guest. "All I want is a quick shower and a long session with you." She tiptoed to brush her lips against Brandy's.

"Resistance is futile," Brandy said, doing her best robot impersonation. "Your wish is my command, Your Majesty."

They showered, made love, and snuggled. "Today was fun." Brandy sighed as Regan rested her head on Brandy's shoulder. "I like Kate a lot. She has a quick wit, and I love her laugh. She's really beautiful when she lets her hair down and enters into the banter."

"It was delightful," Regan said, "but I suspect it was because I was with you. Everyone else just seemed to fade into the background. As the old song says, 'I only have eyes for you.'"

Brandy hummed a few lines of the song as she closed her eyes, imploring all her senses to remember every detail about the woman in her arms.

"I wouldn't make a habit of calling her Kate," Regan advised. "I suspect the woman we hung out with today has been folded up and put away. Do you think Peyton is dating her?"

Brandy frowned as she thought about it. "I don't think so. I can't see Peyton with the Ice Queen. I believe she invited her because she knew the chancellor would be alone on Thanksgiving. She's a widow, you know?"

"I did read that somewhere," Regan said. "That's a shame. There is something very sensuous about her. She'd make someone a good bed partner."

"The only bed partner I care about is you." Brandy hugged her closer. "I do love you, Regan."

"I know, darling, and I love you."

Chief Pat Sawyer sat in her patrol car at the end of the street that harbored Regan Shaw's home. The gathering of cars in front of her house had caught Pat's attention when she was making her rounds.

Pat knew each car parked at the gathering. It was her job to know who belonged and who didn't. The shiny BMW belonged to Joey Sloan. The burnt-orange Jeep Wrangler belonged to Agent Peyton King, and the sleek black Mercedes belonged to Chancellor O'Brien. She didn't wonder where Brandy's car was. She knew it had been parked in Shaw's garage for more than two weeks. She wondered what O'Brien would say if she knew the author/professor was playing house with her student. *More power to Shaw,* she thought. *I wouldn't mind hitting that myself.*

The front door opened, and people began pouring out of the Shaw house. All the people who apparently had nowhere else to go for Thanksgiving were laughing and hugging each other goodbye. *I wonder if they even thought of inviting me to their little feast.* Pat tried to squelch the bitterness that welled up in her.

A striking blonde caught her eye. Joey walked beside her, carrying a small child. Peyton's family loaded into her Wrangler as she stopped the blonde and spoke to her.

Pat studied the woman. She looked familiar. It took her a minute to put a name with the face. "Paula Lambert," she said out loud.

She's more mature and even more attractive than ever, Pat thought. *I wonder why she's back in Austin. If she's talking to Peyton, it can't be good.* She contemplated informing Radford but decided to stay out of anything Agent Peyton King was handling. She was just thankful that King was letting her testify against the abusers in the athletic department in exchange for no jail time. She'd throw them all under the bus and walk away scot-free.

Chapter 27

Regan lay quietly listening to Brandy's soft breathing. She was on her side, facing away from her lover, and Brandy was wrapped around her. It felt safe and warm in Brandy's arms. She wondered if Brandy would still love her when she was sixty-six and Brandy was fifty-two—or even worse, when Brandy was sixty and she was seventy-four.

Right now their sex drives were equal, but that would diminish with age. She knew she would always love the perky blonde, but at what age would Brandy notice women closer to her own age? At what age would she lose interest in sex while Brandy was in her prime? The way she felt now, she would always want to make love with the blonde goddess sharing her bed. She truly couldn't imagine a world where she would lose her desire for the young woman.

She knew Brandy was a natural nurturer by the way she had mothered her after Robin Chase had attacked her. *I love her too much to condemn her to playing caregiver to me in my old age,* Regan thought. *I'll have the time of my life this year and then return to New York and forget about Grace Brandywine.*

Brandy mumbled Regan's name in her sleep and pulled her closer. "I love you so damn much," Regan whispered into the night.

##

Regan was slipping from their bed when strong fingers wrapped around her wrist. "I told you I don't like waking in an empty bed." Brandy's sleepy, husky voice sent a shiver through Regan.

"I'll be right back." Regan leaned down and kissed her. "I want to brush my teeth."

"I should do that too," Brandy said. "I'm planning on some quality bed time with you this morning."

"I was hoping you'd say that." Regan giggled as she slipped from Brandy's grip.

They made love, talked, and made love again. Brandy fell onto her back, taking big gulps of air. "God, I love loving you," she said, moaning. "You're like no other woman I've ever known."

"And just how many women have you known, Miss Brandywine?"

"Enough to know that you're truly someone special, Regan. Someone I'd like to spend the rest of my life with."

Regan's noncommittal sigh left Brandy's suggestion hanging.

"Let's go out for breakfast," Brandy grumbled.

"I can cook breakfast for us."

"No, I need to get some fresh air." Brandy stood and pulled on her jeans. "Do you see my bra?"

"Even if I do, I won't tell you," Regan teased. "I rather like the view as it is right now."

A smile ghosted Brandy's lips as she tried to remain upset with the brunette.

"I've hurt your feelings," Regan said. "I didn't mean to."

"You just made it pretty clear that you don't want to spend the rest of your life with me." Brandy scowled. "I love you, Regan. You're damn right, you hurt my feelings."

"I can't promise you a lifetime." Regan bowed her head for a second before raising her eyes to meet Brandy's furious gaze. "But I'd love it if you'd move in with me this year."

"Give me one year"—Brandy grinned confidently—"and you'll throw rocks at every other woman out there."

Regan laughed out loud. "The thing that made me fall in love with you was your cockiness."

Brandy let her jeans pool around her ankles and slipped back into their bed.

"I thought you were hungry," Regan whispered as she pulled the blonde on top of her.

"I am, but my appetite just changed. I'm hungry for something else."

Chapter 28

Peyton studied the crime photos of Paula Lambert. It was clear that she had been beaten and probably raped. She wondered why Chief Sawyer had dissuaded her from continuing with her complaint against Radford. The Austin police had been willing to accept the case. A hard knock on her office door made Peyton close the folder and slip it into her lap drawer.

"Come in," she called out as Pat Sawyer pushed the door open and entered the room.

"Did you have a nice Thanksgiving?" Pat's amicable smile put Peyton at ease.

"I did, and you?"

"Oh, yeah, great," Pat said. "I worked so more of my men could spend the day with their families. It was quiet. It always is when everyone goes home for a holiday."

"What can I do for you?" Peyton asked.

"I thought I saw Paula Lambert on campus the other day. Are you questioning her?"

"No, she stopped by to see me," Peyton said. "She may be able to assist me in my investigation."

"I'd be careful with that one," Pat said. "She kinda went crazy after what happened to her."

Peyton snorted. "I can understand that. She was beaten and raped."

"I wouldn't be too sure about that. We didn't have any proof to back up her claim."

Peyton stared at Pat until the chief became uneasy and started shuffling from one leg to the other.

"I've read the file," Peyton said, her voice ice-cold. "It looks to me like you were doing your usual cover up. I think you need to address that on the recording you're making for me. Record the truth, not the lie you were pushing. How's the recording coming, by the way?"

"I'm almost finished," Pat growled. "It's rather therapeutic. Sorta like going to confession."

"You know what they say—confession is good for the soul." Peyton stood. "Come on, I'll buy you a cup of coffee."

"Still, I'd be careful of the Lambert girl," Pat continued. "She swore she'd get even with Radford and his minions, if it was the last thing she ever did.

"She could be the one behind these murders. Tucker and Robin Chase were there when Radford supposedly raped her, and they swore it never happened."

"Humph. Who do you truly believe?"

Pat shook her head. "I don't know. From past experience and knowing Radford, I'd believe the girl."

"My sentiments exactly," Peyton jeered.

##

"You really like her," Brandy said to Joey as they had coffee in the SUB. "I can tell by the way you blush when I mention her name."

"At least I'm not sleeping with her," Joey declared.

"What's that supposed to mean?"

"You know." Joey grinned. "You're practically living at the professor's place."

"I am thinking about moving in with her," Brandy confided in her brother. "I love her, Joey."

"What does she think?"

"It's her idea. She asked me to."

"Damn, Brandy, you get all the gorgeous women. I can't believe the professor is a lesbian. Or did you turn her?" he added, tongue in cheek.

"Don't make me hurt you, Joey," Brandy growled. "It's not like I'm a vampire that can turn women into the same thing I am. You know that."

"I'm just jerking your chain, Sis. Don't get all defensive. But damn, she's hot."

"I had to tell her who we are. She didn't want to get involved with me if I was sleeping with you."

"So you threw me under the bus to get into the professor's bed." Joey chuckled. "Did you tell Peyton that the professor knows we're undercover agents?"

"Not yet. I'm heading over there after I finish my coffee. She's with Chief Sawyer right now. She'll probably rake me over the coals."

"Yeah, but I have a feeling Professor Shaw is worth it." Joey hugged his sister's shoulders.

"Your little Texas sidestep isn't going to work," Brandy quipped. "Do you like Paula Lambert?"

"What's not to like?" Joey wrinkled his brow. "She's drop-dead gorgeous, incredibly intelligent, witty, and kind. She's also a terrific mom. I'm as crazy about Trent as I am about her.

"I spent the week with them. Only not as intimate as your week. I went home to an empty dorm every night."

"So . . . man-to-man,"—Joey snickered—"what's it like with Professor Shaw?"

Brandy sobered. "I'm not discussing my sex life with you, you big idiot. But I will tell you she is like no one I've ever known. She's the one, Joey. I want to spend my life making her happy."

"I'm happy for you, Sis," Joey said. "Really happy that you've found the right woman."

Now if I can just convince her I'm serious about a lifetime commitment, Brandy thought.

Chapter 29

Peyton perused her file one more time. She felt confident she had enough evidence with Paula's statement and Trent's DNA match to get the district attorney to file charges against Bob Radford, providing Chancellor O'Brien the opening she needed to start interviewing for a new athletic director.

"Are you ready to do this?" She smiled confidently at Paula as she slipped the file into her briefcase and stood.

"As ready as I'll ever be," Paula said.

They chatted about mundane things as Peyton drove to the DA's office. She pulled the car into a reserved parking space in front of the building that housed the offices of the district attorney and the cubbyholes of the public defenders.

"This could get rough," Peyton told Paula one more time. "It's not too late to change your mind."

"I want the bastard to pay for what he did to me and scores of other women seeking a college degree." Paula opened her car door. "Let's get this over with."

District Attorney Beverly Barnes was ecstatic over the evidence and statements Peyton had compiled. "You have no idea how many women have sought justice over this arrogant asshole's behavior," she said. "I'd like nothing more than to put him behind bars for twenty years. He thinks he's untouchable. With this file I'll have my hands all over him, especially around his throat.

"I'll get a warrant for his arrest and pick him up today. By Friday, he'll be someone's girlfriend in the county jail. Give him a taste of his own medicine."

"You know he'll come at you with a bevy of attorneys," Peyton warned.

"Will the college stand behind him with their legal department?"

"I'm fairly certain I can convince Chancellor O'Brien to take a hands-off approach to this."

"She's a sharp cookie," Barnes said. "I've met her on several occasions at various functions. I've always been impressed with her. I'm sure she will steer the university away from this."

Peyton agreed. "It's a nasty business."

AD Barnes personally managed the arrest of Radford, timing it so he was picked up at seven in the evening at his home.

The arrest happened after the normal day's news cycle had completed and attorneys had gone home. Picking Radford up from his home avoided a scene on campus and forced him to spend the night in jail before his attorneys could arrange bail. By noon he was out of jail and storming into Chancellor O'Brien's office.

"You're responsible for this," he said, shrieking like a wounded banshee. "You've been after my job from day one."

Agent Peyton King arrived at the office shortly after Radford. "You need to leave, Coach," Peyton suggested politely.

"I don't need to leave, and I don't need to take orders from you," Radford stormed. "You're just her lap dog."

"I'm going to do you a favor," Peyton said. "I'm going to count to three. If you haven't left this office by the time I reach three, I'm arresting your butt again. Of course, you probably enjoyed being in jail with all those big, burly men. One!"

Radford took a step backward toward the door. "You don't scare me."

"Two!"

Radford rushed to the door and slung it open. It bounced off the wall with a loud bang. "You and Paula what's-her-name will rue the day you came after me." He whirled around and was gone.

"That went well." Katherine snickered as Peyton closed the door. "I believe I owe you a dinner, Agent King. We can go out or I can cook. Your choice."

"What's for dessert?" Peyton grinned impishly.

"My house it is," Katherine said, chuckling as she gathered her purse and laptop.

Chapter 30

Peyton was late getting into work the next morning and was surprised to see Paula's car parked in front of her makeshift office building.

"Good morning, Paula," Peyton said cheerfully. "How are—"

Paula burst into tears and held out a sheet of paper to Peyton. "He's . . . he's—"

"The son of a . . . ." Peyton stopped short of cursing a blue streak as she read the paper Paula handed her.

"It's a subpoena," Peyton muttered. "He's subpoenaing you to bring Trent to court. He's filing for his parental rights as Trent's father. He's filing for custody of Trent."

Paula sobbed louder as Peyton read the information she'd handed her.

"He's trying to take my son," Paula wailed.

Joey knocked on the door and then peeked around it at the two distraught women. "What's going on?" He immediately moved to provide Paula a shoulder to cry on, and she accepted it.

Peyton frowned. "It's a long story. Why don't you take Paula for a cup of coffee while I make a few phone calls?"

Joey put his arm around Paula's shoulders and guided her out the door. Peyton waited until she saw them heading across the campus before she picked up the phone and called Chancellor O'Brien.

"Katherine, I need to see you immediately," she said when Kate's sultry voice came on the line.

"My door is always open for you, Agent King. Come now. I'll have fresh coffee waiting for you."

Peyton reached Katherine's office in record time. As promised, a cup of steaming hot coffee awaited on the coffee table. "I thought we'd relax on the sofa," Katherine said as she motioned for Peyton to sit next to her. "Now tell me what's so important it couldn't wait until tonight."

Peyton sipped her coffee and tried to clear her mind. Her leg brushed the chancellor's, sending an unexpected thrill through her. The contact was soft and warm, and Katherine didn't seem to mind.

Peyton explained what was happening with Paula Lambert and Bob Radford. "The bottom line is, Paula is trying to do what's right, and Radford may very well end up taking away the only thing she cares about—her son."

"If he admits Trent is his son," Katherine reasoned, "he's admitting he raped her."

"He's now swearing they had consensual sex and that he has the right to his son." Peyton squinted, trying to stave off a vicious headache. "He's produced five witnesses that will swear that Paula flirted with him all night and then pulled him on top of her on the sofa."

"So he lied in the statements he gave to the Austin police," Katherine noted. "He said he'd never seen Paula before and never had sex with her.

"Go visit him. See if you can hold him off until after Christmas." Katherine patted Peyton's knee. "Maybe we'll have a Christmas miracle."

Speaking of Christmas miracles, I wouldn't mind finding you in my Christmas stocking, Peyton thought. She suppressed a smile as a vision of the well-endowed chancellor popping out of a Christmas stocking flashed across her mind.

"Why do I feel your mind is somewhere else?" Katherine chided.

"What makes you ask that?" Peyton mumbled, clearing the lump that had formed in her throat.

"That foolish grin on your face," Katherine said, elbowing her.

Peyton called Radford from the car as she headed to his office. His secretary assured her that he would be there all afternoon. She wanted to talk to him as soon as possible to head off Paula's problems.

Peyton tried to think of ways to present her proposal to Radford that would convince him to give up his claim on Trent, but her mind kept going back to Katherine O'Brien. She wondered if Katherine ever gave her a second thought.

Radford was on his phone when Peyton entered his office. He pointed toward a chair in front of his desk and continued his conversation.

"That was the father of our best receiver." Radford scowled as he slammed down the phone. "He's threatening to pull his son out of UT and send him to Alabama. This sex scandal shit you're stirring up is destroying my recruiting efforts."

"I think the sex scandal is your baby," Peyton huffed. "Don't try to lay that at someone else's feet. Besides, I believe the murders of your head coaches are what brought your sordid mess to the forefront."

"And now you've dragged up that little tramp Paula Lampley—"

"Lambert," Peyton corrected.

"Whatever." Radford waved his hand as if shooing away a gnat.

"I wanted to discuss Paula Lambert with you," Peyton said, plunging ahead. "I have over a dozen women who are willing to testify in court that you raped them"

Radford batted his reptilian eyes and shrugged.

"I have witnesses and one of the men who supplied you date rape drugs on a regular basis." She continued to bluff.

Radford began to squirm in his leather chair. "Look, Agent King, can't we solve this without the university suffering? I mean, this crap is destroying our football program."

"You could resign or retire, or whatever it takes to get you off this campus," Peyton advised. "I'll try to get Paula to drop her charges."

Radford leaned across his desk. "You don't seem to understand, Agent King. I want that little boy. I have no children, and I want him. Just for the record, I intend to die in this job."

Peyton glared at the despicable man, trying to rein in her temper. "Why don't we all back off and get through the holidays? No sense in destroying everyone's Christmas. I won't take any further action right now, and we can get together in January and work out something that works for everyone involved."

Radford nodded thoughtfully. "I can agree to that."

Chapter 31

"Paula, please tell me what's wrong," Joey pleaded as he drove Paula home. "Is Trent okay? I mean, he isn't ill, is he?"

"No, Trent is fine. It's all very complicated, Joey, and I have to decide what to do. You've been so sweet. I appreciate everything you've done for Trent and me."

"This is beginning to sound like the big kiss-off," Joey mumbled.

"Believe me, you don't want to get involved in my problems. You're the star quarterback. You need to go play football and worry about graduating. Trent and I will only be a distraction."

"A very beautiful and precious distraction," Joey said, trying to cheer her up.

"I . . . I just need some time to think." Paula forced a weak smile.

"Just remember that I'm here for you and Trent," Joey reassured her. "Please call me."

"I will," Paula said, getting out of the car and running toward the house before Joey could walk around and open her door.

As he pulled his car from the curb, Joey pushed the button on his steering wheel and instructed his system to call Brandy. She didn't answer until the fourth ring.

"Are you still in bed?" Joey marveled. "Is Professor Shaw with you?"

"Yes, and yes." Brandy giggled.

"I need to talk to you about Paula Lambert," Joey said. "Can we meet for coffee—just you and me?"

"Sure. Give me time to shower. How about the Greek Spot across from the campus in an hour?"

"Make that an hour and a half," Regan whispered in her ear as she slipped back into bed.

"Joey, better make that an hour and a half," Brandy repeated. She rolled over and pulled Regan into her arms.

Regan collapsed onto Brandy. "I love laying right here," she said, trying to catch her breath.

"I love you laying right here." Brandy tightened her arms around the brunette's waist. "You're so gorgeous. I love the way you look in the morning, with your hair all mussed and your sleepy, bedroom eyes."

Regan purred as Brandy rubbed her back. "Is everything alright with Joey?"

Brandy snickered. "Paula Lambert has him chasing his own tail. He is really smitten with her and Trent."

"What is she doing with Peyton?" Regan stretched like a big cat and rubbed against Brandy.

"I don't know. I know that Peyton is interviewing everyone who ever filed a complaint against Radford. She's trying to nail his butt to the wall. When something is rotten in any program, it usually comes from the top."

Regan stretched again. "I have to go teach a class. I'll see you this afternoon in English lit. I suppose you and Joey will come in acting like hormonal teenagers."

"That drove you crazy, didn't it?" Brandy laughed out loud.

"You have no idea, dear." Regan considered making love to the blonde one more time but knew she'd be late for class. "Now, the only thing that drives me crazy is you."

##

Joey had secured a booth in the deepest corner of the Greek restaurant. "I ordered baklava and coffee," he said as he stood and hugged his sister.

"Baklava?" Brandy cocked an eyebrow at him. "You're eating sweets? This must be serious."

Joey got straight to the point. "Tell me what you know about Paula."

"No more than you," Brandy said. "I know she filed a complaint against Radford about four years ago, but other than that I know nothing. Have you talked to Peyton?"

"Yeah." Joey snorted. "Peyton just says that Paula and a dozen other girls and two men are involved in her ongoing investigation of Radford. Do you think the son of a bitch molested her?"

"I don't know. I'll talk to Peyton and see if I can find out anything more," Brandy said.

"Thanks, Sis. This means a lot to me."

The alarm on Brandy's cell phone sounded, and she smiled. "Almost time to go to English lit."

"I've never seen you look so happy about going to a class," Joey said, teasing his sister. "You have it bad, girl."

"I know." Brandy shrugged. "I'm just not sure Regan feels the same way about me. Something is holding her back. I can feel it."

"She's giving a pop quiz today," Joey blurted.

"How do you know? She didn't say anything to me about it."

"My roommate called me on my way to meet you and gave me a heads-up. He said the quiz has one question on it."

"What?"

"Write a line from *The Twelfth Night*. Have you read it?"

"Once, but I remember a couple of lines that hit home."

"Give me one," Joey pleaded. "I haven't cracked the book open."

" 'Many a good hanging prevents a bad marriage.'"

"I'll use that." Joey grinned.

"Okay. I've got another one just as apropos. 'Love sought is good but given unsought is better.'"

"I don't know," Joey said, "I think the harder we have to work for it, the more we treasure it."

##

Regan didn't look up when Brandy and Joey entered her classroom. She knew the look in her eyes would give away her feelings for the young woman. The rest of the class laughed at their antics as Joey kept putting his hand in Brandy's hip pocket, and she continued to slap it away.

Regan got to her feet. "Joey Sloan, Miss Brandywine—enough! Joey, I want you to sit on the far right of the front row, and Miss Brandywine, you sit on the opposite end." *Or in my lap,* she thought. She hid the smile that threatened to give away how delighted she was to see her sassy blonde student.

"How many of you read *The Twelfth Night* over the weekend?"

Everyone's hand went up.

"I'm impressed. We're going to have a quick quiz over it," Regan informed the class. "Then we'll review for the midterm exam, which is next Monday."

A groan went up from her students as they pulled out their notebooks. "This is simple," Regan continued. "Write one quote from *The Twelfth Night*. One simple line. You have ten minutes."

She sat down in the chair behind her desk and observed her students as some scribbled like crazy and others stared at the ceiling as if waiting for divine guidance.

"Your ten minutes are up." Regan's heels clicked on the tile floor as she walked to the front of the classroom. She handed each row a stack of paper. "These are your study guides for Friday's test. Take one and pass the others back.

"Please pass your quiz papers to me. Mr. Sloan and Miss Brandywine, hold on to your papers." She moved across the front row of students, collecting everyone's papers except Joey's and Brandy's.

"Mr. Sloan, please stand and read your line to the class."

Joey stood, graced the class with a beautiful display of his dimples, and then snorted with laughter. "You guys are going to love my line," he gloated. "'Many a good hanging prevents a bad marriage.'"

The class broke out in wild laughter as Joey swept his arm across his chest and bowed at the waist.

Regan controlled the laughter that welled up in her. "You may be seated, Mr. Sloan. Miss Brandywine, what line did you write?"

Brandy didn't take her eyes from Regan's face as she recited her line. "'Love sought is good but given unsought is better.'"

Silence fell over the class.

"You've probably never sought love, Professor," she said. "Love would always seek a woman like you."

Regan tried to tamp down the heat rushing up her body but failed as her face flushed bright red. "Class dismissed. We'll have our review Wednesday."

Regan gathered her laptop and briefcase and escaped to her office as Joey and Brandy started their usual banter.

Regan relaxed in her desk chair as she thought about Brandy. She had expected the girl to follow her into her office, but she hadn't. As Regan graded the quiz her students had just taken, she wondered what Brandy was doing. *Hopefully she'll be at my house when I get home,* Regan thought as she gathered her things to teach her last class of the day.

Chapter 32

Regan was delighted to see Brandy's car in the garage when she pulled hers in beside it. Missing the blonde had left a dull ache in her body most of the day. She hated being away from her.

Brandy met her as she got out of the car and leaned down for a soft, lingering kiss. "Let me help you carry your things," she said, gathering Regan's laptop and briefcase from the back seat.

"Mmm. Something smells good," Regan said as they walked into her home office and deposited her things on the desk. "You didn't tell me you were cooking dinner."

"It's so cold outside. I thought you'd prefer eating in tonight."

"It smells incredible. May I taste it?"

"Of course." Brandy beamed. "It's a Weight Watcher's Mexican dish."

"What's in it?"

"Shredded chicken, corn, salsa, and taco seasoning simmered in the crockpot. I just stirred in the yogurt. You put it in these little Tostitos dipping chips and presto—the perfect bite every time." Brandy held up one of the chips filled with the aromatic mixture. "Open wide."

Brandy gazed into Regan's dark eyes as she placed the morsel into the brunette's mouth.

"Oh my God, that's delicious!" Regan's eyes sparkled as she swallowed the food. "You're an amazing cook."

"I'm glad you like it." Brandy slipped her arms around Regan's waist. "It's a Texas tradition to kiss the cook if one really likes the food."

Regan wrapped her arms around Brandy's neck and tilted her head, savoring the moment Brandy's lips would touch hers. "I love you, baby," she whispered.

"I bet you say that to all the women who cook for you," Brandy teased as she placed soft kisses on lips she had thought about all day. "I love your lips."

##

After dinner, Brandy listened as Regan talked to her agent, Mel Denton, on the speakerphone. "Just send me the rejection in writing," Regan insisted.

"You don't need it in writing," Mel growled. "Take my word for it. I'm not hawking that book, and the publisher has no desire to market it. I'm telling you, Regan, it will be detrimental to your career to publish a lesbian murder mystery."

"Are you at your computer right now?" Regan asked.

"Yes."

"Then send me an email saying that you reject *Dressed to Kill,* and I'll never mention it again."

Less than thirty seconds later, an email dinged into Regan's computer. "Did you get it?" Mel barked.

"I have it. Thanks."

Mel moved on to a happier topic. "So, when can I expect your next book?"

"When I finish this school year," Regan said, indifferent. "I can't teach and write too."

"I'm not sure your readers will survive a whole year without a Regan Shaw murder mystery," Mel said as he tried to cajole Regan into a better mood.

Regan hung up the phone and printed out the email. "Now I have proof that Mel rejected *Dressed to Kill*."

"What's so important about that?" Brandy asked.

Regan picked up a stack of stapled papers from her desk and handed them to Brandy. "You're the law student. Tell me what my contract says about me publishing with another agent and publisher."

Brandy read the contract as Regan carried her iPad to the sofa in front of the fireplace.

"It says that the contract is binding and that you cannot publish a book without first offering it to Mel Denton and Night Owl Publishing Company. So, the email you just received from Mel frees you to publish *Dressed to Kill* anywhere you want."

"Exactly." Regan hugged herself. "I'll contact publishers over the Christmas holidays."

"It'll be a bestseller." Brandy took her place on the sofa, and Regan wiggled between her legs with her iPad on her lap. "I can't wait to hear who did it. At this point in time, I have no idea."

Regan leaned back against the softness of the blonde and began to read.

"I never saw that coming," Brandy squeaked as Regan finished *Dressed to Kill*. "She is the last person I would have pegged as the killer. I guess that's why they call you the Queen of Surprises."

"Did you like it?" Regan asked shyly.

"Like it? I loved it. This may be the best novel you've ever written."

"I think so too, but sometimes the writer is barn blind." Regan giggled.

"Who are you going to offer it to first?"

"I'm thinking about offering it to Just for Women Publishing. It's a lesbian novel, so a lesbian publishing company should do well with it."

Brandy kissed the back of her neck and nibbled at her shoulder. Regan turned her head slightly to give Brandy easier access.

"If it's a big hit, can I come out of the closet and be your significant other?" Brandy murmured.

Regan stiffened. "I . . . look, I—"

"You don't have to answer that question right now," Brandy whispered. "We'll cross that bridge when we come to it."

"You know I love you." Regan turned in Brandy's arms and kissed her until she moaned.

"Prove it," Brandy said, moving her hands up and down the brunette's body. She wrapped her legs around Regan and crushed their bodies together. "You have the rest of the night to prove how much you love me."

##

The Texas sun had melted the minuscule amount of snow that had fallen during the night, leaving the morning still and crisp. Brandy backed her car from Regan's garage and let a tremor run through her body as she thought about the night she'd spent with the beautiful woman she'd left sleeping. The way Regan had made love to her left no doubt in Brandy's mind. Regan was deeply in love with her. *Maybe Regan is afraid of commitment,* she reasoned.

Regan's first class was at ten, but Brandy's Spanish class was at eight. She decided she would sprint from her Spanish class to Regan's English class and sit in on her creative writing lab. *Then we can have lunch together,* she mused. *I'll make myself so much a part of her life that she won't be able to imagine life without me.*

Chapter 33

Wednesday morning, Brandy stared at the test grades posted by her Spanish professor. Regan nudged her aside so she could see the board.

"Baby, what happened?" Regan said. "How did you get an incomplete on your Spanish test?"

"I . . . I don't know." Brandy frowned. "Obviously I'm not grasping what you're teaching me in our tutoring sessions. I must have left some of the questions blank."

"Ask the professor to let you have the test. I can look at it and ascertain what's causing you trouble," Regan suggested. "Then we can concentrate on that."

Brandy nodded. "I took that test yesterday morning. I may have had other things on my mind."

Regan cocked her head, asking for clarification.

"That was the morning after you . . ." Brandy looked around to make certain no one was close enough to hear and then whispered in Regan's ear.

Regan blushed from head to toe. "We did do that, didn't we?"

"Yes, ma'am, we did,"—Brandy beamed—"and I couldn't stop thinking about it. I couldn't concentrate on anything else."

Regan took a deep breath as she tried to control the ache in her lower abdomen. "I'll have to remember to ask about your test schedule before we do that again."

Brandy laughed out loud. "I'd lie."

"You would, you little devil," Regan said, bumping Brandy with her hip.

"I've got a meeting with Peyton," Brandy said. Her sparkling eyes rivaled the clear waters of the Caribbean. "I'd love to kiss you right now, but I'll wait until we're not in a crowd."

"I have some errands to run." Regan touched Brandy's arm. "I'll see you at home tonight."

##

Joey scowled at Agent King. "Come on, Peyton. We're all working the same case. Can't you give us information on Paula Lambert?"

"Are you dating her?" Peyton asked.

"Sort of." Joey blushed.

"Sort of? What kind of answer is that?"

"Yes, we're seeing a lot of each other. But every time I think she's at ease with me, she stiffens and pushes me away. I'm not talking about sex. I'm talking about holding her hand or taking her elbow to guide her through a crowd."

"It's her place to share with you, Joey. Not mine."

Just then, Brandy burst into the room. "Sorry I'm late. I was with . . . uh . . . checking on my test grade."

"If you two can pull yourselves away from your love lives for a few minutes, we need to discuss where we are on this case." Peyton smirked, turning on her laptop and flashing the information onto the electric whiteboard.

"Did you look at the videos I gave you?" Joey asked. "They should be enough to put Radford and a few football players away for ten years."

Peyton scowled. "Where'd you get the videos?"

"They came from my frat brothers."

"Good. I'd hate to think you'd stand by videoing while a girl was being molested."

"Obviously you don't know me very well," Joey fumed. "I'd never let that happen. I'm disgusted that the guys videoed the occurrences instead of stopping them."

"Some of Joey's frat brothers are real assholes," Brandy chimed in. "One of the videos was posted on Facebook. What kind of degenerate does that?"

"I have warrants to arrest them all," Peyton informed them.

"Radford too?" Joey asked.

"That's a little more complicated."

"He's the head of the serpent," Brandy said. "You have more than enough evidence to get a conviction in any court."

"I'm treading carefully with Radford. More than his reputation is at stake here. The university could end up with a black eye if we mishandle this.

"The day before the university closes for Christmas, we'll quietly arrest twenty-two athletes and Coach Clint Wayne. He was the star of one of your videos."

Photos of Coach Danny Tucker and Women's Athletic Director Robin Chase flashed onto the whiteboard. "We still have no clue who murdered these two," Peyton said. "I know your focus is on sex crimes, but the two murders activated my assignment to this case.

"There were no witnesses to Coach Tucker's murder, and no one saw anyone drive Robin into the bonfire. It's incredible that this was pulled off without anyone seeing it, given that there were swarms of people everywhere."

Brandy and Joey nodded. "You've found plenty of people with motive," Brandy pointed out. "Tucker and Chase molested a lot of girls over the years. Maybe one of them has returned for revenge."

"I have only one who is willing to come forward and have her name dragged through the dirt in order to convict Radford," Peyton said. "Even she is having second thoughts. Men who prey on women count on them being too ashamed to prosecute. They know the women will keep quiet to avoid public embarrassment."

"What about Chief Sawyer?" Joey suggested. "She's cleaned up the athletic department's messes over the years. We know they were blackmailing her. Maybe she decided she couldn't be a part of what was happening to the girls on this campus."

"She's at the top of my list," Peyton said, "but I'm not sure. I have no evidence that would connect her to the murders."

"I could flirt with Radford and then shoot him when he makes a move on me," Brandy said with an impish grin. "That would solve our problem."

Peyton tried her best to look appalled but couldn't stop the smile that ghosted her lips. "The courts might see that as entrapment, Agent Brandywine." She chuckled.

"Are you two going to the chancellor's Christmas party tomorrow night?" Peyton asked.

"It's a masquerade party," Brandy declared. "We have to dress as elves or Santa or comic book characters. Joey and I are going just to keep an eye on things."

"Is Professor Shaw going?" Peyton asked.

"I'm pretty certain she's going with Professor Bolen," Brandy said. "I think she's going as an elf. I saw a black bodysuit in her closet and a black mask. But she did say something about Wonder Woman.

"Joey and I are going as Superman and Supergirl," Brandy said with a laugh. "We'll wear masks, so no one should be able to identify us. What are you wearing?"

"I haven't decided." Peyton shrugged. "I may go as FBI Agent Peyton King."

Regan's heart fluttered as her garage door went up and Brandy's BMW came into view. *I love it when she beats me home. I hate entering an empty house now that I've gotten used to her being here.*

As usual, Brandy was at her car door in a flash, gathering her briefcase and laptop. Regan stood and tilted her head back for the kiss she had become accustomed to.

"Do you have your Spanish book here?" Regan asked as she opened the door for Brandy to enter the house.

"Yes, but it's too late for that. Professor Arturo will probably fail me."

"I had coffee with her this afternoon and convinced her to retest you tomorrow morning."

"Seriously? That's awesome," Brandy gushed as she dropped Regan's things in her office and pulled the brunette into her arms.

"No, no," Regan said, pushing her away. "No distractions tonight. All we're going to do is study."

"Study all night?" Brandy groaned.

"Until you know all the answers. Then we're going to sleep, so you will be rested and have a clear mind tomorrow."

Regan followed the aroma of something cooking. "What are you making?"

"Something simple," Brandy said as she followed Regan. "You have the sexiest walk." She giggled.

"Get your attention off my backside and onto your Spanish," Regan teased her. "What gourmet delight have you prepared for us tonight?"

"Lemon pepper chicken, scalloped potatoes, and green beans," Brandy said as she pulled the chicken from the oven.

"Grace Brandywine, you are the woman of my dreams." Regan slipped her arms around the blonde's neck and pressed the full length of her body against Brandy.

"Have mercy on me, Professor." Brandy moaned as she pulled the brunette into a long, burning kiss.

They finished dinner and settled in front of the fireplace to study. "Your biggest problem seems to be with verb conjugation," Regan noted. "Let's try something a little different."

"Something a little different?" Brandy winked at her. "Those are the same words you said to me last night."

Regan burst out laughing. "Not gonna happen tonight, baby. Your grades are too important."

After two hours of struggling to use the correct verbs, Brandy tossed the Spanish book on the coffee table and pulled her teacher onto her lap.

"Jeez, Regan, they taught a gorilla sign language faster than I'm learning Spanish."

"Why don't we take a break?" Regan meant to kiss the blonde chastely, but somehow the touch of their lips inflamed them both. "Baby, you've got to ace that test in the morning."

"I will. I promise. Only right now I need—" Firm lips cut off her rambling as Regan explored Brandy's lips and then engaged her tongue in a heated dual of lust.

They made love on the sofa, and Brandy pulled the throw blanket over them. "I love how soft and smooth you are," she murmured in Regan's ear. "Your skin is like silk, only warmer and more luxurious. I've never touched anything as pleasing as your body."

"You feel the same," Regan whispered. "I can't keep my hands off you."

"That's a good thing." Brandy hugged her tighter. "A very good thing."

"I'm going to get a couple bottles of water," Regan said, pulling her sweater over her head. "Why don't you find the rest of our clothes?"

"Could you leave your bra off? I love caressing you."

Regan laughed softly. "No. You know how that turns me on. We're going to study, and that's all."

By midnight, Regan deemed Brandy prepared to take the Spanish test. They showered and slipped into bed. Regan rested her head on Brandy's shoulder.

"I'm surprised Professor Arturo agreed to let me retake the test," Brandy mumbled, stroking Regan's back. "How did you swing that?"

"She's married to one of her former students," Regan answered. "She understands how distracting love can be."

"Hmm. Did you tell her why I couldn't think straight?"

"No, just that we'd had a long night, and your mind was elsewhere." Regan kissed the blonde on the side of the breast. "Go to sleep, darling."

Chapter 34

Joey counted the ringtones. He was anxious to talk to Paula. Just to hear her voice would make his day. His heart sank with each additional ring.

As he was about to give up, a breathless Paula answered the phone.

"Paula, this is Joey. Are you okay?"

"Give me a minute to catch my breath," Paula gasped, taking deep breaths and exhaling slowly. "That's better. Now I can talk."

"Are you okay?"

"Yes, you caught me at the end of my run. I try to run every day to keep in shape."

"I'd say you do a darn good job of staying in shape." Joey chuckled.

"You are so sweet, Joey Sloan."

"Have you and little man had breakfast?"

"No," Paula answered without hesitation.

"Neither have I. May I pick you up and take the two of you to breakfast? I can be there in thirty."

"Make it forty-five so I can take a quick shower, and you have a deal. I know Trent will be thrilled to see you."

"What about you?" Joey dropped his voice to a soft hum.

"I'd love to see you, Mr. Sloan."

"Forty-five minutes," Joey sang into the phone.

##

As he drove to Paula's home, Joey tried to pinpoint the moment she and Trent had become so important to his happiness. It had evolved gradually. Scenes flashed through his mind: Trent climbing into his lap and talking to him about football; Paula reaching across the table to gently touch his hand; pulling both under his coat to protect them from falling raindrops; Trent clutching Joey's shirt in his tiny hands because Santa Claus scared him. Of all the moments in his life, the ones containing Paula and Trent were the most important.

Joey knew that Paula cared about him. She showed it in so many ways: cooking his favorite meal; putting ice packs and heating pads on his football injuries; reaching for his hand when they walked; leaning against him; the happiness in her voice when he called. But when it moved beyond hand-holding—when he tried to kiss her—she turned away.

Joey knew he was dealing with something beyond his comprehension. He wished she would talk to him, tell him what was wrong and how he could help.

He turned onto Paula's street and hummed a few bars from *My Fair Lady*. "There's no place I'd rather be than on the street where you live." He knew his words weren't quite right, but the meaning was spot-on.

Trent chattered to himself, absorbed in his eggs and toast. Paula smiled and held Joey's hand across the table. "Do you have any special plans for Christmas?" he asked as the waitress refilled their coffee cups.

"No, just Trent and me."

"Would you like to spend it with me at my dad's ranch? Brandy and Professor Shaw will be there. You'll love my dad. He's great and will dote on Trent. Of course, you and Trent would have your own room.

"We have horses and a few baby goats that little man would love."

"Baby goats?" Trent perked up, momentarily forgetting his food. "I play with baby goats?"

"Oh, I can see how this is going to go, Joey Sloan. The guys against the girls, and I'll always lose. He will follow your lead on everything."

Joey laughed out loud as Trent nodded enthusiastically. "Trent loves Joey," the boy jabbered.

"It's settled then," Joey said. "This will be the best Christmas ever."

Chapter 35

Joey knocked on the door and then turned the handle. "Paula?" he called into the house.

"I'm in the kitchen, honey. Come on in."

"Wow! It smells amazing here." Joey bent to kiss her on the cheek as he handed her a bottle of wine. "I believe this is your favorite."

"It is," Paula said. "It will go perfectly with dinner."

Joey moseyed into the living room and looked around.

"Are you looking for something?" Paula asked.

"Mini me." Joey grinned. "Is he hiding from me?"

"No. He isn't here."

"Where is he?" Alarm filled Joey's voice. "Is he okay?"

"Wanda took him home with her. Last minute call. I have to be at work early in the morning and didn't want to wake him and drag him out. Wanda has a TV repairman coming in the morning, so we thought it best for her to take him home with her. He was so excited about an overnight at Wanda's."

I would be excited about an overnight with you, Joey thought, but immediately dismissed the idea. If he wanted her to feel at ease with him, he had to be on his best behavior.

"If you'll point me toward the wine opener, I'll uncork the wine and let it breathe."

Paula opened a drawer and handed Joey the corkscrew. He opened the wine and volunteered to set the table.

"You are much more domesticated than I expected," Paula teased.

"Seriously," Joey said, laughing. "Have you met Brandy?"

"Your girlfriend?" Paula raised an eyebrow.

"My . . . no." Joey suddenly realized that he had never explained his relationship to Brandy. "She's—"

"She's gorgeous," Paula mumbled. "I can't see you trading her for a woman with a small child."

"She's a lesbian," Joey blurted. "I act as a boyfriend for her so she doesn't have to deal with the idiots who are convinced she's just never met the right man."

"I did notice she paid more attention to Professor Shaw than you during Thanksgiving. Are she and Shaw lovers?"

"They live together."

Paula nodded as if that explained everything.

"The plates are in the cabinet behind you, and the silverware is in the drawer on your left."

They made small talk over dinner, discussing the university and Joey's upcoming bowl game on New Year's Day.

"Who'll coach the game?" Paula asked.

"It'll have to be Radford." Joey scowled. "He's all that's left. He's not very good."

"Did you ever join in his celebration parties after the games?" Paula narrowed her eyes.

"Not really," Joey said. "I was usually physically exhausted. The quarterback gets the hell beat out of him during a game."

Paula placed her hand on his forearm. "I'm glad you aren't planning to go pro. I hate to see you so abused."

"Why don't you bring Trent to the game?" Joey suggested. "He'd love to watch me play."

Paula glanced away. "It'll probably be too cold, and I've already promised Wanda we'll spend New Year's Day with her."

"I'll get you seats in the skyboxes. I can get a ticket for Wanda too," Joey pleaded. "It would mean a lot to me if you brought the little man to see me play. This will be my last year of football."

Paula clenched her jaw. "No. I don't want to discuss it anymore."

They finished dinner in silence. Joey carried the dishes to the sink and cleared the table, while Paula put things in the dishwasher.

"We make a pretty good domestic team," Joey said.

"If all else fails, we can always get jobs cooking and cleaning for the rich and famous," Paula said, doing her best to join in his joshing.

Joey caught her by the shoulders. "Paula, I didn't mean to upset—"

She jerked from his grasp and backed away from him like a terrified rabbit. "You need to leave. Leave now! This was a bad idea. I shouldn't have put myself in this situation."

"What situation? Paula, I don't understand. Why—"

"Don't touch me," she screamed. "Don't touch me."

Joey backed away from the hysterical woman. "I don't understand."

"Please, just leave," she gasped, trying to pull herself together.

Joey walked calmly to the kitchen counter, poured two glasses of wine, and carried them to the living room. He placed them on the coffee table, sat down, and looked up at her.

Paula watched him, prepared to bolt at the slightest indication he might try to touch her. After several minutes, she looked around, squeezed her eyes tightly shut, and let the tears run down her cheeks.

"Talk to me," Joey begged. "Please just talk to me. Don't send me away without an explanation. Surely you must know I've fallen in love with you."

"I'm so sorry, Joey. I never meant to hurt you."

"I think you have feelings for me too," Joey said softly. "Can we just talk?"

Paula sniffled. "You never ask me questions. You never ask about Trent or who his father is or—"

"Because it doesn't matter," Joey interrupted. "I don't care who his father is. I don't care if you're an unwed mother or a divorcée. I don't care. What I do care about is making you my family, taking care of you and Trent. I love him too."

"God, I don't deserve you," Paula mumbled as she sat in the chair across from Joey. "Don't interrupt me. I'll only tell this story once."

Joey sat in shocked silence as Paula related the sordid details of Trent's conception. Finally, she stopped talking.

"Bob Radford is Trent's father?" Joey said. "Does Radford know?"

Paula nodded. "I went to Agent King and volunteered to give testimony to help put Radford behind bars. The next thing I knew, Radford showed up with his lawyer, claiming the sex was consensual and saying he wanted custody of his son. He had five other people willing to testify that I was more than willing. His attorney said he was already drawing up a court order demanding that Trent be placed with Radford. I'd kill him before I'd let him take Trent."

"As would I," Joey growled. "What did Agent King say?"

"She talked Radford into waiting until after Christmas break to do anything. She said she's weighing our options."

Joey clenched his fists trying to control his temper.

"Joey, I can't lose Trent. I can't let a monster like Radford raise my son."

"We'll take Trent and disappear before we'll turn him over to Radford," Joey declared.

"You'd do that for me? Even after what I just told you . . . what another man did to me?"

Joey dropped to his knees in front of Paula and carefully took her hand. "I'd do anything for you, honey. You've been through a lot. Give me the chance to show you that all men aren't like Radford. Give me the chance to show you and Trent what true love is—to build a safe, happy life for us all."

Paula pulled Joey's hand to her lips and kissed each knuckle as if it were precious. "I will, Joey. Please just be patient with me."

"I'm the most patient man in the world," Joey said, flashing his dimples.

"God, I love you," she whispered as she pressed her lips against his. "How'd I ever get so lucky?"

Chapter 36

Peyton arrived two hours before Chancellor O'Brien's masquerade party. She wanted to check out the security and make certain the extra campus officers working the party knew what to do if anything went wrong. Chief Pat Sawyer had insisted on helping with the security.

"We'll keep in contact wearing these earbuds," Peyton informed them as she and Pat handed out the small devices. "If you get even a whiff of trouble, notify me immediately."

Katherine O'Brien entered the ballroom. "Agent King, Marisa said you were here. May I have a word with you in private?"

"Of course." Peyton followed the chancellor to her quarters. "Is something wrong?"

"No," Katherine said coyly. "I need help with my costume."

"What character did you choose?"

"Cat Woman. Is that too risqué?"

"I can't wait to see you in costume." Peyton licked her lips, trying to return some moisture to a mouth that suddenly felt like it was stuffed with cotton.

Katherine closed and locked the door to her enormous bedroom/sitting room and walked to the bed where her costume waited. Peyton followed close behind. "Would you mind unzipping me?" Katherine said as she backed up to Peyton.

Peyton overcame the desire to kiss the nape of Katherine's neck as she unzipped the dress. She also pushed the button to turn off her earbud.

"Please unfasten my bra too," Katherine requested. "The bodysuit has a built-in bra for smoother lines."

Peyton steadied her hands as she fumbled with the bra hooks. Katherine pulled the pins from her long auburn hair, letting it float softly onto her shoulders. She turned to face Peyton as she slipped her bra straps down her arms.

Peyton held her breath as she surveyed Katherine's perfect breasts. The chancellor stood still for several moments, until Peyton slowly let her gaze drift from Katherine's breasts to her emerald-green eyes.

"I . . . I . . ." Peyton's tongue wouldn't work properly.

"You what, Agent King?"

"You're so gorgeous," Peyton whispered as she realized Katherine's breast showcased nipples that were erect and begging to be touched.

"I'm glad you think so," Katherine murmured, taking a step toward Peyton.

Peyton threw caution to the wind and took Katherine by the shoulders, pulling her close and kissing her. Her kiss was tentative, praying for a response. Katherine slowly moved her full, pink lips against Peyton's. Peyton pulled her into her arms and deepened the kiss, seeking an invitation to entangle her tongue with Katherine's.

Katherine moaned softly and began unbuttoning Peyton's shirt. Peyton caught her hand and stopped her. "No, Kate. This isn't wise. You need to get dressed, and I need to have all my faculties firing at a hundred percent. I don't want any more dead bodies on this campus. Especially at Christmas time."

Katherine pressed her body hard against Peyton's. "Are you refusing me?" she whispered, brushing her lips across the agent's.

"Never," Peyton declared. "I'm just postponing the inevitable. I've wanted you from the first moment I laid eyes on you."

Katherine nodded and backed away. "Please help me put on my Cat Woman bodysuit."

Peyton smiled. "I'd love to. And I'll stay after the party to help you take it off."

Katherine laughed softly. "I'll look forward to that, Agent King."

Chapter 37

Peyton surveyed the ballroom, making note of who was at the party. Brandy was dressed as Supergirl, and Regan was dressed as Wonder Woman. *Figures,* Regan thought, laughing to herself.

Suddenly, she heard a loud noise and moved quickly toward a disturbance in the corner. "What's going on here?"

"Radford is drunk." Disgust dripped from Supergirl's words. "He fell down."

"I didn't fall," Radford growled as he used Peyton's arm to pull himself from the floor. "You pushed me, you little tart."

"You were groping Wonder Woman," Supergirl said, giving him another shove that sent him back to the floor.

"Get out of here," Peyton commanded Supergirl. "Go get some punch or something."

"What's going on?" Joey, dressed as Superman, caught Brandy's hand and pulled her away from the others.

"Radford's here, and he's drunk as a skunk."

"Maybe I should get rid of him," Joey hissed.

"Good idea. Take him back to his apartment so he can sleep it off."

Joey consulted with Peyton and then pulled Radford up, all but dragging the inebriated man toward the back exit.

Brandy returned to Regan. "Does Wonder Woman want to dance with Supergirl?" She flashed a devilish grin as she pulled Regan into her arms.

"Lord, you're an incredible dancer," Regan said, relaxing into Brandy's body and letting the blonde lead. Her senses were overcome by the fragrance Brandy was wearing.

"I think you'll find I'm pretty good at anything physical," Brandy murmured in her ear. "I can feel your heart beating. I like dancing with you. This is as close as I can get to you wearing clothes."

"I love your arms around me," Regan whispered. "You're very strong. I like strong women."

"I like soft, warm women," Brandy said. "Soft, willing women."

Regan realized she was clutching the back of Brandy's cape in an effort to pull the woman closer. "Miss Brandywine," she said, fighting to control her breathing, "I believe you're working both of us into a state unfit for the chancellor's party."

Brandy looked away, her eyes quickly scanning the room.

"What's wrong?" Regan whispered.

"Nothing. Joey is having trouble with Radford."

"Does he need your help?"

"No." Brandy chuckled. "Joey is quite capable of handling the likes of Radford."

A hush fell over the partiers as Radford stumbled back into the room. He was covered in bloody scratches and mumbling incoherently.

Peyton instructed Chief Sawyer to call for an ambulance as Radford collapsed to the floor.

"What happened?" Peyton asked Joey as she checked Radford's pulse.

"The lush fell off the porch and into the chancellor's prize rose bushes." Joey cursed under his breath. "Grab his feet. Let's get him out of here." The two carried the unconscious man to the front porch.

"You didn't shove him into the rose bushes, did you?" Peyton raised a questioning brow at Joey.

"No, but I might have if I'd thought about it," Joey scoffed. "He yanked his arm from my grip and fell backward off the porch. I do admit I laughed for several seconds before pulling his sorry butt from the bushes."

The ambulance pulled into the circular drive of the chancellor's mansion. Peyton waved the paramedics toward them and explained what had happened.

"He does look like a clowder of cats got hold of him," one paramedic observed, chuckling. "Got drunk and fell into the chancellor's prize rose bushes, huh? This guy's a piece of work."

"Yeah." Peyton snorted. "A real piece of work. Take him to the campus facility so he can sleep it off."

##

Regan watched Brandy as she consulted with Peyton and Joey. A soft touch on her arm drew her attention to the person dressed as Zorro.

"Let me guess who you are," Zorro said in fluent Spanish.

Regan chuckled. "Professor Arturo. Are you having a good time?"

"I am," Sofia Arturo replied. "I see you're with Supergirl."

"Yes." Regan sighed. "Dare I ask how she did on her test?"

"Aced it," Sofia said. "She didn't miss a thing. You must be a good teacher."

"She's a good student. She's very smart, but for some reason she was struggling with verb conjugation."

"That's what they all have trouble with, but you must have taught her something that made it all fall into place. When you have time, I'd like to discuss how you approached it. It might help me in my classroom."

"That's very flattering," Regan said. "I'm sure you know all the little teaching techniques. I'm afraid Brandy just wasn't listening."

Sofia scanned Wonder Woman's body. "I'm sure she had other things on her mind."

"I must go to the University Health Services," Peyton informed Katherine O'Brien. "Your athletic director took a nosedive into your prize rose bushes. I had the ambulance take him to UHS. I want to make certain no one tries to blame Joey for the accident."

"But you'll be back." Katherine looked up through long lashes, a tiny smile playing at the corner of her mouth.

"Stampeding longhorns couldn't keep me away," Peyton promised. "I know what's under that Cat Woman costume."

"I appreciate the way you and your team have contained Radford tonight," Katherine said. "Few people are even aware he was here. He's such an embarrassment. Please hurry back. I'll miss you."

Peyton entered the clinic as the ambulance drivers were returning to their vehicles. "Is he okay?" she asked.

"Yeah, they just put him in a room to sleep it off," the driver replied. "He's still covered in his own vomit."

"Do you know what room he's in?"

"I heard the orderly talking about room 302," the paramedic responded. "We told them he fell into a bunch of rose bushes."

Peyton thanked them and moved toward the elevator. The clinic was quiet. She knew that many of the students had already left campus for the Christmas holiday, and the facility was operating with a skeleton staff.

The driver's information was correct, and Peyton found Radford snoring loudly. "You'll have one hell of a hangover tomorrow," she muttered as she watched the man sleep.

Chapter 38

When Peyton returned to the mansion, the masquerade ball was in full swing. She searched out Katherine and approached her. "Everything is under control," she reassured the chancellor. "Your party seems to be a tremendous success."

"Yes, it is." Katherine beamed. "With no animals from the athletic department in attendance, everything is running smoothly. Thanks to you."

Peyton looked around the ballroom, locating the security team. Pat Sawyer was strutting around as if she were important. *I wonder how she sleeps at night*, Peyton thought as she mentally went through all the sexual violence cases Chief Sawyer had covered up or destroyed evidence from to prevent prosecution.

Joey and Brandy were in deep conversation about something that was obviously infuriating Brandy. Peyton stifled a smile as she watched Brandy turn from totally furious to meek as a lamb when Professor Shaw returned from the bar with two glasses of wine. *She's got it bad*, Peyton thought.

"Has anyone guessed who you are?" Peyton asked Katherine.

"Not a soul." She chuckled. "It's fun to be incognito in plain sight."

##

As planned, the Christmas party ended at midnight. Peyton and the rest of the security team herded stragglers toward the front door, where Katherine wished everyone a Merry Christmas. After the last guest left, Katherine closed and locked the door. She fell back against it and closed her eyes for a few seconds.

"You look tired," Peyton whispered. "I'd better be going too."

"You promised to help me out of this suit," Katherine said, her voice soft and sultry.

Peyton followed the chancellor upstairs and locked the bedroom door behind them. Katherine stopped inside the room and waited for the agent to unzip her costume.

Peyton's downward pull on the zipper was excruciatingly slow. She stopped midway and placed soft lips on Katherine's shoulders and neck.

"Please," Katherine moaned.

The zipper continued its downward trajectory, as Peyton slipped her hand inside the suit and let her fingers walk toward the redhead's taut breast. She teased the nipple, causing Katherine to throw her head back against Peyton's chest. Peyton cupped both of Katherine's breasts and pulled her tighter against her.

"I've thought about this all night," she whispered in Katherine's ear.

"As have I," Katherine murmured, turning in Peyton's arms. "I fear you won't think of me as a lady after tonight."

"What will I think of you?" Peyton said as their lips brushed together.

"I want you to think of me as the woman you can't love enough," Katherine whispered. "The woman you will always turn to for fulfillment of your fantasies and your needs."

##

It was five in the morning when Peyton slipped from the bathroom into Kate's bed. She lay on her back and replayed her night with Kate O'Brien. The stories she'd heard about redheads were true. They were demanding and satisfying lovers. Heat pooled between her legs as she thought about the way Katherine had begged and screamed her name, as if it were a mantra for sexual release.

Katherine snuggled into her and muttered, "You're cold, darling. Wrap around me."

Peyton spooned against the woman who now consumed her heart and mind. She inhaled the scent of Katherine and slipped into a dreamless sleep.

The ringing of Katherine's phone made both jerk awake. It took them a minute to untangle their naked bodies. "Hello?" Katherine's sleepy, sensuous voice made Peyton want to make love to her one more time.

"When did you discover this?" Katherine asked. The sleep was gone from her voice, and she became Chancellor O'Brien, university lioness. "Have you called Chief Sawyer? . . . "Yes, please call her, and tell her to call me as soon as she knows anything. . . . Thank you."

"What's going on?" Peyton asked as she turned on the bedside lamp. A lump formed in her throat as the dim light danced in Kate's emerald eyes.

"Radford's dead," Kate mumbled. "They think he aspirated and choked to death on his own vomit."

"I can't say I'm sorry." Peyton pulled Kate back into her arms. "It solves everyone's problems."

"Mmm, yes it does," Kate murmured as she pulled Peyton's hand where she wanted it.

Chapter 39

"I'm telling you the security cameras show someone dressed as Batman going into his room and coming out a few minutes later." Chief Pat Sawyer was pacing the floor. "I think Radford was murdered."

"Now you start acting like a real police officer?" Peyton scoffed. "Do you have the security footage?"

"The clinic is pulling a copy for me now." Sawyer grunted. "You know, Radford's death solves a lot of problems for a lot of people."

Peyton frowned. "Yeah, and the timing couldn't have been better. Football season ends with the bowl game. His death frees Chancellor O'Brien to begin the search for a reputable head coach and athletic director.

"Paula Lambert is free to live her life without the specter of Radford haunting her and her son. You really screwed her over, by the way."

"I did what I had to do to survive," Pat said.

"I've spent the last four months tracking down the women who filed rape complaints against Radford, his staff, and his athletes," Peyton said with a sigh. "Do you have any idea how many of them committed suicide after dealing with you?"

Pat had the decency to look down at the floor. "I meant them no harm. I was just staying afloat in a world of corrupt politics."

"Corruption you permitted to grow like a cancer on this campus." Peyton snarled in disgust. "How did you see all this ending?"

"Honestly, I didn't see it ending," Pat muttered. "But it has. Thanks to someone who had the guts to kill Tucker and Chase and maybe Radford."

"Keep that to yourself until we get a close look at the security video," Peyton instructed. "Triple murders tend to send up a serial-killer flare. The last thing we need is the news media crawling around our campus sensationalizing the three deaths.

"You really can't stand up to close scrutiny," Peyton added.

"When are you going to put me into witness protection and let me start living a new life?" Pat asked.

"As soon as I wrap up these murders." Peyton inhaled deeply and let the air escape her lungs slowly. "I've already made the arrangements. I have your written and audio confession about the atrocities committed by the athletic department and covered up by you. It was easy to convince the brass that your life will be in danger when I start rounding up the people you are testifying against.

"Christ, this goes back twelve years. One of the perps is a state senator now. That's gonna hit the fan."

"I know," Pat mumbled.

"Have you arranged an autopsy on Radford's body?" Peyton asked.

"Not yet. I guess I should do that," Pat said. "They don't usually do an autopsy when someone dies in a hospital facility. The coroner declared his death an accident. He asphyxiated on his own vomit."

"Hold off on the autopsy," Peyton instructed. "Don't release his body until I tell you to."

Chapter 40

"Give me this assignment," Leslie Winters pleaded with her new boss. "I promise you I'll bring back one hell of a story."

"People are fascinated by Texans and their frontier justice." William Porter steepled his fingers in front of his face. "I'd like nothing better than to embarrass their smug, conservative asses. Can you stay off the booze long enough to handle this?"

"I've been sober 369 days," Leslie said, scowling. "You took a chance on me and gave me this job. I won't let you down. You know I'm a damn good investigative reporter."

"I know you used to be," Porter said. "Okay, but if you screw this up, I'll see that you never work in this town again."

Porter pushed the intercom button and instructed his secretary to book Leslie on the next flight to Austin, Texas. "Tell accounting to cut her a check for her first month's salary. She'll pick it up in about ten minutes."

"I figure you're flat broke," Porter said. "Keep track of your expenses. We'll reimburse you."

"Thanks." Leslie tried to appear humble, something that was difficult for her.

Porter scrutinized his newest employee. She was still one hell of a good-looking woman. She was the whole package—brains, beauty, grit, and an instinct for a good story. She had the tenacity of a tiger and would get down in the dirt to get a good story. Rumors of a third death at UT had sent her flying to his office, declaring there was a serial killer loose on the college campus.

"We'll give you five minutes of airtime every night. Fill it with juicy info, and there may be an anchor spot for you on late-night news. Don't screw this up, Leslie. If you do, the only place for you will be in a breadline."

Leslie leaned her head back as the big jet tore down the runway, picking up enough speed to catapult it into the sky. She couldn't wait to see Regan Shaw. A flash of heat zipped through her body as she recalled nights with the sexy brunette. *What was I thinking*—she chastised herself—*trading a bottle of whiskey for nights with Regan?*

She licked her lips at the thought of a whiskey shot burning its way down her throat. She quickly returned her thoughts to Regan. She knew this was her last chance at the once-glorious career and loving woman she had thrown away because of alcohol. She had never lost track of Regan, cheering her on from afar as her writing career continued to soar. Now that her own career was about to be back on track, she wanted the only woman she had ever truly loved back in her life.

She was confident Regan would be thrilled to see her and hoped they could pick up where they'd left off.

"Dammit!" Regan slung the letter across her desk.

"What's wrong, Babe?" Brandy said as she entered the room carrying two cups of coffee.

Regan took both cups and placed them on her desk. She took Brandy's beautiful face between her hands. "What did I tell you about calling me Babe?"

"Err . . . um, that it made you want to throw me on the floor and fu—"—firm lips interrupted her—"me silly." Brandy finished her statement before pulling Regan into her arms. "Which I'm totally okay with."

Regan forgot about the letter, the coffee, and everything else in the world except the beauty exploring her body with both hands. "God, you drive me crazy," she whispered, moaning as Brandy lowered her onto the sofa.

They made love, and Regan dozed off in the warm arms of the woman she adored.

Brandy gently stroked Regan's back. They had been living together since before Thanksgiving, and she'd loved every minute of it. She couldn't imagine her life without Regan. Her life before Regan seemed distant, memories that belonged to someone else. She truly couldn't remember life without the brunette.

Regan stirred, and Brandy kissed the top of her head. "I love everything about you, Babe," Brandy said. "The way you feel, your scent . . . and, Lord help me, the way you kiss makes me weak in the knees."

"Obviously you have no effect on me at all," Regan murmured.

"What were you cursing about when I entered the room?"

"Did I curse?"

"As much as you ever do." Brandy chuckled. "That's just one of the many things I like about you. You are every inch a lady."

"I'm glad I am your lady," Regan snuggled deeper into Brandy's arms.

"You're avoiding my question."

"I received another rejection notice," Regan said. "The third one this week. They all love the book but don't want to get into a legal battle with Night Owl Publishing. Everyone knows I have an ironclad contract with them. They don't know about the refusal clause and don't want to take any chances."

"May I try something?" Brandy asked.

"What?"

"Let me market it on Amazon."

"Amazon?" Regan pulled back to look into smoldering green eyes. "Only writers who can't get a publishing house to sign them use Amazon."

"Au contraire, my dear," Brandy said in her most sophisticated voice. "One of the great lesfic writers of our time is an indie author and only offers her books on Amazon."

"She's a fluke," Regan snorted.

"No, she's a hell of a good writer, and people read her books—just like they read yours. She's one of the top ten bestselling authors this year. She appeals to lesbian and mainstream readers. I've studied her marketing strategies, and I think I could do the same thing with your book."

"I don't know," Regan muttered.

"What do you have to lose?"

"My career. What if Mel's right? What if people stop reading my mainstream books when they find out I'm a raging lesbian?"

"Raging, huh? I like the sound of that." Brandy scooted under Regan. "Making love to you is often like walking into the eye of a raging storm, and I love it."

"My book—like my body—is yours," Regan murmured. "Do whatever you want with them."

Later, Regan collapsed on Brandy's body. She lay still, trying to stop the pounding of her heart and catch her breath. "If you're as good with my book as you are with my body, we should make millions from it."

"Your book isn't quite as exciting as your body," Brandy murmured as she wrapped her arms around Regan and held her tightly. "I just can't get enough of you."

"You know the feeling is mutual." Regan raised her head from Brandy's chest and inched her body up Brandy's until their lips were touching. "Never enough!"

"What do you have planned for today?" Regan asked as she folded the throw and hung it over the back of the sofa.

"Let me see," Brandy mused, searching for her bra. "You've taken care of items one, two, and three on my list, so we can move on to whatever you'd like. Right now, I'm thinking a cup of hot coffee."

"The second-best way to start any day." Regan tiptoed to kiss the blonde, who bent down to meet her lips.

"Why don't you turn on the weather, and let's see what kind of day we're going to have. I'll make raisin toast and coffee." Brandy picked up the two cups of cold coffee and headed for the kitchen.

Regan flipped through the channels until she found her favorite meteorologist on one of the top cable TV stations.

The anchor asked viewers to stay with them for the upcoming weather report. Using the usual hook to keep people from channel surfing, he added, "We have a surprise for our viewers after the weather. Don't touch that remote."

Brandy joined Regan on the sofa, putting her arm around the brunette and snugging her into her side. They talked as the meteorologist forecast a warm, sunny day. The station cut to a commercial as they finished their toast.

"Do you play tennis?" Regan asked.

"Yes, I do," Brandy said, a lopsided grin on her face, "but you probably don't stand a chance against me. I was state champion."

"And you're a lot younger than me." Regan knitted her brows. "We'll see."

Brandy's heart ached when she saw the look in Regan's eyes. "Honey, I didn't mean that. I just mean that I'm very good and three inches taller than you."

Before Regan could respond, the TV anchorman reappeared on the screen. "And now for our surprise," he said as the photo of a gorgeous blonde filled the screen. Her eyes were a mesmerizing, dark denim-blue. Her lips and facial features were perfect.

Brandy jerked her head around to see how Regan was reacting. "Isn't she—"

"My ex? Yes." Regan nodded.

"I didn't realize her eyes were that color," Brandy said.

"Contacts," Regan huffed. "Her eyes are hazel."

"Miss Winters will be reporting live tonight from the University of Texas campus," the anchor said, continuing his spiel.

"Why is she coming here?" Brandy turned her body to face Regan.

"I have no idea," Regan said defensively. "Why are you asking me? You saw the same thing I just saw."

Brandy grabbed her cell phone and jabbed at a number on her speed dial. "Are you watching the news? . . . Uh-huh. . . . Why is Leslie Winters coming to our campus? . . . Tell me that isn't true." Her shoulders sagged. "Yeah, I'll be there in thirty."

"What's wrong?" Regan could feel the anxiety radiating from Brandy's body.

"Your girlfriend is coming to investigate the serial murders on our campus."

"Serial?" Regan squeaked. "But there have only been two—"

"Radford died last night," Brandy said, scowling. "The cause of death has been declared asphyxiation. He choked to death on his own vomit, but that idiot Pat Sawyer told a local newsman that Radford might have been smothered with a pillow. You know . . . three deaths—"

"And the perp becomes a serial murderer." Regan shook her head.

"Chief Sawyer has got to be the biggest screwup east of the Pecos," Brandy muttered. "What the hell was she thinking? The FBI is handling this case. Why was she even talking to the news media?"

Brandy stood. "I've got to meet with Peyton and Joey. We've got to head this off."

"May I go with you?" Regan asked

Brandy snorted. "So you can see your girlfriend?"

"That's the second time you've called her that," Regan said, seething. "She's not my girlfriend. That ended years ago."

Brandy shrugged as she pulled on her boots.

"Grace Brandywine, don't you dare pull this on me! You, and you alone, are my only love."

Brandy gazed into Regan's dark, stormy eyes. "I hope so, Regan, because I can't live without you."

They arrived at Peyton's office as a local news van pulled up. Brandy hopped out and sprinted around to open Regan's door. They stood facing each other. "I love you," Regan whispered.

"I know you do. And I love you. I'm sorry I was such a brat."

Regan tiptoed to kiss her. "My brat, I'll have to spank you when we get home."

"I think you should." Brandy's grin overshadowed the morning sun.

They entered Peyton's office while Leslie Winters and the local camera crew were getting their gear assembled. Joey and Paula were with the blonde FBI agent.

"Gather around," Peyton said, waving Brandy and Regan over to their huddle. "Quick strategy on handling Leslie Winters. No matter what Winters says, our only comment must be, 'We're waiting for the forensic report. At this time, the coroner has declared it an accident.'

"She'll try to separate us and interview us individually. Don't use Radford's name. That humanizes his death. Use the words 'it' and 'he,' but don't say his name.

"Everyone have a seat. I want this to look like a gathering of concerned friends. Also, that will leave no chair for Winters.

"Paula, don't ever repeat you're glad Radford is dead."

Paula blushed and nodded.

"I've placed Chief Sawyer under arrest for her own protection. She may be a target of the killer—or she may be the killer." Peyton swallowed the lump in her throat. "Under no circumstances is she to talk to Leslie Winters."

A loud knock on Peyton's office door announced the arrival of the reporter. "Come in," Peyton called.

As always, Leslie made a grand entrance, charging to the desk where Peyton was standing and extending her hand. "I'm Leslie Winters with—"

"Miss Winters, I'm FBI Agent Peyton King. What a pleasure it is to meet you." Peyton let her eyes rake Leslie from head to toe. "You're even more beautiful in person than on TV. What brings you to the Wild West?"

Leslie lost her train of thought as the agent fawned over her. It had been a long time since a beautiful woman had looked at her the way Agent King did. She didn't notice when Joey closed the door, blocking her cameraman's entrance.

"I . . . uh . . . you've had three murders on campus since the fall semester started. That makes the homicides the work of a—"

"No, we've had only two homicides here," Peyton interrupted. "That's why my office is involved. One victim lived in Oklahoma and worked in Texas. You know, crossing state lines—that sort of thing."

"But yesterday a third body was discovered," Leslie blurted.

"I wouldn't say 'discovered'. The UT athletic director—who is a notorious drunk—choked to death on his own vomit at a local clinic where he was being treated for his drunken behavior. Hardly a reason to send an investigative reporter of your caliber flying from New York to Austin." Peyton flashed her most engaging smile. "But I'll be happy to talk with you. Have you had lunch?"

Leslie looked down at the floor, fighting to regain her composure. She hadn't anticipated the sexy agent, and the information she had been given said nothing about Radford choking on his own vomit. She decided to risk exposing her informant.

"I'd like to speak to the university chief of police," Leslie said.

"Everyone's gone for Christmas vacation. Even the chief gets a vacation occasionally. I can have her call you."

"What about Chancellor O'Brien?" Leslie pushed. "I'd love to speak with her."

Agent King's demeanor changed with the mention of the chancellor. "As I said, I'm in charge of this case. You can ask me anything you wish."

"I insist on speaking to Chancellor O'Brien." Leslie narrowed her eyes at King. "Unless the university has something to hide, I'd think the chancellor would want to speak with me."

"Chancellor O'Brien doesn't do off-the-cuff interviews with anyone," King said, glaring at the gorgeous reporter. "You may interview me or pack up and leave."

"You . . . you can't refuse me access to O'Brien," Leslie growled.

Peyton walked around her desk to confront Leslie. "Miss Winters, I'm in the middle of two murder investigations. The entire campus is closed for the Christmas holidays. If you'd like to come back in mid-January when everyone is back in their office, I'm sure Chancellor O'Brien will try to work you into her very busy schedule."

Leslie clenched her fists, trying to control her anger. "Who the hell do you think you are?"

"I know who I am," Peyton scoffed. "I know my job and the authority that goes with it. What in the world makes you think you have the authority to barge in here and demand anything?"

"I'm a reporter," Leslie bellowed.

"And . . . ?" Peyton waited, but Leslie was momentarily speechless.

"We'll see what the public thinks of your authority when we air this little exchange, Agent King. Did you record all this?" For the first time Leslie whirled around to discover her cameraman wasn't in the room.

She had been so furious with Peyton that she hadn't realized there were others in the office. Her eyes moved from face to face until they settled on the one that haunted her sleeping and waking hours. A loud gasp escaped her lips.

"Miss Winters, allow me to introduce my friends: Professor Regan Shaw, Grace Brandywine, and UT's star quarterback Joey Sloan and his girlfriend, Paula Lambert."

"Regan, I was hoping to touch base with you," Leslie said. "Perhaps when I'm through here?" She closed her eyes for a second, trying to erase the sight of Brandy sitting on the arm of Regan's chair with her arm draped possessively around Regan's back. Regan was resting her hand on the blonde's jean-covered thigh.

Regan looked up at Brandy. "Would that be okay, honey? We could take Leslie to lunch."

"Of course," Brandy said. "Whatever you want to do."

Leslie could feel her interview and career spinning out of control. "I'd hoped we could share some alone time."

"I have no secrets from Brandy," Regan said as she patted the young woman's leg. "She's my—"

"Lover." Brandy smirked. "A position I hope to fill for the rest of my life."

Regan stood, clasping Brandy's hand. "Why don't you tell your camera crew to take a lunch break, and we'll take you to a restaurant I know you'll love."

Leslie nodded and headed for the door. With her hand on the knob, she turned to Agent King. "Perhaps you'd like to join us."

Peyton smiled. "Sure! Only a fool would pass up the opportunity to dine with three gorgeous women." She was glad Leslie had given Joey and Paula a cursory nod and dismissed them.

"Honey, I'll give you two some time alone," Brandy offered, pitching Regan her car fob. "I need to discuss something with Agent King. We'll ride in her jeep."

"She must feel very confident about your feelings for her," Leslie noted as she fastened her seatbelt.

Regan shrugged. "She should. I adore her."

"What does she teach?"

"Oh, she . . . she's not a teacher," Regan said. "She's a student."

"Did I hear you correctly?" Leslie jeered. "Did you say you're dating a student?"

Regan raised her chin. "Yes. Brandy is in my English lit class."

"May-December romances always end badly for the older woman," Leslie declared.

Regan glared at her ex-lover. "Same-age romances don't fare well either. You're a walking testament to that."

"Regan, I—"

"Why are you here, Leslie?"

"I think there's a hell of a story here . . . and I wanted to see you," Leslie answered truthfully. "I miss you, Regan."

Regan said nothing as she pulled Brandy's car into the parking space in front of the restaurant.

"This place has wonderful Italian food," Regan said as she opened her car door. "I know how you love Italian food."

Leslie caught Regan's wrist, holding her in the car. "You know all the things I love," she murmured.

Brandy appeared at Regan's car door. "Is everything okay here?" She glared at Leslie, noting the grip the newswoman had on Regan's wrist, and extended her hand to her lover.

Regan yanked her wrist from Leslie's grasp and placed her hand in Brandy's. "We were just talking," Regan said.

During lunch, Leslie tried every trick in her repertoire to glean information about the deaths of Danny Tucker and Robin Chase, but her dining partners steered the conversation in every other direction possible.

"I'd like to take you out to dinner," Leslie said to Regan. "We have a lot to talk about. A lot has changed since you left me."

Regan frowned. This wasn't a conversation she wanted to have, especially in front of Brandy and Peyton.

"I know your current heartthrob is cute as hell, but that won't last," Leslie continued.

"Pardon me," Brandy quipped, putting her hand over her heart. "Regan's current heartthrob is sitting at the table with you."

"Leslie, I have nothing to discuss with you," Regan said. "That plane has cleared the runway. Please move on to another subject."

"We need to go," Brandy said as the waitress placed their check on the table. She insisted on paying for lunch, and Peyton proclaimed it her duty to take Leslie to her hotel.

"Truth is, I haven't checked into a hotel yet." Leslie glanced sideways at Regan, who pretended not to hear her. "Can you recommend a good one?"

"Are you on your own dime or the station's expense account?" Peyton chuckled. "If you're on an expense account, I'd recommend the Sheraton downtown. If it's coming out of your pocket, I'd stay at the Courtyard by Marriott."

"I guess the Marriott," Leslie muttered. "If I don't bring back a sensational story, I'll probably end up eating my expenses."

"I'm sorry to hear that, Miss Winters," Peyton said, "but I'm afraid there's no story here."

Leslie turned to Regan. "I don't suppose you have a guestroom."

Brandy jumped in. "We do, but we're leaving this afternoon to spend Christmas at my dad's ranch."

"When will you return?"

"After New Year's," Regan replied. "Excuse me. I need to powder my nose."

"She always does that when she wants to end a conversation," Leslie said, watching Regan walk away.

Peyton pushed back from the table. "If you're ready, I'll take you to the Marriott."

"I should visit the ladies' room before we leave." Leslie shoved back her chair and was gone before Brandy could decide what action to take.

Peyton caught Brandy's arm. "Let them talk," she advised. "Regan's a big girl. She can take care of herself."

"Leslie Winters is one pushy broad," Brandy grumbled.

"Trust Regan."

##

When Regan walked from the bathroom stall, she was shocked to see Leslie propped against the sink. She shot her a go-to-hell look.

"Regan, I know you're still angry with me," Leslie said.

"I'm not angry with you, Leslie. I honestly never gave you a second thought. By the time I was able to pack up and leave you, I was over you."

Leslie caught Regan by the shoulders. "I know you don't mean that. I know I was a lousy partner those last two years, but I've changed, Regan. I'm the woman you fell in love with. I'm off the bottle, and I've landed a great job. If this assignment pans out, I'll get an anchor position on the late-night news."

"I'm happy for you, Leslie. I really am. I hope everything works out and that you're happy."

Leslie shook Regan by the shoulders. "You can't tell me you've forgotten the good times. How I made love to you. The way I touched you. I don't believe this student of yours can compare to—"

"This student of mine loves me more than you could ever comprehend. And believe me, Leslie, if you'd ever once made me feel the way she does every time she touches me, I'd still be with you!"

"That's good to know," Brandy said, grinning as she let go of the door so it could close. "Miss Winters, if you don't take your hands off my woman, I'll be forced to break both of your wrists."

Leslie released Regan as if she were a hot iron. Something about the look in Brandy's eye told her the young woman was quite capable of doing her bodily harm.

Brandy caught Regan's hand and turned to Leslie. "Neither of us are fans of yours. Don't come around her again."

Leslie watched the two as they left the bathroom. *Don't think I'll give up so easily, little girl. I still have a few tricks up my sleeve,"* she thought.

Chapter 41

Paula laced her fingers through Joey's as he drove her home. "You have such nice, strong hands. I love them."

Joey smiled. "I'm glad, because I love everything about you."

Paula sat in silence for a long time before she spoke again. "I know I'm not supposed to say this out loud, but I'm thrilled that Bob Radford is dead."

"It's okay to talk to me about it," Joey said. "I know you didn't kill Radford. You were with me."

Paula nodded. "I wonder who I have to thank for making that bastard disappear from my life."

"It's almost as if a guardian angel is watching over us," Joey pointed out. "Coach Tucker was murdered after he tried to roofie Professor Shaw. Then Coach Chase was burned in the bonfire after she tried to molest the professor. Now Radford is dead—hopefully from natural causes."

They stopped by Wanda's and picked up Trent. Joey carried the tot on his shoulders as they walked to the car. "I giant," Trent squealed.

"What are your plans for Christmas?" Paula asked Wanda.

"I had hoped to go to my daughter's. She sent me a bus ticket, but when I called to confirm departure time this morning, I was told the bus I need to take is overbooked. Unfortunately, they have nothing available until after Christmas."

"Where does your daughter live?" Joey inquired.

"Amarillo."

Joey took out his cell phone and made several calls. "I couldn't get you on a plane, because they're all booked too, but I have arranged for a town car to pick you up in the morning and drive you to Amarillo. You'll have use of it the entire time you're there, and she'll drive you back when you're ready to return home."

"I . . . I can't afford that." Tears filled Wanda's eyes.

"It's my Christmas gift to you," Joey said. "You deserve to spend time with your daughter. I'm texting you the name and number of your driver now."

"I can't believe you would do that for me."

Joey grinned. "I have an ulterior motive. I'm hoping Paula and Trent will spend Christmas with me at my dad's ranch. We have plenty of guestrooms, so it's not a problem, and Trent will love the horses. We even have some baby goats."

"Baby goats?" Trent started bouncing up and down on Joey's shoulders. "I wuv baby goats."

Joey opened the car door and buckled Trent into the car seat that had become a fixture in Joey's car.

The toddler caught Joey by the ears and kissed his cheek. "I wuv baby goats," he whispered.

"So do I." Joey laughed and kissed him back.

They had barely left Wanda's driveway when Trent fell asleep. Joey placed his hand in Paula's lap, and she wrapped her hands around his.

"That was a very nice thing you did for Wanda," she said softly.

"I'm happy to do it," Joey said. "Did it work? I invited you a while back and have given you time to think about it. Will you and Trent spend the Christmas holidays with us?"

"Who is 'us'?" Paula asked.

"There is something you should know. Brandy is my sister. I'm enrolled in school under an alias. Brandy and I are undercover FBI agents gathering evidence about the unlawful sexual activity connected to the athletic program. It is necessary for us to maintain our cover until we wrap up our case."

"Why didn't you tell me this sooner?" Paula demanded.

"Does it matter?"

"Yes. It matters a lot. Do you have any idea how many sleepless nights I've spent over you and Brandy?" Paula looked away. "I know you said you were her beard, but there was a closeness between you that was more than that. I never thought you might be siblings."

"Are we okay?" Joey frowned. Sometimes women failed to make sense to him.

"We're more than okay," Paula said. "Now back to my original question. Who—besides baby goats—will be at your family home for Christmas?"

"My dad, Brandy, and me. Brandy's invited Professor Shaw. We lost Mom sometime back, so it's just the three of us and those we care about."

Paula mulled over the invitation for several seconds. "Trent would love the animals, and I would love the company. Okay, it sounds like fun."

Joey sighed deeply. He knew Paula had been through a lot, and it would take time to have the relationship they both wanted. He knew she loved him, and God alone knew how much he loved her and the little boy sleeping in his back seat.

Chapter 42

Alone in her apartment, Peyton watched the security video from the hospital. Sawyer was right; it was plain as day that someone dressed as Batman had visited Bob Radford's room in the clinic. She jotted down the time on the video. Batman was in Radford's room for ten minutes.

She pulled the medical examiner's report from her briefcase. He had put Radford's death at between four and five that morning. Batman had been in Radford's room during that time.

I've got to wrap this up, she thought. *The last thing Katherine needs is the university smeared all over national TV.* She wondered if there was any other story that might capture Leslie Winters' attention. She knew the woman was desperate to take something sensational back to New York.

She popped the DVD out of her computer and opened the spreadsheet she used to organize information on her cases. Beside each victim's name were the names of the people who stood to gain the most from their death.

Only two names were beside all three deaths: Chief Pat Sawyer and Chancellor Katherine O'Brien. Peyton knew Katherine hadn't murdered Radford, because she'd been in her bed that night. The only one with no alibi was Sawyer. *I've granted immunity to the person most likely to be the killer. All the evidence points to Pat Sawyer. That's a good thing. Now all I have to do is wrap up this mess.*

The knock on Peyton's door surprised her. She looked at her watch, wondering who could be visiting her after midnight. She picked up her Glock and crept to the door to look out the peephole. Katherine O'Brien, in all her glory, fidgeted in the hallway outside her door.

Peyton opened the door and pulled the chancellor inside. "Merry Christmas, darling," Katherine said. She slipped into Peyton's arms and kissed her until she couldn't breathe.

"I was afraid you wouldn't come," Peyton said, trying to catch her breath. "I'd decided you couldn't get away."

"I would have come no matter the hour," Katherine said. "I've ached for you all day. Just knowing I'd see you sooner or later made my entire day wonderful."

Peyton kissed her again and then realized she still had her coat on. "Let me take your coat."

The devil danced in the redhead's eyes. "Um, maybe you should open it in your bedroom. It's the wrapping for your Christmas present."

Peyton's breath caught in her throat, and her knees weakened as a wave of lust swept over her. "I can't wait to open it."

Peyton grabbed Katherine's hand and led her to a beautifully decorated room. Soft lighting from two bedside lamps illuminated the king-size bed, the covers already turned back. Katherine smiled as she turned to her lover.

Savoring the moment, Peyton slowly removed the pins that held Katherine's long, glorious hair in a proper chignon. Peyton kissed her neck and nipped at her shoulders as the hair slowly fell to her full breasts. The blonde tangled her hands in Katherine's hair and pulled her head back, giving her complete access to the pounding pulse point in her neck.

Katherine moaned loudly. "Are you getting even with me for making you wait?"

"No, I'm simply enjoying every second of opening my present." Peyton smiled to herself as the chancellor began to breathe harder. She liked that she could make Katherine lose control.

"Hmm. Let's see what we've got," she whispered in Katherine's ear as she unbuttoned the top button of the coat and kissed her way to the first exposure of cleavage.

"Oh my, Chancellor, I believe you are beautifully endowed." She unbuttoned the second button. "Um, yes." She kissed between Katherine's breasts. "So perfect," she murmured, making her lips hum against Katherine's silky skin.

"Peyton!" Katherine gasped as the blonde sucked a nipple into her mouth. "Oh Peyton, it's okay to rip the wrapping off a package."

"I'm enjoying this." Peyton teased Katherine's other breast with her tongue and caressed the first one she'd uncovered.

Katherine's breath was coming in sharp, frantic gasps, as Peyton took her time worshiping the body that dreams were made of.

Peyton dropped to her knees as she released the last button. She ran her hands down Katherine's waist, clutching her buttocks and placing warm, soft kisses on her stomach. Katherine squirmed, dropping the coat to the floor.

"I believe you're ready for me, Chancellor," Peyton teased.

"Oh God, yes!" Katherine cried out.

##

Much later, Katherine lay in Peyton's arms, running her fingers through Peyton's shoulder-length hair and reveling in the scent of the blonde. "I love your hair," she whispered. "It's so soft and fragrant.

"Sometimes when you come by my office to report about what is happening on campus, you lean over my shoulder and place something on my desk. The soft fragrance and nearness of you makes me want to run to my door, lock it, and make love to you right there on my office sofa."

Peyton laughed softly. "It's good to know my little ploy works."

"Especially when you lean down and let your breasts rest against my back," Katherine said with a sigh. "But you know what you're doing, don't you?"

"Yes," Peyton admitted. "But you do a damn good job of pretending I have no effect on you at all."

"I've fallen in love with you, Agent King." Katherine undulated against Peyton's body, clutching her closer. "I can't stand being away from you."

"You know I adore you," Peyton whispered as she kissed Katherine's ear and down her neck. "All I want is to make love to you."

"How do we handle this?" Katherine groaned as Peyton slid her hand down her back to the top of her thigh.

"What do you mean?"

"I want to be with you all the time," Katherine said. "I want to fall asleep in your arms every night."

"That's for you to decide." Peyton pulled back so she could look into dark jade eyes. "I'm pretty honest about who I am and my proclivity for women. You're the one we must protect. You're the chancellor of a major university, the keeper of the next generation's morals, the example for young women all over the world."

"I'm very aware of the burden I carry," Katherine said. "Being a lesbian doesn't change my moral character.

"Peyton, I've lived a lonely existence for years—all my life, actually—because my sexuality didn't fit the job description. I love what I do. I love that I can guide our youth and clean up a corrupt athletic program. I've been given the opportunity to clean up corruption that has been eating at the heart of this campus for decades.

"Everyone will know that there is zero tolerance for sexual misconduct at our university. They will know that monsters aren't real."

"Oh honey, monsters are real, and they're disguised as people," Peyton said. "They will always be lurking in the shadows, waiting for crusaders like you to disappear so they can slink back in."

Katherine shuddered.

"I love what we have," Katherine said. "Would you be willing to continue our relationship under our present conditions?"

"You mean slipping around after midnight? Pretending that we only interact with one another on a work basis? Keeping it a secret from the world that the most wonderful, glorious creature in existence is in love with me, and I love her?"

Katherine rolled over on her back. She knew the answer to her question. "You're the only one I've been with since my husband died. I thought I could live a celibate life, because men don't appeal to me, and women were not in my realm of possibility.

"Then you came along and made life and love and happiness possible. I don't know how I'll—"

"Yes!" Peyton rasped.

"What?" Katherine couldn't believe her ears.

"Yes, I'll live any way you need me to—in secret, in a dark cave. Any way I need to live if I can fall asleep in your arms. I don't want to face a life without you in it, Katherine. I'd do anything to protect you and keep you and your reputation above reproach."

"We can make that happen." Katherine wrapped herself around Peyton. "We'll find a way, my love."

They clung to each other, running through scenarios that would make it possible for them to be together without becoming the center of campus gossip.

"Pat Sawyer," Katherine said. "If she's out of the way, the university could hire you as the chief of campus police. We'd have an excuse for constant contact."

"I think Sawyer is the killer of Tucker and Chase," Peyton replied. "And possibly Radford. Just a few more I's to dot and T's to cross and I'll be able to arrest her."

"I'll leave that in your very capable hands," Katherine said, snuggling closer. "May I feel those hands on me one more time?"

Chapter 43

"What do you mean you can't get an interview with anyone of importance?" William Porter roared over the phone line.

"I mean this place is a ghost town," Leslie explained to her boss. "Everyone's gone for Christmas. The chancellor and campus police chief are gone until January 19th."

"Something an experienced investigative reporter should have taken into consideration," Porter huffed. "What are you going to do, waste four weeks hanging around Texas or return to New York?"

"Expense-wise it's a break-even deal, and I might learn something. I'll keep digging here."

"You haven't hooked up with that writer, have you? Everyone in this town knows you two—"

Leslie snorted. "No chance of that."

"If you're just staying there to warm her bed—"

"William, she won't even talk to me. She certainly isn't letting me warm her bed."

"I'm warning you, Leslie. This better be the story of the year."

"It will be. I'll keep in touch."

Leslie racked her brain, trying to figure a way to get Regan alone. Regan's current paramour was like a beautiful pit bull—gentle until aroused. Leslie suspected that Brandy could be deadly when provoked.

I'm a fool, Leslie thought. *I had it all with Regan and let it slip away.*

##

Leslie called an automobile rental, requested an economy car, and had it delivered to her hotel. She spent the week exploring UT's 423-acre campus. It was a beautiful campus, with everything one could imagine in a world-class university.

She located the office of the *Austin American-Statesman*, Austin's leading newspaper, and parked her car beside the building. She showed the girl at the front desk her press credentials and requested use of their archives and photo morgue.

The girl looked up from the game she was playing on her cell phone long enough to point toward a door marked "Archives."

"You'll have to sign in here," the girl said, pushing a clipboard toward her. "Be sure to include the name of the paper you work for."

Leslie nodded. Her press credentials clearly stated the network name of her employer, but the girl hadn't even looked at that. Leslie decided to write the name of a struggling New York newspaper. No reason to draw attention to her investigation.

She thanked the gods that the archives were electronically stored and easily searchable. She'd had visions of searching through musty newspapers.

As she researched, she became more and more impressed with Chancellor Katherine O'Brien. A stunning red-haired beauty, O'Brien had closed deals and accomplished things that had brought worldwide recognition to the university. Her track record surpassed most men, and she was still in her midforties.

Widowed in her twenties, O'Brien had never remarried, turning all her energy toward her profession instead. The more she read about O'Brien, the more determined she was to meet her.

Leslie spent the entire day searching for articles on sexual misconduct related to the university. The only black mark on the university's stellar reputation was the high number of sexual assault complaints filed by students.

She researched Chief Pat Sawyer, who seemed to be affable but ineffective in reducing the number of sexual assaults on her campus. Four years ago, Sawyer had arrested the man responsible for the rape and murder of a coed. Leslie's instinct told her there was more to the story than that. She decided to pursue the conviction and get an interview with the man.

She searched for information on FBI Agent Peyton King. A former sex-crimes profiler, King was a decorated officer and was known for closing cases quickly. Coach Danny Tucker had been murdered four months ago, and Robin Chase had died under suspicious circumstances around the same time. Leslie was certain King had some idea who the killer was.

She closed the newspaper computer and decided to give King a call. She was tired of eating dinner alone in her hotel room. She was disappointed to find that Agent King had disappeared for the holidays along with everyone else.

Chapter 44

Brandy packed the last of her belongings in a duffle bag and walked from her dorm room. By the time Regan got home, she would have all her things put away and dinner on the table.

She knew Regan would be tired. The first day back at school was always hectic. Brandy's first class was tomorrow, and she was looking forward to it. Sitting in Regan's classroom was like an aphrodisiac. Watching the brunette teach and interact with the class members was arousing and always made Brandy's heart beat faster.

A text dinged into her cell phone. "Can you meet me at the SUB for lunch?"

"I'd love to," Brandy replied. "I'll get us a table in the corner." Her day had just gone from good to awesome. She thought about the holidays they had enjoyed together.

Christmas at the ranch had been a series of enjoyable days and incredible nights. Joey and Trent had shared a room, giving Paula a chance to relax and sleep late without a little finger poking in her eye or up her nose.

Everyone had fallen in love with Trent, and the little fellow had become Joey's shadow, following him everywhere. She hoped things worked out between Paula and Joey, because she knew Joey had fallen in love with both the Lamberts.

Regan had been delightful, and Brandy's father loved her. "Why can't I find a woman like you?" Grayson had lamented.

When they had returned to campus, Brandy had been disappointed to find Leslie Winters was still in town. She had been on her network doing background bits on Austin and continually talking about the murders of Tucker and Chase. She'd had the good sense not to deem as murder Radford's asphyxiation by vomit.

The day after Christmas, Brandy had uploaded Regan's rejected book to Amazon, and it had taken off like a rocket. It shot straight to the top and was rated number one in Amazon's mainstream books and every category in the lesbian genre. Both Mel Denton and the publisher were begging Regan to pull the book from Amazon and let them run with it, but Regan refused to do that.

"Don't forget your contract is up this year," Mel had threatened. "This is a fluke. You won't have the same success with your next book."

"You made this happen," Regan had told Brandy as they lay in each other's arms. "You get the credit for the success of *Dressed to Kill*."

"You're too quick to credit others with your genius," Brandy said, beaming. "The only reason your book shot to the top is because it's a damn good book."

Brandy secured the table in the corner farthest away from the crowd milling around in the SUB. She opened her laptop and began checking Regan's stats on *Dressed to Kill*.

The book had been on sale for three weeks and was averaging 500 books sold per day. Barnes & Noble had ordered a pallet of books and had put them on their bookshelves in every store. Brandy quickly did the math on her computer calculator. If the sales held steady, Regan would make over a million dollars on the book in a year.

Brandy looked up from her computer. She could always feel Regan's presence before she saw her. It only took her a second to locate the gorgeous professor as she made her way toward their table. Brandy stood and took Regan's books, touching her hands as she slipped the things from the brunette's grasp. She really wanted to kiss her but taking her books let Regan know how she felt.

"I know, darling," Regan whispered as she sat down.

"How's the first day back?" Brandy asked.

"Good. It's amazing how quickly everyone gets back into the swing of things. How was your morning?"

"Nice." Brandy looked away. She couldn't hide the desire she felt for the professor. "I picked up the last of my things from my dorm and let Kiki know I wouldn't be back."

A slight tremor shook Regan's body. "We're actually doing this, aren't we? Moving in together."

"Are you having second thoughts?"

"None at all, baby." Regan caught her hands and held them across the table. "None at all."

"On another note, your book is still number one," Brandy said. "If it follows the trajectory of your other books, you'll net over a million this year."

"You mean gross?" Regan laughed. "By the time I pay the commissions, advertising fees, promotion fees, and everyone involved, I'll be lucky to see a hundred thousand."

Brandy frowned. "No, there's no one else involved. Amazon takes their cut for posting it online, but the sales figures we see are the net profit. There is no one else to pay.

"I've handled all the advertising through social media, so the sales amount is all yours."

Regan tilted her pretty head to one side. "Seriously? You may be the best agent I've ever had. We need to discuss this when I get home tonight. Right after I properly thank you."

"Uh-huh." Brandy giggled. "I will work for sex!"

Chapter 45

As students returned to campus, Leslie tried in vain to catch up with Agent King or Chief Sawyer. She tried to make an appointment with the Austin police chief, but he was still on vacation too. After a dozen phone calls and flirting with as many policemen, she was put through to Lt. Eldon Wilde. Wilde had handled the Jamie Wright case and was more than willing to help her. He informed her that the case had never felt right to him, and he suspected that Pat Sawyer had manipulated the evidence to get a conviction against a mentally deficient homeless man named Manuel Vargas.

Wilde arranged for her to visit the Beauford H. Jester Psychiatric Unit in Richmond, Texas, where Jamie Wright's killer was housed. The trip took three hours one way, but Leslie figured she had nothing better to do.

Compared to the northern states, Texas was flat and barren. Leslie thought she'd never seen more desolate country.

##

Leslie was surprised by the size of Vargas. As the guard led him in, she noticed that he was less than five feet tall. He had thick black hair and dark eyes. From the looks of his teeth and the scars on his face, he hadn't fared well in prison.

"Mr. Vargas, I'm Leslie Winters. I'd like to talk to you about Jamie Wright."

The man shook his head.

"You don't want to talk about Jamie Wright?" Leslie used her smoothest voice.

Vargas shrugged. "I don't know Jamie Wright. I can't talk about somebody I don't know."

"Do you know why you're in prison?"

"I did something bad,"—Vargas furrowed his brow—"but I can't remember what."

After talking to Vargas for thirty minutes, Leslie was certain he could be of no help to her. She was also certain he was not strong enough to overpower Jamie Wright, who had been five-eight and on the swim team. *She had to be strong*, Leslie thought. *If nothing else, I'll turn this trip into a crusade to release Manuel Vargas, who is serving time for a crime he didn't commit.*

On her way back to Austin, she decided the key to her investigation was Chief Pat Sawyer. *I'll talk to her as soon as she returns to campus.*

##

After lunch, Leslie got Regan's schedule from the registrar's office and decided to visit one of her classes. She knew Regan wouldn't cause a scene in front of her students. *She's too prim and proper for that*, Leslie thought.

She sat on the back row, as far away from the front of the classroom as possible, hoping Regan wouldn't notice her. About midway through class, the professor locked eyes with the reporter.

Regan stumbled over a few words but quickly regained her composure. "Everyone read the first fifty pages of *Hamlet,* and we'll discuss it in class Friday. Be prepared to tell the class what you think of the main characters and their motivations. Since this is our first day back, I'm going to dismiss you early. You may use the time to read *Hamlet*."

Regan waited until her classroom was empty before turning her attention to Leslie. "Miss Winters, are you enrolled in my class?"

"No." Leslie chuckled as she walked down the aisle toward Regan. "I had to see you alone. This was the only way I could spend time with you without your lovesick puppy."

"You may talk to me," Regan said, "but keep your nasty comments about Brandy to yourself."

"How old is she? Ten, fifteen years younger than you?"

"What do you want, Leslie?"

"I want you to give me a second chance. Come back to New York with me. Surely you don't see a future with Bambi."

Regan ignored Leslie's intended slur at Brandy's name.

"I have a contract with the university," Regan said. "I'm not like you. I honor my commitments."

"Ouch." Leslie flinched as if Regan had struck her. "I deserved that, but it still hurt."

Regan exhaled hard and pressed her fingers to her temple. "I don't know how long Brandy and I will last," she said, "but I will stay with her as long as she wants me.

"Every day with her is new and exciting, and I know I've only scratched the surface. Right now, she is enthralled with me and that's enough. I love her."

"That's all that matters." Brandy's voice echoed in the empty classroom as she walked toward Regan, followed by the handsome young man Leslie had met in Agent King's office.

"You left your lesson plans on the nightstand," Brandy said, a sly smirk on her face. "I thought you might need them. You were pretty adamant about finishing them last night before we . . . um—"

Regan blushed slightly. "Thank you, darling. Do you and Joey have time for a cup of coffee?"

"And a cheeseburger," Joey chimed in.

"I'll always make time for you." Brandy's eyes twinkled as she picked up Regan's laptop and books. "Good day, Miss Winters."

Leslie stood alone in the empty classroom. She had never felt so desolate. She knew she'd never be a part of Regan Shaw's life again unless she did something drastic to force the brunette to come to her.

Chapter 46

Peyton and Chief Sawyer watched as the coaches and athletes who had been arrested over the Christmas holidays were brought before the judge for arraignment. They all pleaded not guilty, but the mountain of evidence compiled by Joey and Brandy was irrefutable.

"When this hits the fan, all hell will break loose for the chancellor," Sawyer grumped. "And me too."

"Just keep your mouth shut and don't talk to anyone," Peyton reminded her. "Especially that Leslie Winters. If our carefully laid plans come unraveled, you'll find yourself behind bars with your buddies."

"When will I go into witness protection?" Sawyer asked.

"Tomorrow or the next day," Peyton said. "I've got it all arranged. I'm just waiting for a call from the federal marshals who will be handling you. With your testimony and the way these rats are already squealing on each other, this will be a slam dunk."

"Do you know who killed Tucker, Chase, and Radford?" Sawyer asked, glancing at Peyton's face.

"Yes, I do. The person in the Batman suit."

Sawyer laughed as Peyton left the observation room.

##

Pat Sawyer seriously thought about throwing one last monkey wrench into Chancellor Katherine O'Brien's perfect life. If she could only figure out a way to tell Leslie Winters that O'Brien and Agent King were lovers without getting herself involved, she would do it. But every plan she concocted always incriminated her.

I'll just behave and let King get me out of here, she thought. *I wonder where they'll relocate me.*

She watched through the one-way glass as attorneys and parents showed up to get the criminals out of jail. She smiled when federal agents sent them packing.

Slipping on her jacket and pulling the hood over her head, she snuck out the back door of the police station. *I'm going to give our uppity chancellor a piece of my mind before I ride off into the sunset.*

Katherine was surprised when Chief Sawyer pushed her way past her secretary and entered the chancellor's office.

"Chancellor, I told her—"

"It's okay, Debbie. Please close the door behind you and hold my calls.

"Chief Sawyer, what can I do for you?"

"It's more like what *I* can do for *you*," Pat said.

Katherine frowned. "I don't understand. What are you talking about?"

"You and Peyton King." Sawyer's twisted grin made Katherine think the woman was unhinged.

"Again, what are you talking about?"

"You're lovers," Sawyer blurted.

Katherine laughed out loud. "Have you completely lost your grip on reality?"

Sawyer took a step backward. Katherine seemed astounded by the idea that she was having an affair. *Maybe I'm wrong. I haven't actually seen them together, only*

Peyton coming and going from the chancellor's mansion at all hours of the night.

"You need to leave my office." The cold disgust in Katherine's voice would make hell freeze over. "Don't ever enter my office again without an appointment."

Sawyer fled the office, wishing she had kept her suspicions to herself. *If Peyton finds out I pulled this stunt, she'll have me sent to Barrow, Alaska*, she thought.

Peyton waited until she was certain Sawyer was gone before coming out of the restroom in the chancellor's office. "Did you hear her?" Katherine gasped.

"Don't worry, honey. I've made arrangements for her. She'll be out of your life in a couple of days." Peyton locked the office door and returned to hold Katherine. "I'll never let anything hurt you."

By the time Sawyer returned to her office she had worked herself into a panic. The sight of Leslie Winters sitting in her waiting room almost made her vomit. She pulled herself together and tried not to scream at the pushy newswoman.

"I'm sorry," she said. "I don't have time. I have a meeting in a few minutes. If you'll leave a number with my secretary, I'll call you tomorrow."

"This won't take long, Chief," Leslie said. "I just need to ask—"

"What part of 'I don't have time' do you not understand?" Sawyer snapped. "I'll call you tomorrow. Please leave my office."

Leslie stood in shocked silence as Sawyer slammed the door to her office and locked it.

She handed her business card to the secretary. "My cell number is on it." She almost ran to her car. She had never been treated so rudely.

What the hell is going on in this town? She seethed as she fastened her seatbelt and put the car in gear.

##

"Is she in?" Peyton asked Sawyer's secretary, Margaret Lews.

"Yes, but she has the door locked." Margaret knocked on Sawyer's door. "Chief, I'm leaving for the day, and Agent King is here to see you."

The door unlocked, and Sawyer pulled it open. "Drive carefully," she cautioned her secretary. "Come on in, Peyton."

Peyton eyed the prescription bottles on Sawyer's desk. "What are those?"

"New refills," Sawyer snorted. "This one is for depression. This is for insomnia, and the big one is for high blood pressure. I swear, Peyton, this job is killing me." She opened her bottom drawer and tossed the medications into it.

Peyton heard Margaret lock the entry door as she left. She joined Sawyer at her desk and pulled a fifth of expensive scotch from her coat pocket. "I need a drink. How about you? Although I'm not sure you should ingest liquor after taking those pills."

"That's the best suggestion I've heard all day." Sawyer grimaced as she pulled two glasses from her desk drawer. "It's a myth that drugs and alcohol will kill you."

Peyton poured two glasses of scotch and held hers high. "A toast to the new life you're about to begin," she said, grinning. She sipped her drink as Sawyer gulped down the golden liquid.

Peyton refilled her glass. "I'm going to leave this with you." Peyton pulled the legal pad that contained Sawyer's confession from her briefcase. "A federal agent from the marshal's office will come by in the morning and go over everything with you. He'll need your recorded information too."

"It's right here on a thumb drive." Sawyer placed the drive on top of Peyton's legal pad and poured another drink. "I can't believe I've come to this," she slurred. "I had such a stellar career until I got involved with that woman." She chugalugged her drink and refilled the glass. "I'm going to get stinking drunk tonight, Peyton. But before I do, I want to thank you for all you've done for me."

"I only wish I had met you sooner. We could have stopped all this from happening," Peyton said.

"You're a good friend, Agent King. I admire you."

Peyton filled Sawyer's glass to the brim and watched as she drank it like water. "How can you do that? It would take away my breath."

"Practice," Sawyer mumbled. "How do you think I've lived with myself all these years?"

Peyton got to her feet. "I'm going to leave you to it. I'll lock the door on my way out."

"Leave my door open. Just lock the main entrance." Sawyer spilled the scotch as she sloshed more into her glass. "Good night, Peyton."

Peyton's thoughts had already gone to Katherine as she closed the entry door to the offices. She fought the urge to go to the chancellor's mansion and headed her car toward her apartment instead.

Chapter 47

It was after three a.m. when the darkly clad figure slithered through the shadows to Chief Pat Sawyer's office. A gloved hand turned the doorknob and prayed it was unlocked. It was.

The lamp on Sawyer's desk cast a light on the Batman figure that moved with the precision of a well-oiled machine.

Sawyer was almost comatose. Batman gagged at the stench of alcohol that was on Sawyer's desk and her clothes.

Batman quickly pulled the syringe with a tiny needle from a hidden pocket. The masked figure felt Sawyer's neck, smiling when the blood pulsed beneath searching fingertips. The needle slipped easily into the carotid artery, making a soft sound as purified distilled water was injected into Sawyer's bloodstream, causing her red blood cells to rupture.

Rummaging through Sawyer's desk drawer, Batman found the prescription drugs. Within seconds the bottles were emptied and tossed on the desk and floor after their contents were flushed down the commode.

After pushing the button that would lock Sawyer's office door, the figure sprinted to the front door and peeked out to make certain no one was in sight. With the coast clear, the intruder pushed the button that would secure the door, slipped outside, and disappeared into the shadows.

##

"Are you certain?" Peyton gasped into her phone. "I'll be right there."

The agent threw on her clothes and broke speed limits getting to the UT sheriff's office. A coroner's van was already on the scene, and Peyton recognized Lt. Eldon Wilde from the Austin Police Department.

"What's going on?" Peyton flashed her badge to the patrolman securing the scene.

"Chief Sawyer, ma'am. I think she's dead."

Peyton pushed her way past the officer guarding the door. Margaret was sobbing uncontrollably. Peyton dropped to one knee in front of Margaret and consoled her.

"She's dead," the woman cried. "I found her this morning when I came to work. She killed herself."

"No! No way. Why would she do that?" Peyton patted Margaret's arm. "Why would you say that?"

"Because she left a signed confession and copious notes," Lt. Wilde said as he motioned for Peyton to enter Sawyer's office. He closed the door behind him.

"The doors were locked when Mrs. Lews came to work this morning. She unlocked the entry door and went to work. When she heard Sawyer's cell phone ringing, she unlocked her office door and discovered the body."

Wilde picked up the yellow legal pad and held it up so Peyton could see as he read it. "It is with a heavy heart that I must put on paper the evil deeds I've been a party to . . ."

Peyton stopped listening as she realized that Wilde mistook the information Sawyer had written for her as a confession Sawyer had written before committing suicide.

"I won't go on," Wilde said, pulling Peyton's attention back to him. "It is obviously a suicide epistle she had to get off her chest before taking her own life. There is also a thumb drive with copious recordings of the crap she was mixed up in.

"She probably knew you were closing in on her and decided she'd rather die than face the music."

Peyton nodded. "I had tracked enough back to her that I considered her my prime suspect. She was probably trying to eliminate anyone that might point the finger at her."

"The biggest thing she admits is that she did frame Manuel Vargas for the murder of Jamie Wright." Wilde flipped to the page where Sawyer had given detailed descriptions of several illegal activities.

"Eldon, we may be able to clean up several trash heaps with this suicide letter," Peyton suggested. "How would you feel about giving this story to Leslie Winters? It would provide the coup she is looking for and let her go back to New York as the crusader who helped free an innocent man from prison."

Wilde nodded. "Good idea. She's been hanging around the police station. Maybe this will get her out of our hair."

"You take the credit on this case. And why don't you give Winters a call and fill her in on what has happened?"

Peyton's magnanimous gesture cinched Wilde's high opinion of her. "You're a real straight shooter," he said, clapping Peyton on the back. "Every other FBI agent I've encounter fought for all the credit. Are you sure you're okay with this?"

"You're the one who found her confession and put a lid on this until the ME makes his ruling. You deserve the credit." Peyton held out her hand. "It's a pleasure working with you."

##

The next day Peyton received confirmation from the ME that the death of Chief Pat Sawyer was caused by mixing drugs and alcohol. She thought for a few minutes and then called Chancellor O'Brien.

"You need to post openings for all the jobs in the athletic department and for a new chief of campus police."

"I'll start assembling a hiring committee today," Katherine said. "It's a shame about Pat Sawyer. I never trusted her and certainly would have fired her, but I never wished her dead."

"Fate moves in miraculous ways," Peyton replied. "Sometimes karma takes care of things mere mortals are afraid to confront."

"Why don't you come to my office around six this afternoon and give me a full report?"

"I'd be happy to do that, Chancellor," Peyton assured her.

Chapter 48

Leslie Winters couldn't believe her ears. Lt. Eldon Wilde had been the only one in this godforsaken state willing to help her, and now he was handing her every investigative reporter's dream.

"Why don't you come down to the station, and I'll let you see Sawyer's confession?" Wilde volunteered.

"I can be there in fifteen minutes," Leslie quipped.

"Park in the officers' parking lot. I'll meet you there with a parking pass that will be good for the duration of your stay."

Leslie made it to the police station in twelve minutes and was surprised to see Lt. Wilde striding toward her with an official Press Parking pass. *Maybe this town isn't so backwoods after all,* she thought.

Wilde spent the day with Leslie, answering all her questions and digging up information she needed to flesh out her story. By the end of the day, both were exhausted.

"I'd be happy to take you to dinner," Wilde said as he pushed his chair back from his desk.

"That's very kind," Leslie said, flashing a brilliant smile, "but I want to go back to my hotel room and organize all these notes. I'd like to get a teaser on the show tonight and then unfold the entire story on my show tomorrow night. My editor is demanding a big send-off for this story. We will run it for a week. It's huge."

"I understand," Wilde said. "If you need anything just give me a call."

"There is one other thing that would pull this story together," Leslie said.

"What?"

"Do you have any influence with Chancellor O'Brien? I would kill for an interview with her."

"No, but I know someone who does."

Wilde punched at his cell phone and held it to his ear. "Peyton, this is Wilde. I need a favor. Leslie Winters wants to interview Chancellor O'Brien about the Pat Sawyer case."

"I'm on hold," Wilde informed Leslie. "She's trying to get in touch with the chancellor now.

"Yes. That's terrific," Wilde said when Peyton came back on the line. "I owe you one.

Wilde ended the call and grinned at Leslie. "You can meet with Chancellor O'Brien in thirty minutes."

Peyton King was in Katherine O'Brien's office when Leslie walked in with her camera crew. "Please, come into the chancellor's office," Peyton said. "She's wrapping up a meeting in another building right now, but that will give you time to set up your cameras and prepare for her."

Leslie was amazed at how accommodating everyone had become. "I guess Pat Sawyer's confession took a lot of pressure off all of you," she mused as Peyton led the way into O'Brien's office.

"It certainly brought closure to a lot of problems and closed a nasty can of worms for the university," Peyton said.

The cameraman finished adjusting his light settings and was ready to record when Katherine O'Brien entered the room.

"Miss Winters," she purred, her low, sensuous voice sending a shiver up Leslie's spine, "it's a pleasure to meet you in person. I'm a fan of your work. I'll never forget your story on the New York brothels owned by one of the city's councilmen."

Leslie blushed with pleasure as the chancellor praised her work. She found herself fawning over the woman, wanting to please her.

"We won't take much of your time, Chancellor. I wanted to get you on camera answering a few quick questions to set the stage for my story. This will be a live interview."

"Where should I sit?" Katherine asked, letting Leslie take control.

"We took the liberty of rearranging these two lovely chairs." Leslie led Katherine to the small staging area her lighting man had arranged. "If you could sit in that one, and I'll sit across from you. Do you want me to go over the questions before we go live?"

"Is that a common practice?" Katherine asked.

"No, I just didn't want to—"

"Treat me as you would anyone else," Katherine insisted. "If you catch me off guard, shame on me." A smile ghosted her lips as she straightened her skirt and crossed her perfect legs.

Leslie did her introduction routine and then launched into her questions. "Chancellor O'Brien, did you have any idea Chief Sawyer was so deeply involved in the misconduct you were trying to clean up?"

"Yes. I called in FBI Agent Peyton King before school began this year. She coordinated with our local police, Lt. Eldon Wilde, and they had compiled enough evidence to arrest Chief Sawyer."

"Chief Sawyer's handwritten confession is common knowledge now," Leslie said. "Were there any surprises in the confession?"

"Yes. A year before I was hired as chancellor, a homeless man was convicted and imprisoned for the murder of a coed. We now know that he was framed by Chief Sawyer to protect personnel in the athletic department. That poor man. I feel so awful for him."

"Chancellor, you were hired specifically to clean up the sexual scandals in the athletic department. It appears that Chief Sawyer has taken care of that for you."

Katherine looked down at her hands folded in her lap. When she looked back up, her eyes glistened with unshed tears. "I would have preferred the culprits face justice in the courts, not death at the hands of a vigilante police chief. But as someone once told me, karma moves in miraculous ways."

"What do you have in mind for the future?" Leslie asked, giving Katherine a chance to put a positive spin on the situation.

"We're in the process of forming a hiring committee to rebuild our coaching staff and hire a new campus police chief.

"I was hired for many reasons and look forward to leading our university into the twenty-first century—the first century of the third millennium. I can assure you things will not get out of control during my tenure!"

"After getting to know Chancellor Katherine O'Brien, I'm certain of that," Leslie said, addressing the camera and signing off for the evening.

Leslie's cell phone instantly started ringing. She answered right away when she recognized her boss's number.

"You did it, Leslie. Oh my God, you did it. How did you manage to get an interview with the Ice Queen? She never gives interviews."

"Karma moves in miraculous ways, boss." Leslie smiled as William Porter informed her that she had a first-class ticket waiting for her online.

"You'll be back in New York before noon tomorrow," Porter crowed. "We need to get ready for your big debut tomorrow night. Makeup, hair, clothes—the whole works. Nothing's too good for my new star anchor."

Chapter 49

The four friends drank coffee in the SUB as they discussed graduation and the events of the past year. "You always suspected Sawyer," Brandy noted as Peyton, Joey, and Regan nodded in agreement.

"I never thought she would commit suicide," Peyton said. "I still feel responsible for her death. I took her that fifth of scotch. I had a drink with her and left the bottle. If I hadn't done that, she wouldn't have overdosed."

"She had a lot of skeletons in her closet," Brandy pointed out. "It was inevitable."

"I suppose so." Peyton sighed. "Still, I feel guilty."

Joey led the conversation toward happier thoughts. "I'm just looking forward to this school year being over. Paula and I are doing so well. I want to propose to her. Do y'all think it's too soon?"

"Joey, that's great," Brandy said.

Joey blushed. "She's incredible."

"How about you two, will you be back?" Peyton asked.

"No, we're getting too old to pose as crazy students," Joey said, chuckling. "The agency is bringing in two new replacements for us. We'll be reassigned. I've accepted a job with a top engineering company. This undercover stuff is dangerous. I'll have a family to consider."

"Aren't we cocky?" Brandy teased. "You must be sure Paula will accept your proposal."

"After this weekend, I'm certain she'll have me. We discussed it a lot. I just need to get a ring."

"I wouldn't mind putting a ring on it," Brandy said, her eyes on Regan, who had remained silent during their conversation.

"What are your plans, Professor?" Peyton inquired.

"I must return to New York and take care of some business there," Regan mumbled.

"That's the first I've heard of that," Brandy huffed.

"It just came up. I need to renegotiate my contract with my publisher. Thanks to the great job you did with *Dressed to Kill,* they're offering me a larger piece of the pie. Of course, I'll be required to go on more book tours and do TV appearances."

Brandy clenched her jaw as she glared at Regan.

"What about you, Brandy?" Peyton turned the conversation to the blonde.

"I've had an incredible offer from an international law firm. I'm considering it. They have offices everywhere." She turned to Regan. "Even New York."

"What about you, Peyton?" Regan avoided Brandy's glances. "What are your plans?"

"I guess I'll go on to my next assignment," Peyton replied, "but I must admit I'm tired of moving around. I'd like to find a job in law enforcement where I can stay in one place."

"The university is looking for a new chief of campus police," Joey informed her. "Why don't you apply for that?"

"I don't know." Peyton shrugged. "I'd be working directly under Chancellor O'Brien. She's pretty haughty and strictly business."

"Yeah," Joey said, "but you must admit she's hot."

Peyton laughed. "I must admit that, Joey."

##

They rode home in silence. Brandy didn't take her eyes from the road, and Regan looked out the side window. She was miserable. She couldn't stop the ache that was gnawing at her heart.

Brandy followed Regan into their living room. "When were you going to tell me you were going back to New York?"

"I just heard from them this morning," Regan explained. "I haven't had time to discuss it with you."

"Discuss it? It sounds like your mind is made up."

"Brandy, I . . . our age difference. I don't think—"

"Regan, you're worried about being left alone and heartbroken. I'm the one taking the chance. I know I'll always be at your side, as long as you'll have me. I'd never leave you or hurt you or cause you a moment's angst. You will always have me.

"You're a little older than me, so chances are I'll outlive you. I'm the one who will be left alone to wander this earth until I can join you. I'm the one who will suffer the devastating emptiness of one who has lost their soul mate. I'm the one taking the chance, but you're worth it. One more day with you is worth everything. At the end of every night, just promise me one more day. Do you love me?" Brandy demanded.

"You know I do, more than anything." Regan sobbed. "But I think—"

"Then don't think." Brandy pulled Regan into her arms and held her tightly against her. "Don't think of anything but how much I love you and you love me. I want to marry you."

"I need time to think, Brandy." Regan pulled from the blonde's arms. "I can't think when you're holding me."

"Why not, Regan? Why can't you think when you're in my arms?"

"Because you make my entire body tremble. You make my stomach do somersaults. I can't think, because all I want is to . . ."

"To what?" Brandy said softly.

"To make love to you."

"There's nothing wrong with that." Brandy reached for her, but she skittered away.

"I'm going to make a pot of coffee," Regan said.

Brandy slipped onto the stool at the kitchen island. "Take me to New York with you. School's out, and I haven't started work yet. I'm taking a month off to relax and get reacquainted with the world. Take me with you."

"Why do you want a woman older than you?" Regan said. "You're just enamored of me because I'm your professor. When you get out into the real world, you'll change."

"I promise I won't," Brandy declared. "I'll always love you. Can't we live in the moment? Can't we relish each day we spend together and love as if the world will end tomorrow?"

"And if it doesn't end? What then?" Regan sniffled. "Don't promise me the stars. Promise me something real. What guarantee can you give me that we'll always be as happy as we've been this past year?"

"Regan, the only stars I can guarantee you are the ones in my eyes when I look at you. The only love I can promise you forever is mine. The only touch I need to complete me is yours. Please don't take it away from me."

Regan placed her coffee cup on the island as Brandy pulled her between her knees and kissed her gently. "I want you," Brandy whispered. "I'll always want you."

"God help me, I love you with every fiber of my being, Grace Brandywine. I can't live without you, and this is so unfair to you."

"There is something I must tell you." Brandy gasped for breath as Regan kissed her and caressed her body with hands that left a line of fire as they trailed down her back.

"Later," Regan insisted. "Right now, I just want to make love with you."

The ringing of her phone pulled Regan from a satiated sleep and Brandy's arms. "Hello, Mel. . . . No, I won't be returning to New York. . . . No, I have a new agent. . . . I'm hanging up now. Goodbye, Mel."

Brandy pulled the brunette back into her arms and thrilled to the feel of her. "You hired a new agent?"

"Yes, one I trust." Regan kissed between Brandy's breasts.

"I need to read your contract before you sign it," Brandy said, warming to the idea. "Have you already negotiated percentages and book promotions and all that? What percentage are you paying them?"

"Nothing." Regan snuggled in closer and kissed Brandy's nipple.

Brandy gasped and tried to control the desire that was running rampant through her body. "No one works for nothing," she squeaked.

"Oh, she works for sex." Regan giggled. "You're my new agent, silly. I'll put you on retainer, and you can handle everything that has to do with my books."

Brandy chuckled. "That'll be a lot of hours. I'll require a lot of—"

"You'll get anything you want, baby. Anything."

Chapter 50

"What kind of function is this?" Regan asked as she slipped her arm through Brandy's.

"I'm being inducted into the Order of the Coif," Brandy answered. "It's a reception for those of us who were selected."

"Order of the Coif?" Regan scowled. "That's the crème de le crème of graduating attorneys. The what—top ten percent of the class?"

"Something like that." Brandy's modest smile made Regan's heart skip a beat.

A light went on in Regan's eyes as she stopped in her tracks. "You're too young to be . . ." She did the math in her head. "To get a law degree you couldn't possibly be any younger than twenty-six."

"Twenty-eight." Brandy beamed.

"Twenty-eight? You're twenty-eight?"

Brandy nodded. "Still a whole eight years younger than you. Still a younger woman madly in love with a more mature woman."

"Oh, shut up," Regan murmured as she pulled Brandy's head down for a long kiss. "Why didn't you tell me?"

"I tried on several occasions. Then I decided that if you didn't love me enough to stay with me no matter my age, we didn't stand a chance anyway."

"I did stay." Regan smiled as she looked at the wedding band on her finger. "I had to."

"Yes, you did stay, and I love you for that decision. Now, may I go get my recognition so we can get on with the rest of our lives?"

"To us, darling." Katherine O'Brien raised her wine glass and tapped it against Peyton's.

Peyton sipped her wine and then leaned forward. "I'd rather taste the wine on your lips," she said, smiling.

"I'm sure that can be arranged." Katherine kissed her.

"You were brilliant in the meeting," Peyton commented as she slipped off the floor-length gown she wore and hung it in the closet. She twirled her finger, motioning for Katherine to turn around.

"Um, as I recall, this whole thing started with the unzipping of your dress." Peyton kissed the back of her neck. "There is something so sexy about unzipping a beautiful woman's dress."

Katherine let her gown fall to the floor, stepped out of it, and walked toward her bed. Peyton followed, carrying their wine.

"I'm delighted everyone was as excited as I that you accepted the job as our new police chief," Katherine said as she sat on the side of the bed and reached for her wine. "With our new coaching staff and you, nothing can stop the progress of our university."

"You did surprise me by announcing that you plan to marry me." Peyton chuckled. "Did you see their faces?"

"I did." Katherine laughed out loud. "But they knew that only you and I had kept a lid on what could have been a devastating scandal for the university. They trust us to lead the school into the future.

"So, when are you going to make an honest woman out of me?"

"You set the date, honey, and I'll be there with maracas. You'll have no trouble finding me. I'll be the one with a smile as big as Texas and shaking two brightly colored gourds."

"Right now, all I want you to shake is the earth under my feet." Katherine lay back on the bed, holding out her empty wine glass for Peyton to take.

##

Katherine and Peyton's wedding had been the social event of the year, and Peyton had settled into her new job creating a safe environment for all students. Katherine had initiated a zero-tolerance policy for sexual misconduct.

"This is the last of your boxes," Katherine called out as Peyton carried two containers from the garage. "What's in them?"

"Clothes, I think." Peyton opened one of the boxes as Katherine opened the other.

"What's this?" Katherine said, holding up a costume.

"Oh, I wore that for Halloween one year." Peyton shrugged as Katherine unfolded the costume's mask.

"You went as Batman?" Katherine laughed and kissed her wife. "You should wear it at the masquerade ball this year. I bet you're a heart-stopper in spandex."

Peyton pulled the costume from Katherine's hands. "I think I'll donate it to Goodwill. It's served its purpose."

The End

Thank you for reading my book. I hope you enjoyed it as much as I enjoy writing for you.

Learn more about Erin Wade
and her books at www.erinwade.us
Follow Erin on Facebook
https://www.facebook.com/erin.wade.129142

**Other #1 Best Selling Books
by Erin Wade**
Too Strong to Die
Death Was Too Easy
Three Times as Deadly
Branded Wives
Living Two Lives
Don't Dare the Devil
The Roughneck & the Lady
Wrongly Accused
The Destiny Factor

Coming in 2019
Assassination Authorized!
Java Jarvis
Dead Girl's Gun
Doomsday Cruise

The following Erin Wade novels are on Audio

Three Times as Deadly
Living Two Lives
Don't Dare the Devil
The Roughneck & the Lady
Wrongly Accused
The Destiny Factor

Assassination Authorized
By Erin Wade

Below are the first four chapters of *Assassination Authorized*. I hope you enjoy them. *Assassination Authorized* will be released in the second quarter of 2019.

Again, thank you for being a reader of Erin Wade novels.

Chapter 1

Dr. Mecca Storm took the familiar white envelope from her patient, a handsome, muscular man in his midforties.

She removed the card from the envelope and glanced at it. She knew, without looking, what the card said. "Please take care of this gentleman for me," was neatly printed in black ink on the stark white card.

"I truly appreciate you seeing me after hours," the man said.

"Who recommended me to you," she asked.

"A friend of a friend," the man flashed a smile and lowered himself into the chair across the desk from her. "I was told you are the best in the business." His easy manner and relaxed demeanor told her he was a man confident of his place in the world. A place she knew he might not occupy for long.

"Mr. Reynolds, how may I help you?"

"Please, call me Tom," he flashed his easy smile again.

A heavy silence weighed on the room as she waited for him to begin talking.

"Tom, how may I help you," she prodded.

"If you read the papers, you already know who I am and why I'm here." For the first time, he seemed uneasy.

"You're a United States Senator and a person of interest in the disappearance of your wife and three children." Mecca spoke softly, watching his face for any emotions her words might elicit. "You're the ranking Republican on the Ways and Means Committee. You're a very powerful man and are considered the top contender in the next election for president."

"I see you have done your homework." The easy smile was back.

"Did you kill your wife and children?"

His head snapped back as if she had hit him with a hard uppercut. The smile disappeared from his face. "No! God, No."

"Well, now that we have that out of the way, how may I help you, Tom?"

After Tom Reynolds left, Mecca looked at the stark white card with its perfect lettering. She called patients bearing the card her "special patients" and she had received more special patients than usual this year.

Mecca was still replaying her visit with Tom Reynolds in her mind when the cab stopped in front of her Upper West Side apartment. She paid the driver as the doorman opened the cab door greeting her warmly. "You're home late tonight, Dr. Storm."

"It's been a long and interesting day, Paul," she smiled.

Alone in her apartment, she ordered Chinese food, poured a glass of wine and walked out onto her terrace. She never tired of her view of the Hudson River. She collapsed onto the lounge, leaned her head back and reveled in the unseasonably cool breeze.

Tom Reynolds. The man's face flashed before her as she recalled the distress in his eyes as he discussed the disappearance of his family. She wasn't sure whether the distress was caused by the disappearance of his family or the investigation of him as a suspect.

Reynolds' wife and three daughters had disappeared during a shopping trip in New York; just vanished. Their driver had dropped them at Macy's Herald Square before noon. When they failed to call him at the appointed time, he began calling Mrs. Reynolds' cell phone. After several calls, Mrs. Reynolds answered and told him they had taken a cab back to the hotel. She would call him tomorrow. On closer questioning, he couldn't swear it had been Mrs. Reynolds' voice.

Authorities traced the family's movements through credit card purchases, which stopped at the restaurant where they had dinner. No one recalled seeing them after that. A check of the cab companies showed no pickup of four women from Macy's. It was as if they had eaten, paid the bill, and vanished.

Reynolds had been in his office in Washington. Although most of his colleagues had deserted the "The Hill" early for their Fourth of July vacation, he had stayed late to finish dictation on several matters he needed his office staff to handle while he was gone. Both his secretary and an assistant had reported he had not left his office, as they could hear him dictating the information he later gave the secretary. His secretary had reported that he had left her office a little after nine, handing her dictation drives he had just finished. A check of the thumb drive showed the data had been entered during that period.

The doorman rang that the deliveryman was on his way up. As Mecca sat down to dinner, she turned on her laptop. A quick check of her Swiss account verified that the usual quarter-million dollars had transferred into it. It was time to go to work on Tom Reynolds.

##

Chapter 2

Jericho Parker pulled Mecca Storm's file from the double locked drawer in the heavy metal desk. Jericho had been protecting Mecca for over five years. An honor student, graduating at the top of her class, Mecca had received numerous scholarships from medical schools that recognized her genius and wanted to add her name to their list of distinguished alumni.

Her work in the field of therapeutic hypnosis had received rave reviews from the psychiatric community. She had finished her bachelor's degree in two years and a medical\law degree at Harvard in four years. She was editor of the Harvard Law Review. Graduating Summa Cum Laude, the top psychiatric hospitals had vied for her to do her residency in their facilities. After her residency, she devoted seven more years to research, honing her knowledge and absorbing everything she could from those considered the elite in her field. Wherever Mecca went, lucrative government grants followed to fund her research. The psychiatric community was surprised and disappointed when she suddenly left research and opened a private practice.

Fluent in five languages, Mecca worked with wealthy, influential patients from all over the U.S. and other countries. Her client load was heavy, and she often worked ten hours a day.

Jericho flipped through the photos of Mecca Storm. At 5'8", she was an imposing figure, tall and slender. A true natural beauty with long dark hair, she looked more like a movie star than a doctor.

Both of Mecca's parents were doctors with a successful practice in Albany, NY. Mecca and her older sister Teagan were highly regarded in their chosen medical fields. She adored her parents and her sister and visited them as often as possible. She often commented that the Hudson River tied them together.

Jericho's job was to keep her safe and make certain no one interfered with her work. Her file gave no indication why she was so important to the United States Government. Although Jericho knew all there was to know about her, they had never met.

##

Mecca never took anything for granted. When patients told her their stories, she listened attentively, watching for the telltale signs of half-truths or outright lies. After one session, she could tell if a patient was being open and honest with her, or guarded and secretive. She was never wrong. As his second session with her began, she knew Tom Reynolds was hiding something.

"Tom, I feel you are holding back information I need to know in order to help you," Mecca spoke softly but firmly, carefully articulating each word as if he were a child that might not understand what she was saying. "I can't make a recommendation to the DA's office unless you are completely honest with me. We are all working hard to get your name removed from the suspect list, so you can get on with your life."

"Dr. Storm, I believe I am being framed and I don't even know how to stop it. Miriam and I have certainly had arguments over living in Washington. She wants to raise the girls in Texas, but she would never just leave me."

Someone has gone to a lot of trouble to make it look like Miriam took the girls and left me or worse," Tom cocked his head to one side and glared at her. "Supposedly she cleaned out our savings account and the girls' college fund; almost a million dollars. Why would she do that?"

"Did you give this information to the police?" Mecca asked.

"Of course! They interviewed the bank officer who handled the transactions. Miriam withdrew the cash over a three-month period. The bank official called me a couple of times to alert me to the withdrawals, but I was too busy to be bothered with our personal household issues. I was sure it wasn't important. I never returned her calls.

"I looked at the security tapes of Miriam's transactions and honestly, I don't believe the woman on the tapes is my wife. She resembles Miriam, and everyone keeps insisting it is, but it isn't."

Mecca made a note to obtain a copy of the police report and the tapes. She didn't like being fed bits and pieces of information whenever Reynolds deemed it necessary for her to know something.

"What do you think is happening, Tom?"

"Dr. Storm, my wife is an heiress. She didn't need the piddling amount of money in our savings account, but I do. I barely have enough money to retain a lawyer. Most people think I married her for the money, but that's not true. I love my wife and I love my daughters. I would never hurt them. I am worried sick about them.

"You've seen what a media circus this has become. It has eclipsed the presidential election and I believe that is the intent of whoever is behind this. I think my family has been murdered and I'm being framed for it in order to give the other party an excuse to drag my name through the mud and cost us the election. These people are ruthless, and nothing will stop them. They wouldn't think twice about killing my family. Yes, I'm hiding something; sheer terror!"

Mecca closed her eyes. "Your family has been missing almost a month. Has there been a ransom demand?"

"No."

"Who inherits your wife's estate in the event of her death?" Mecca asked.

"It is to be divided evenly among the girls," Reynolds said, "If all of them preceded me in death, I would inherit everything, billions; a great motive for murder, right?

"As long as Daniel Devon is alive, he will be the sole administrator of the estate," Tom added.

The intercom on her desk buzzed reminding her of her next appointment. "Same time next week," she smiled.

Tom Reynolds left by the private entrance to her office. An entrance used only by clients who presented the white referral card. She usually handled two such patients a year. Their names never appeared on her calendar or in her accounting. As far as the records of Dr. Mecca Storm showed, such patients never existed.

##

Jericho loved it when Mecca went to Broadway plays or musicals. Though not so fond of the opera, it was beginning to grow on the bodyguard. Jericho was even beginning to recognize songs from the various operas they had attended over the years. Of course, only Jericho knew they were a couple. Mecca was completely oblivious to her shadow's existence. If she ordered tickets, Jericho automatically received a ticket for the seat directly behind her. For the more popular theaters, she had standing box seats and so did Jericho. Mecca's apartment was right above Jericho's, so the agent was very aware of those times the doctor paced the floor. On occasion, Jericho silently removed threats to her: a friendly drunk, a not so friendly mugger, and a stalker that had become obsessed with her. The drunk and mugger had simply faded into the crowd when Jericho shoved the Ruger into their back, but the bodyguard had been forced to kill the stalker.

Mecca was in great demand both professionally and socially. She attended many benefits and political black-tie events, moving easily among senators, governors and visiting royalty. She had many suitors who escorted her around town, but she never took any of them home with her. For that, Jericho was thankful. She was the epitome of what a proper, chaste woman should be.

Five years ago, when assigned the job as Mecca Storm's invisible bodyguard, Jericho was upset. Life as Jericho knew it ceased. Mecca's life became Jericho's life. Where she went, Jericho went. Where she dined, Jericho dined. Jericho was thankful Mecca disliked sushi. Although Jericho hated to admit it, life's best hours were the ones spent watching Mecca. Sometimes during a play or musical, Jericho had to suppress the urge to reach out and touch her hair. The agent couldn't imagine life without Mecca Storm and she didn't even know Jericho existed.

A former member of the Air Force's Special Operations Team, Jericho had escaped the war with only a small metal plate in her head. She was tall, beautiful and completely devoted to her country. Extremely intelligent, fluent in seven languages, and an expert in all forms of combat, she had never failed a mission. Her transition from special ops to secret service agent had been an easy one. She was considered one of the nation's top assets when it came to protecting her assignments. She did whatever it took to keep her charge safe. Although she preferred intimidation, killing came easily to her when all else failed.

Jericho had no idea why Mecca was so important. She did know not to ask questions. It was a sweet assignment for her. Mecca was so important the government wanted to keep Jericho as happy as possible in her assignment. The government paid all her expenses. Everything she did charged to a limitless credit card, and she had received a clear deed to her five-million-dollar apartment. Of course, she knew the only reason her apartment was so grand was because she had to be below Mecca's. Funds were automatically deposited into accounts for her homeowner's association, utilities, etc. Every two years a new black vehicle appeared in her parking place with a title and insurance card in her name in the console. She banked her annual income of $200,000 in a savings account. In exchange for being a kept woman, she gave up all semblance of a personal life. Twenty-four hours a day, seven days a week, she belonged to Mecca Storm.

Mecca dialed the phone number she had always called when she needed information on her special clients. The same voice she had heard for the past five years answered. "I need a copy of the police files on Tom Reynolds," she said.

"You will have it tomorrow," the voice replied.

"Please, don't hang up," Mecca pleaded, but Jericho knew the dangers of engaging in conversation with her. The line went dead.

Mecca watched a sailboat on the Hudson and slowly lowered the phone from her ear. She had made every search imaginable to find the owner of the number she called when she needed information. As far as the phone company knew, the number did not exist. More than anything she wished the voice would talk to her. She needed someone to talk to when she was sent these patients. She recorded every conversation she had with her unknown contact. She couldn't tell if the mechanically altered voice was male or female, but she knew that if she ever heard that voice—even in a crowd—she would recognize the speech pattern.

The information on Tom Reynolds arrived at her office before noon. The courier had strict instructions to release the manila envelope containing a flash drive to Dr. Storm and no one else.

Mecca instructed her secretary to hold her calls for an hour and spent her lunchtime reading the Reynolds' file and viewing the bank's videos.

Miriam Devon Reynolds was a beautiful woman. Her daughters were equally beautiful. They looked like money; the right clothes, the right haircuts, the same bright, wide smiles and long blonde hair. Miriam Devon was the sole heir of one of the wealthiest oil families in Texas. Like so many who grow up with great wealth, she had no idea what it meant to earn a living but was certain she could help run America. Running on the Republican ticket, armed with a law degree and Daddy's money she had easily won the race for U.S. Representative in her state. She spoke Arabic, Spanish and French. Her second year in Washington she had met and married Senator Tom Reynolds, a rising star in the Republican Party. With Miriam's money behind him, the party soon began grooming the charismatic senator for the presidency.

Miriam and Tom had three daughters: 8, 10, and 12. When Tom wasn't working, he was with his family. He doted on his wife and daughters. It was no secret, Miriam desperately wanted to get her family out of Washington politics and return to Texas to raise her daughters. "Washington is no place to raise children," she said often.

It was also no secret; Tom Reynolds wanted to be president.

While a massive manhunt was underway, the police were scrutinizing Tom and his whereabouts when his family had disappeared. His alibi was solid, and the police had no leads at all on Miriam and her daughters.

Everyone connected with the case wanted to know why Tom had waited so long to report his family missing. He insisted he thought Miriam had taken the girls and gone to Texas. He had gone to his home office to finish reading a house bill and fallen asleep at his desk. When he awoke the next day, he had discovered his wife and daughters had never made it home the night before.

He tried Miriam's cell phone and left messages. He finally called her father and learned that Miriam was not in Texas.

He had called the chauffer and learned his wife and children had taken the train home from the city. He then called the police and reported them missing. Tom told the police he and his wife had been arguing for months over their lives in Washington, but it was nothing they couldn't work out. He hoped that Miriam had simply packed up the girls and gone to Texas but calls to Miriam's family turned up no trace of Miriam or the girls.

There was no evidence of foul play, and there was no trace of the Reynolds women. Daniel Devon, the administrator of Miriam's family trust, had arrived in Washington within six hours of learning of his daughter's disappearance. He had immediately demanded the arrest of Tom Reynolds. According to Devon, a divorce was imminent. Miriam had told Reynolds she was leaving him and taking the children. The shopping trip had been to purchase items for the trip to Texas. Devon had drafted the prenuptial himself, so Reynolds would never get a cent of the family fortune if Miriam divorced him.

Prior to his family's disappearance, Reynolds had been the top contender for president. Wildly popular with most Americans, the charismatic senator had won his own senate re-election by a landslide. He consistently polled as the most popular member of congress.

Reynolds had swept the Republican primary, winning 1580 delegates. The Republican National Convention was just a fanfare to solidify national support for the candidate.

Republican Committee Chairman Mark Thornton had scheduled a press conference following the national convention Wednesday to celebrate the committee's nomination of Reynolds.

Mecca closed the file. She wondered why Reynolds had been sent to her. Certainly, he had a motive, but there was no evidence of foul play. Reynolds had agreed to take a polygraph to rule him out as a suspect. By the time of their next appointment, she would know the results of the test.

##

Chapter 3

Mecca stayed an hour after her secretary left. She meticulously filed her cases of the day and cleared the top of her desk. She jumped when her phone rang. A quick glance at the caller ID told her it was Teagan. "I was about to give up on you," she answered.

"What a day," sighed Teagan. "I can't wait to sit down and have some handsome young waiter pour me a glass of wine. Can we go to that Italian restaurant? You know the one that opens the sliding glass doors, and it feels as if we are sitting right on the sidewalk."

"Of course," laughed Mecca. "I can be there in thirty minutes."

"Great, we can people watch, while we catch up," Teagan said.

##

Jericho took an obscure table next to the wall, so she could observe the sisters. They laughed and giggled like two schoolgirls. No one would ever think them two of the best medical minds in the country. Teagan was a top neurosurgeon and Mecca a groundbreaking psychiatrist. Both were graduates of the Harvard Medical School, Mecca had been awarded the DuPont-Warren Fellowship for advanced study and research in psychiatry and had proven her theories that had been previously shunned by the psychiatric community. Both chose Johns Hopkins in Baltimore, MD for their residency because the hospital was ranked number one in the U.S. in both their fields. Teagan had settled at New York's Presbyterian Hospital and Mecca opted for private practice.

"I need your help with a patient," Teagan finally moved their conversation toward work. "She was brought into the hospital last week with TBI and is in a coma. Poor thing she was suffering from malnutrition and dehydration. No telling how long she has been in that condition. She was literally starving to death. She's coming around, but still has serious trauma."

"Traumatic Brain Injury," Mecca shook her head. "That's really more your specialty, Sis."

"The injury part is going to be okay," Teagan nodded, "but she was badly beaten, and I had to remove some bone fragments from her skull. Dr. Davis had to work on her cheekbones and nose, so she could breathe comfortably. She is regaining consciousness but doesn't know her name or where she is. Her trauma is now more mental."

"Oh, one of your famous penniless patients," Mecca tried to lift the somber mood that had fallen over them.

Teagan laughed. "No, her perfect teeth and manicured everything tells me she isn't destitute. The hospital reported her to the police, but she doesn't match any missing person's reports. I am just hoping we can get her to remember something—anything."

"You know I'll be happy to help in any way I can," Mecca patted her sister's hand.

"She is going to require more facial surgery. Nikki said some one really did a number on her face, but that must wait until she heals more. In the meantime, I need your magic." Teagan tipped her wine glass as if toasting Mecca.

Dr. Nikki Davis was one of the best facial reconstruction surgeons Mecca had ever encountered.

She was excited about working with two doctors she highly respected. "Just tell me where and what time. I'll clear my calendar and be there," Mecca reassured her sister.

Back in her apartment, Mecca called the number. The phone was picked up, but no one answered. "I need the results of the polygraph Reynolds takes tomorrow," she said.

"You'll have them tomorrow evening." The dial tone signaled the end to the conservation.

Mecca pushed the remote to turn on the TV. Tom Reynolds' handsome face flashed across the screen of CNN News as the commentator rehashed the situation with his missing family. The liberal news media had opened its airwaves to Daniel Devon who was all too happy to try Reynolds on public television. He blamed his son-in-law for Miriam's disappearance.

Mecca wondered what would happen to Miriam's fortune if she and her daughters were dead and Tom was found guilty of their murder. Who else stood to benefit from the deaths of the Reynolds women?

Mecca's thoughts turned to her sister. As teenagers, Teagan had teased her about her fascination with hypnosis.

Their mother had taken them to a medical conference when Mecca was 14. One of the seminars was devoted to psychiatry and hypnosis. Teagan and Mecca convinced their mother to let them go to the seminar while she attended her seminar on internal medicine.

When the girls arrived in the seminar, they were surprised to find 40 mats with pillows neatly arranged 10 to a row. The speaker had discussed various forms of hypnosis ending with mass hypnosis. Mecca and Teagan scoffed at the idea. The speaker asked everyone to ascertain the time. He then asked everyone to turn off all cell phones. He explained the dangers of a hypnotized subject hearing a loud noise or ringing. He asked everyone to lie down on the mats. "You don't have to close your eyes," he said, "just relax and get comfortable. If you do happen to fall asleep, you will awaken when I clap my hands."

He had continued in an even, comforting tone, "When I arrived here today, I was delighted to find so many signed up for the seminar. It is always nice when one's subject is received favorably. I hope you have found my research interesting and relaxing. If your eyes are feeling heavy, it is okay to close them. Just relax and..."

Mecca and Teagan awoke at the same time. Looking around them, they had discovered that everyone in the room was just awakening from a deep, restful sleep.

The speaker told them to look at their watch to verify that they had been asleep for forty-five minutes. "What you have just experienced is mass hypnosis on a small scale," he smiled.

Mecca's passion was born.

As her fascination with hypnosis grew, so did her determination to become a psychiatrist. She devoured every book ever written about hypnosis. She found that she could hypnotize a subject very quickly with or without their cooperation.

She became convinced that the 1978, mass suicide of 909 members of the Peoples Temple in Jonestown, Guyana had been the result of mass hypnosis perpetrated on his followers by Jim Jones.

An avowed communist Jones had been a leader in the Democratic Party in California where he was appointed Chairman of the San Francisco Housing Authority Commission as a reward for the important role he played in the mayoral election victory of George Moscone.

First Lady Rosalynn Carter personally met with Jones on multiple occasions and corresponded with him about Cuba. She spoke with him at the grand opening of the San Francisco Democratic Party Headquarters where Jones received louder applause than she did.

Jones enjoyed the protection of his Democratic Party friends in high places until the IRS began looking into his Peoples Temple. To get away from the media scrutiny and the IRS investigation he moved his followers to Guyana and established Jonestown.

His drug addiction and indulgence in sex with young girls in his congregation caused the unraveling of his self-proclaimed deity.

In November 1978, U.S. Congressman Leo Ryan butted heads with the local Democratic establishment and the Jimmy Carter administration's State Department in order to investigate allegations of human rights abuses of U.S. citizens in Jonestown. Ryan's delegation included relatives of Temple members, an NBC news crew and reporters from various newspapers.

Ryan's visit to Jonestown was cut short when a Temple member attacked Ryan with a knife. Congressman Ryan and his people quickly left taking fifteen People's Temple members, who had asked to leave, with them. Jones did not attempt to prevent their departure.

As Ryan's delegation began boarding planes to depart, they were gunned down by Temple members

The next morning the Guyanese army cut through the jungle to Jonestown. They discovered 909 inhabitants, dead from ingesting poisoned Kool-Aid. The individuals died in what was declared a "mass suicide/murder ritual"

At Harvard, Mecca had set the psychiatric world on fire and made headlines when she gave the last speech of the commencement ceremony. She hypnotized everyone in the room: graduates, faculty, staff, parents, relatives, etc.; all 3,000 of them.

In an experiment prearranged through the research department, small cups of grape Kool-Aid were passed out to everyone in the hall. At Mecca's suggestion, everyone drank the Kool-Aid. Mecca then told her audience that when she blew a whistle they would be fully awake. That the graduates were to leave the auditorium as practiced and then others could follow. She suggested that no one involved with her experiment would ever sue anyone associated with it. "Remember to put the cups in the trash cans on the way out and tell your friends what an awesome speaker I am." She couldn't resist the last statement just for the fun of it.

She blew the whistle and the procession proceeded as practiced, with proud parents following to find their graduates.

Every single cup was placed in the trash receptacles. Not even a scrap was dropped in the auditorium. There was never a single complaint from anyone over being hypnotized. Mecca had made them drink the Kool-Aid.

Mecca had gotten the attention of every psychiatric research facility in the world and the unwanted attention of the United States government.

The phone ringing yanked Mecca back to the present. It was Teagan.

"How does your calendar look for Friday?" Teagan asked.

"Great," Mecca replied, "I have one patient, but I can reschedule her."

"Good, bring your appetite. I'll cook and the three of us can discuss our patient. Nikki has already pulled x-rays, so you can get some idea of the physical trauma the girl has experienced." Teagan added. "I want you to visit with her, and then you can give us some idea of the mental trauma we're battling."

##

Mecca walked her last patient out of the office. "There is a gentleman holding for you," Julie nodded toward the phone.

Julie had been her secretary from day one and Mecca knew she was largely responsible for the smooth way her office ran.

"Were you able to reschedule Mrs. Lewis?" Mecca asked over her shoulder.

"Monday at three," Julie answered as Mecca closed the door.

"Dr. Storm," she announced herself into the phone receiver.

"The information you requested is in your apartment," the familiar voice said.

"Why don't we go over it together?" Mecca tried to engage her informant. "I suspect you know more about the situation than I."

"No, I'm really puzzled over this one," the voice replied, "But your clients are your business."

"Please talk to me a moment," Mecca wanted a commitment to stay on the phone.

"Okay."

"Who are you?" she whispered.

To her surprise, she received an answer. "A flunky in the police department," the voice lied. "I'm just an information source for you. Good night, Dr. Storm."

The voice mystified Mecca. She could tell from the mechanical sound the person she called used a voice altering app on their phone. She didn't know if she was speaking with a man or a woman.

As promised, the results of the polygraph had been slipped under her door. Mecca came home late from the office. Closing the door behind her, she sat down her brief case and purse on the entry hall table and bent down to pick up the envelope. The hallway light cast a shadow under her door. The shadow hesitated and then it was gone.

Mecca placed the envelope on her bed as she slipped into something more comfortable. Her sheepskin house shoes felt good after wearing heels all day. She carried the envelope to the kitchen and let it sit unopened as she made a chicken salad sandwich. She curled up on her sofa eyeing the envelope as she ate her dinner.

She looked around her apartment. She knew it was Spartan compared to her sister's apartment. She considered it a place to sleep and eat. She hadn't put forth much effort to decorate it.

She knew she was putting off opening the envelope because she was afraid of what she might find. She wanted Tom Reynolds to be innocent, but she was afraid he wasn't.

She studied the polygraph results. It appeared Tom was telling the truth. He had no knowledge of what had happened to his family. If Tom didn't know, then where were they?

Before going to bed, Mecca located her Presbyterian Hospital nametag and pulled out her white Johns Hopkins issued coat.

##

"The Storm sisters," Kadence Pride grabbed her heart feigning an attack. "It would make me the happiest woman in the world if either one of you would marry me," she laughed.

Mecca greeted her friend with a hug and a kiss on the cheek. "How is the world's most gorgeous surgeon," she smiled.

"Better, now that you're here. To what do we owe the honor?"

"Collaborating," Teagan answered. "Remember the Jane Doe that came in last week? Mecca is helping me with her."

"Good luck," Kadence shook her head. "She really took a beating; poor thing. Dr. Marcus had to remove her spleen, and she had multiple cracked ribs. He had to stop the internal hemorrhaging before he could turn her over to your gifted sister. Honestly, Teagan, I didn't think she would live through the brain surgery."

"She is coming out of her coma," Teagan said, "but she is completely uncommunicative. I'm hoping Mecca can help her."

"You know where I am if you need me," Kadence grinned mischievously, "for anything at all."

Kadence had been their self-appointed protector in college. Although the truth was, they had carried her home drunk from many parties and put her to bed. Fortunately, she had outgrown her wild ways. She was an outstanding plastic surgeon. She jokingly referred to herself as the doctor to the stars and royalty.

The elevator stopped on the trauma floor and the two sisters picked up Jane Doe's chart. She'd had a quiet night with no change in her condition.

Mecca watched as Teagan checked her patient. Jane Doe was bandaged from the top of her head to her hips. Both arms were incased in casts.

Dr. Nikki Davis joined them,

"Not a very pretty sight," Dr. Davis, side-hugged Mecca and gently touched Teagan's arm. "She'll be okay. There is nothing the two of you can't fix."

"Who would do such a thing to another human being," Teagan closed her eyes to block out the bloody mess Jane Doe had been in the emergency room.

Nikki caught Teagan's hand and held it as if willing her strength. "A year from now Jane Doe will be completely healed and we will be discussing her case over dinner for years to come."

"Any luck with missing persons matching a name with our patient," Mecca watched the motionless body for any sign of movement.

"Not yet," Nikki said. We got the news stations to run a description of her from what we have. You know brunette, 5'6", and 125 pounds—pretty general description. Someone from the police department is supposed to come by to collect her fingerprints and DNA."

Nikki let go of Teagan's hand, "How about a cup of coffee before we make our rounds?"

Jericho watched the three head for the doctor's lounge and decided Mecca was safe in the hospital. She stepped inside Jane Doe's room. She was sleeping peacefully. She also wondered how someone could beat a woman that badly. She was certain that whoever did it was sure she was dead.

She stepped back into the hall and saw a man at the nurses' station. The bulge beneath the man's jacket caught her eye immediately. Jericho walked away from the room listening to the footsteps of the man. When she was certain the man was inside Jane Doe's room, she turned and quickly stepped inside too.

The man had placed a pillow over the helpless woman's face. He was aware of Jericho's presence for only a few seconds before his neck was snapped.

Jericho called her contact at the police department and within minutes, two uniformed police officers appeared to carry away the body of the Muslim assassin.

Mecca and Teagan were surprised at the flurry of excitement around Jane Doe's room and the two police officers standing guard at her door.

"Someone tried to kill Jane Doe," the head nurse rushed to Teagan. "The police took him away."

"If he tried to kill her, he must know who she is," Teagan spoke to one of the officers. "Where is he? I must speak with him."

"His neck was broken when he was apprehended," the officer replied.

"I must speak to the officer in charge," Mecca said, "Who is handling the case?"

"Mecca, we are in the middle of something very dangerous," Teagan cautioned her sister. "Apparently our news coverage last night caught the attention of Jane Doe's assailant who came back to finish the job."

"Thank goodness he was apprehended," Nikki strode toward them and put a protective arm around Teagan "Are you ok? I came as soon as I heard the news."

"I'm going to get some water," Mecca had a feeling the body of the assailant was probably in the hospital morgue and she wanted to see his face.

"I need to see the man that was just brought in," Mecca spoke to the morgue attendant.

"Go through those double doors. He is against the far back wall; on the green gurney waiting for the ME's office to pick him up," the intern pointed to the back of the long room. "He's the one right next to the double doors leading to the loading area."

Mecca stared at the killer's face for a long time. She etched every detail of it into her memory, and then she took a picture with her cell phone.

Suddenly a hand went over her mouth and a strong arm encircled her holding her tightly, so she couldn't move or make a sound. A hard body pressed against her back as she was dragged behind a row of file cabinets. She struggled in vain.

"Please, be still," Jericho growled her whisper.

Mecca knew that voice. She knew she was safe. She let herself collapse against her captor and moaned softly.

The person was tall and muscular but smelled faintly of expensive feminine perfume.

"You're a woman," Mecca gasped.

Mecca breathed in the scent of her, the feel of her. She finally had someone to go with the voice. She tried to turn to face her captor but was held tightly from behind.

The double doors leading to the loading area flew open and three armed men rushed to the hit man's body. One hulking brute threw the corpse over his shoulder and in less than sixty seconds they disappeared through the same doors they'd entered.

"Listen to me," Jericho commanded, "Jane Doe is a danger for you. Get away from her. Don't let anyone know you're involved with her.

"Tell your sister to have her moved to the most secure room in the hospital. Don't give anyone information on her. Don't let any information get out that connects your sister or you to her. Guards will be posted at her door twenty-four, seven."

Her lips were so close to her ear. Mecca could feel her warm breath, but her words seemed far away. She struggled to comprehend what she was saying, but her mind was caught up in the sheer strength of her. She tried again to turn to see her, but Jericho gave her a shove forward and was gone.

"Did you find what you needed," the intern walked toward her.

"Yes," she stammered, "yes I did, but someone just took your body."

Chapter 4

The three doctors were silent during the cab ride to Teagan's apartment. Each of them went over the events of the day in their mind, trying to make some sense of what had happened.

Inside the apartment, they all began to talk at once. Nikki poured wine and sat out *hors d'oeuvres* while Teagan preheated the oven.

The table had been set that morning before Nikki and Teagan left for the hospital. All they needed was thirty minutes for the casserole to heat.

Mecca sat down in an overstuffed armchair and kicked off her shoes. "I don't know what to make of this," she said softly. "I looked at the assassin. His neck was broken. He didn't appear to put up a struggle. He was Muslim. Who broke his neck?"

"I don't know," Teagan frowned, "It all happened so fast. Thank heaven someone was there and realized he was trying to kill her. I had Jane Doe moved to the room in front of the nurses' station and the police guard is there."

Mecca wondered if her faceless friend had been the one to save Jane Doe. Hopefully, she would have the opportunity to ask her.

"Someone knows who our Jane Doe is," frowned Teagan. She lowered herself slowly onto the sofa, leaning comfortably against Nikki whose arm encircled her shoulders protectively and pulled her close.

Teagan and Nikki had been together since college and had leaned on each other through the grueling years of med school and residency. Nikki was obviously as much in love with Teagan as ever, and the feeling was mutual. Sometimes Mecca wished she had someone like Nikki to lean on.

After dinner, they scrutinized Jane Doe's x-rays. Using the x-rays as a base, Nikki used a computer program to reconstruct Jane Does face.

"Unfortunately, there's so much damage to her cheekbones and facial structure it is difficult to determine exactly how she may have looked," Nikki frowned. "I have run several options to provide the police."

"But you can make her beautiful," Teagan said.

"Yes," Nikki smiled, "but it will be a long hard road, requiring several surgeries. I have enlisted Kadence's help. She is the finest plastic surgeon in the world, bar none."

"For now, let's keep everything to ourselves," Mecca said. "There are people out there who want Jane Doe dead.

"I wonder if Jane Doe will ever know how lucky she is that you two were on duty when she came into the hospital," Mecca poured herself another glass of wine.

"And that she has the world's foremost psychiatrist to take care of her psyche," grinned Teagan. "I'm glad you have decided to spend the night. You know safety in numbers and all that."

After midnight, Jericho reclined her seat, trying to get comfortable. She hated it when Mecca spent the night somewhere. It always meant a sleepless night in the car for her. No matter how she tried to arrange her six-foot frame, she was cramped.

As the first rays of daylight hit her windshield, a taxi pulled in front of Teagan's apartment building, and the three doctors got in. Jericho started her vehicle and followed the cab to the hospital.

The first stop for all three doctors was Jane Doe's room. Nikki visited with the head nurse. There had been no change in Jane. Just like the day before, she had regained consciousness several times, only to slip back into a deep sleep.

Since it was Saturday, the two surgeons decided to make rounds and check on their patients then head home. They invited Mecca to spend the day with them. She asked for a raincheck. She could tell by the way Teagan kept flirting with Nikki that the two wanted some time alone.

After examining Jane Doe, Mecca knew she would not be able to reach the woman in her present state, so she opted to head home, also. She secretly hoped she would somehow have contact with her silent friend.

After Jericho had watched Mecca safely enter her building, she parked and went up to her apartment. She was so glad Mecca had gone home. She was exhausted. As she unlocked the door to her apartment, her cell phone vibrated. He looked at the caller ID. It was Mecca. She knew she was safely in the apartment above her. She decided not to answer her phone. She didn't trust herself at that moment.

Jericho's sleep was fitful at first, as the scent of Mecca and the feeling of her back pulled tightly against her kept flitting in and out of her dreams. In her dreams, she turned Mecca to face her and kissed her slowly and gently feeling the softness of her.

Jericho awoke to the sound of the shower above her room. Great idea. She would shower with her.

She could hear Mecca blow-drying her hair as she toweled off and slipped her favorite Henley shirt over her head. Jericho decided to watch TV in her panties, so she wouldn't have to decide on slacks or jeans, just comfort.

Jericho was putting cream in her coffee when she heard Mecca's door close and the bell of the elevator.

Doesn't that woman ever rest? She frantically pulled on a pair of slacks and slid on her loafers. She slipped into the holster harness and pulled on a sweater to cover it, as she ran for the elevator.

Jericho dashed out the building door in time to catch a glimpse of Mecca entering the local pub down the street. She walked the block slowly, regaining her composure and waiting for a group of people to enter.

She blended with a group of tourists entering the pub then made her way to a dimly lit table in the corner. She had learned early in her career not to enter a room alone. Her physical appearance drew eyes to her when she walked through a door alone. Tall, slender and stunning she had to work hard to be obscure.

Jericho quickly located Mecca sitting in a booth with Dr. Kadence Pride. Jericho was surprised to find that she was upset to see her with Pride.

"I can't believe you were free on a Saturday night," Kadence signaled a waitress and ordered drinks.

"I often am," Mecca smiled.

"Then please give me an opportunity to remedy that," Kadence smiled back.

"It's by choice," Mecca cooled her down, "I'm afraid I'm a workaholic and often bring my work home with me."

"Believe me, I understand," Kadence sympathized. "How is Teagan's patient?"

"She'll recover, but it will be a long ordeal," Mecca replied.

Kadence raised her glass, and the two toasted, "Here is to long ordeals and even longer friendships," Kadence laughed.

Jericho watched as the two friends reminisced for the next three hours. Her growling stomach reminded her that she hadn't eaten in thirty-six hours, so she ordered the pub's signature meal. Two young women at the bar sent over a free drink, but she politely declined it. She never drank on duty. Which meant she rarely had a chance to have a drink?

Jericho had finished her steak when Kadence paid their check and the two strolled from the restaurant.

She watched from across the street as Kadence walked Mecca home. They stood for a long time in front of Mecca's building. Jericho held her breath. Please don't invite her up she whispered. Kadence bent down and kissed Mecca on the cheek. The doorman ushered her into the building. Kadence walked back and forth in front of the building as if trying to decide if she would be welcomed inside. She finally decided against ringing Mecca and hailed a taxi.

Jericho entered her apartment quietly, listening for sounds of Mecca above. Mecca walked to her terrace. Jericho went out on her terrace and unknown to Mecca they shared a beautiful view of the Hudson River. Mecca touched the button on her cell phone that immediately dialed Jericho's phone.

Jericho's phone vibrated in her pocket making her jump. She moved into her apartment. She didn't want to take the chance her voice might reach Mecca from her terrace.

She pushed the button that connected her to Mecca and held her breath. She had as many questions for her charge as Mecca had for her. Knowing too much could be dangerous for both of them.

"I tried to call you earlier today," Mecca said softly. "I wanted to thank you for saving Jane Doe's life." She closed her eyes and relived the feel of her. She could still smell her perfume.

"I just notified the authorities," Jericho lied.

"Who broke the assassin's neck?" Mecca asked.

"I didn't know his neck was broken," Jericho lied again.

"Will you give me any information you can find out about him?" Mecca continued. "Do you have any way to find out who Jane Doe is?"

"Yes and no," she replied.

"Don't go all woman of few words on me now," Mecca chided her. "I think we may be in over our heads, and I'm concerned about my sister and Nikki."

"How did you happen to be in the hospital just in time to save Jane Doe?" She continued. "And why didn't you let me see your face, and why all the cloak and dagger action?"

The line went dead. Mecca looked at her phone as if it had betrayed her. She hated when she hung up on her. She dialed her number again, but she knew she wouldn't answer.

During the weeks that followed, Mecca kept busy with her patients. The press seemed to tire of Tom Reynolds and his missing family, and the Democrats and Republicans had moved on to discrediting each other's next potential presidential candidate. Although Tom had not withdrawn from the race, pundits were certain of his campaign's demise. The movers and shakers in the Republican Party were quickly distancing themselves from Tom. The police still considered Tom a person of interest.

Jane Doe was still drifting in and out of consciousness. It was almost as if she couldn't face waking up completely.

"So, the big affair at the United Nations is tonight," Julie handed her the invitation she had received a week ago. "Are you going with Dr. Pride?"

"Yes, Kadence wants to rub shoulders with potential donors for the hospital. I swear she is a one-woman fundraising committee. She has single handedly raised more than one third of the research foundations funding this year."

"The fact that she is eye candy doesn't hurt either," Julie winked. "You know she's crazy about you?"

"We have been friends for too many years to be anything else," Mecca shrugged. "I have to admit it's nice to have someone like Kadence on my arm when necessary. Of course, I do the same thing for her."

"Oh great," Julie feigned shock, "you are her wingman."

"Um hum and she's mine," Mecca smiled. "Well, home to dress for the festivities."

Jericho had stepped out of the shower and was scowling at her evening gown when she heard Mecca's door close. Obviously, Mecca had come home early to get ready for the reception at the UN tonight. Most of the members of the Eurozone were in New York for a financial summit. After President Lockleer's seven years of destruction in America, the U.S. dollar was at an all-time low. European leaders were depending on the next American President and the U.S. to help stabilize the world financial market.

Jericho was sure Lockleer would be at the reception bowing and kissing up to world leaders. She thought of the President with great distain. She hoped America would survive the poor leadership of the weak president.

The vibration of her phone interrupted her thoughts. It was Mecca. She answered gruffly.

"I just wondered if you had found out anything about the assassin?" Mecca's voice was almost breathless.

"Nothing yet," she lied. "I will let you know as soon as I have something. How is Jane Doe?"

As soon as the question left her lips, she wished she could get it back. She knew she should not engage Mecca in conversation. She also knew the beautiful doctor was in danger, but she didn't know why.

"She's better," Mecca answered tentatively. She was afraid she would hang up. "I hope to be able to work with her next week."

"That's good," Jericho knew she should hang up, but couldn't. She wanted to hear Mecca's voice just a few minutes more. "Are you home for the night?"

"I wish," Mecca laughed. "I'm afraid I have to spend the evening in the most boring way imaginable; attending a stuffy reception. Want to join me?"

"No, but thanks for asking," Jericho chuckled and hung up.

Jericho was pleased that she had elicited a laugh from her. She was also pleased that she would be at the UN reception, not as Mecca's escort, but as her bodyguard.

Jericho arrived at the reception a little ahead of Mecca and Kadence. She wanted to make certain the German credentials the agency had sent her worked smoothly; as always, they did. She felt a twinge of jealousy as Kadence walked into the ballroom with Mecca on her arm. *God, she is beautiful*, she thought.

The two made their way around the room, visiting with dignitaries and politicians.

A new band took the stage and Salsa music filled the ballroom. The younger partygoers moved onto the floor, and the older dealmakers moved aside.

Jericho watched as Kadence nodded to a man who led Mecca to the center of the dance floor. A beautiful Spanish woman grabbed Jericho's hand and dragged her onto the dance floor. Suddenly her back collided with another dancer.

Mecca recognized her cologne as soon as she bumped into the woman. Catching hold of her arm, Mecca stepped in front of her. "It's you!"

Jericho looked at her blankly then spoke in perfect German, "I am sorry. I do not speak English." *That should kill the conversation,* she thought smugly.

Mecca looked embarrassed. The harsh guttural language was not what she had expected. "I am so sorry," she replied in flawless German, "I thought you were someone else. I didn't mean to be rude. I'm afraid I ruined your dance." Mecca looked around for her partner, but she had moved on to another dancer.

"Where are my manners," she smiled, "I am Mecca Storm, New Yorker."

"I'm Isa Friedman," Jericho smiled. "I'm attached to the German embassy."

"Friedman; peace maker," Mecca cocked her head to one side and studied Isa's blue eyes and magnificent mane of blonde hair. "Are you a peace maker, Miss Friedman?"

Shakespeare Under Cover by Erin Wade

"Mecca, there you are," Kadence strode toward them. "I have to meet with someone for about thirty minutes. Will you be okay?"

"Kadence, I'd like you to meet Isa Friedman. She's with the German embassy." Mecca was still speaking German.

"Nice to meet you," Kadence shook Jericho's hand.

"She doesn't speak English," Mecca informed her friend.

"Would you just keep an eye on my friend?" Kadence's German was impeccable too. "I have to attend to something quickly. I'll be right back, Mecca."

Kadence disappeared as the band started another dance number.

"Would you like to dance?" Jericho asked as Mecca looked up at her. For the first time, she realized Mecca had the deepest blue eyes she'd ever seen. They reminded her of blue ice except for the hint of laughter that made them mesmerizing.

Jericho took both her hands and led Mecca onto the dance floor. Thanks to the agency's insistence that she be able to fit in anywhere, in any situation, Jericho was an accomplished dancer. Although she had complained loudly during her lessons, she did enjoy dancing.

Jericho enjoyed Mecca's look of surprise as she deftly led her around the dance floor. Fortunately, Salsa dancing was not conducive to conversation. The dance ended, and she turned preparing to make her exit, but Mecca caught her hand as the band began playing a slow number.

Everything in her screamed she should not hold Mecca Storm in her arms, but when has good sense ever overcome desire? More than anything, she wanted to hold her.

"How long have you been in New York?"

"No English," Jericho shook her head, and Mecca repeated her question in German.

"Six weeks," she smiled, "I'll be going home at the end of the month."

Mecca stopped talking and enjoyed the pleasure of following a strong dancer. Jericho held her tightly, her hand at the small of Mecca's back forcing her to follow every move her body made. Most of Mecca's partners had a tendency to let her lead. She knew no one would ever lead Isa Friedman.

"Perhaps, I can show you around our fair city," Mecca offered as they made their way to one of the tables on the far side of the dance floor.

"I would very much like that," Jericho smiled. "May I get you something to drink?"

Mecca watched her as she walked away. She was the right height and weight. She had imagined her as dark, but she was blonde. Her German had no American accent. That confused her. If she could get her alone, she would know for sure. She had no qualms about using her abilities to find out the truth when needed.

When Jericho returned with their drinks, Kadence was sitting at the table laughing with Mecca. "With the commitment I just received from the chairman of Toyota, I believe we have enough money for the new wing," Kadence almost giggled. She was as giddy as a small girl with a new puppy.

Mecca hugged her arm, "Kadence, you are amazing. I don't know of anyone as dedicated as you."

"With Lockleer in the White House it has certainly been difficult to get corporate America to open their checkbooks," Kadence commented. "It's hard to get anyone to let go of a dollar. No one knows what will happen next, so everyone is hanging onto their money.

"The Japanese are still furious with him for the phony recall he made right after his election. Everyone knew it was just to pay off the unions for their campaign support. You know, discredit Toyota and encourage Americans to buy U.S. made automobiles.

"It only took the administration two years to admit they could find no fault with the Toyotas on which they forced the recall."

Jericho sat the drinks down on the table and took a chair next to Mecca. Mecca stood and excused herself. "I'll be right back," she said. "Don't go away."

"Your wife is very beautiful," Jericho was trying to gauge the depth of Kadence's feelings for Mecca.

"Oh, I wish," Kadence watched her walk away. "We have been friends for many years. College, med school, and residency. I'm afraid I was quite a hell raiser. Too many times, Mecca and her sister washed the vomit off me after frat parties to consider me marriage material."

Jericho was relieved when Mecca reappeared. She never liked to let the brunette out of her sight, especially at a gathering of politicians. She watched her walk toward them and was surprised to see the President grasp her by the arm and pull her close to him. He was leaning down and talking into her ear so no one else could hear what he was telling her. It was obvious she did not like what he was saying. True hatred flashed across her face and then was gone. Turning to face him, she raised her free arm and placed her hand on the President's forearm. He seemed to freeze in mid-sentence. She spoke several words to him then removed his hand from her arm. She walked away while he was still trying to talk to her. Jericho had no idea that her influence reached presidents.

Mecca rejoined them, sitting close to Kadence. She placed her hand on Kadence's arm drawing her full attention to her. It was like watching a snake charmer.

"Kadence, I'm so proud of you," Mecca said softly, "I don't know what our profession would do without dedicated women like you."

Jericho watched closely, fascinated by the way she had Kadence under her control. Thinking Jericho didn't understand English, she made a suggestion to Kadence, "I know you need to stay and visit with others. I'm ready to leave, and Isa has offered to see me home if you don't mind."

Kadence looked at Jericho as if seeing her for the first time, "Miss. Friedman, I need to visit with some other people, would it be possible for you to see Mecca home?"

Jericho shrugged, "No English."

Kadence repeated her question in German and Jericho smiled and nodded yes. Kadence hugged Mecca, "I'll call you tomorrow and let you know if I still have the Midas touch." She headed for the bar.

"Would you like to go somewhere quiet?" Mecca suggested. "There's a little German pub not far from here. I think you'll like it."

"I would like that very much," Jericho agreed.

As they walked, Mecca looped her arm through Jericho's and asked her about her home. Fortunately, Jericho had been stationed in Germany for three years and was well versed in the history and culture of the country.

"I spent two years in Germany working with one of your top research scientists," Mecca said.

"You're a scientist?" Jericho steered the conversation toward her. She had no idea about Germany's top research scientists.

"Oh, no," Mecca laughed.

Jericho saw German writing heralding the location of "America's best German pub." Mecca was right. The pub was quiet and intimate. They slid into a booth and ordered a drink.

"Have you eaten?" Jericho asked. She knew Mecca hadn't, and she was starving. They ordered the pub's specialty and began the process of getting to know one another. It didn't take her long to realize that Mecca was very private, great at small talk but not one to share important details.

"I couldn't help noticing your encounter with the President," Jericho watched her face for a reaction. "He seemed to be bothering you."

"Oh, no he wasn't bothering me," Mecca lied. "I just don't like anyone who works to destroy my country. He and I have nothing in common. I certainly didn't want him touching me. But enough about me, I want to hear about you."

Mecca placed her hand on Jericho's arm, leaned across the table, and looked into her eyes. Mecca's eyes held Jericho's as she spoke in the same even, soothing voice she had used on Kadence. Jericho knew she could get lost in those blue eyes. The light in them was captivating. Mecca was hypnotizing her. Fortunately, Jericho was not susceptible to hypnosis. Whether it was the small metal plate in her head or the mind techniques she had often used to ease the terror in Afghanistan, there was no way anyone would ever hypnotize Jericho Parker. Nevertheless, it would be good to let Mecca think she was under her power. She sat without moving and let her body relax.

"Do you like America," Mecca said in English testing Jericho's claim to speak only German.

She didn't answer and Mecca repeated the question in German.

"Yes."

"Do you have my phone number?"

"No."

"Were you at the hospital when Jane Doe was attacked?"

"No."

She removed her hand from Jericho's arm and said, "It's late. I should be getting home."

"I'll see you home," Jericho signaled the waitress for the check.

"No need. I will catch a cab," Mecca stood, "It was nice to meet you, Isa. I hope you enjoy our city." She walked out the door before the server returned with Jericho's credit card.

Jericho had the driver drop her a couple of blocks from her apartment building. She didn't want to run the risk of encountering Mecca. As she entered her apartment, her phone began to vibrate.

"Hello," she answered in her sleepiest voice, and Mecca hung up.

Jericho knew she'd dodged a bullet. She was pleased with how she had handled the situation. She was sure Mecca would not connect Isa Friedman with her. She made a mental note to keep as much distance between herself and Mecca Storm as possible. She could hear Mecca pacing the floor above her. The usually calm and collected doctor was angry. Mecca called Jericho again.

"Who are you," she demanded.

"Listen, lady," Jericho used her sleepiest, annoyed voice, "it's after midnight. My job description doesn't include taking late night calls from drunk, spoiled, rich girls. Sleep it off." She hung up.

Jericho unlocked her desk and took out Mecca's file. She had read it from cover to cover but could find no reason the government would spend millions to protect the brilliant doctor. Protect her from what?

From what she had witnessed, Mecca was quite capable of taking care of herself. Jericho perused Mecca's photos for the millionth time. None of them had prepared her for those incredible eyes.

Mecca went onto her terrace. She loved New York, *the city that never sleeps, how appropriate*, she thought. She loved the Hudson River, the Statue of Liberty, Times Square, Central Park and St. Patrick's Cathedral. She had dedicated her life to preserving the America in which she grew up. She wondered what her unknown friend had dedicated her life to; law enforcement perhaps. She had certainly been a wealth of information over the past five years, but she didn't understand why she hadn't been allowed to meet her, know her. Why she insisted on keeping her distance from her.

Mecca was irritated that she had called her a spoiled, rich girl. She wondered if that was what she thought of her or if she was just trying to create a rift between them.

Now that she knew what her informant looked like, maybe she would be able to find her. She was far more attractive than Mecca had expected. Mecca involuntarily shuttered recalling the woman's hand on the small of her back. She tried to push the thoughts of being in her arms from her mind.

Foolish woman! She honestly thought I believed her hypnotized, Mecca thought. For the first time in her life, Mecca had encountered someone she couldn't hypnotize and it made her more curious than ever.

Made in the USA
San Bernardino, CA
12 August 2019